TRIPLE FUGUE

BY

OSBERT SITWELL

PENGUIN BOOKS
HARMONDSWORTH . MIDDLESEX

First published by Grant Richards, Ltd, June 1924
Transferred to Gerald Duckworth & Co. Ltd, June 1927
Published in Penguin Books 1940
Reprinted 1948

AUTHOR'S PREFACE

In humbly presenting the following tales of the Old and New Worlds I should at the same time wish to warn my readers that any character attempting to recognize himself will be immediately prosecuted for libel.

MADE AND PRINTED IN GREAT BRITAIN
FOR PENGUIN BOOKS LTD BY C. NICHOLLS & COMPANY LTD
LONDON MANCHESTER READING

CONTENTS

And though no perfect likeness they can trace;
Yet each pretends to know the Copied Face.
These, with false glosses feed their own ill-nature,
And turn to Libel, what was meant a Satire.

. . . .

For, as when painters form a matchless face,
They from each Fair one catch some different grace;
And shining features in one portrait blend,
To which no single beauty must pretend:
So poets oft, do in one piece expose
Whole "belles assemblées" of "cocquets" and "beaux."

William Congreve.

PENGUIN BOOKS

218

TRIPLE FUGUE

BY OSBERT SITWELL

LOW TIDE

It was an entrance that, however unconscious, never failed of its effect, and one to which the eye could never become accustomed. The two little figures at the top of the steps, though put-in on a large and crowded canvas, inevitably and entirely dominated the scene at this precise moment of the day. Behind them under the pale blue canopy of the sky rose the intricate perspective of steep cliffs, trim but wind-cut trees, and dells of a cultivated wildness; while the sharp cries of the children, as they raced round these, falling down, laughing, and dropping wooden spade or metallic pail, gave a certain poignancy to the otherwise flat blur of the band wafted up from below. The staircase was the culmination of the garden. On to it led every dell, dingle, and asphalt path. With heavy stone balustrades, crushed-down beneath rows of weighty, clumsily-carved, stone vases overflowing with purple petunias and a new, very municipal variety of dwarf sweet-pea – salmon-pink in tone – it held its own with any other feature of the town. It competed successfully for the attention with funicular-trams, which by their movement continually caught the eye as they performed their geometrical operations up and down the cliff with the precision of a drill-sergeant; it outshone the flashing eyes of the band-stand, encased in panes of glass, and even outvied in interest the lion-coloured sands flecked with moving, gaily-dressed people, and spotted with trestles, centres of little groups, on which white-clad figures gesticulated, or opened and shut soundless mouths. On each side of this imposing structure, set in wide sloping surfaces of grass, smooth and green as baize, two enormous five-pointed stars – frilled out at the edges with variegated leaves of iodine-brown, ochre, green-white and lemon-yellow, lined again within by lobelias of a copper-sulphate blue that in their turn enclosed a round pupil of coral-pink begonias and red and purple fuchsias – glowered out to sea like two bloodshot eyes; one Cyclops guarding each side of the steps.

When the first terrace, overlooked by all this glory, was reached, the blur of the music sharpened into focus, settling into so many familiar and machine-made moulds, for its broad platform was level with the gilt knob of the circular cage from which rose all this sound. Under cover of that cage – or glass case – alternately scorched on warm days and frozen on cool ones, the band discoursed the whiskered, military joviality of Waldteufel or in a sudden frenzied modernity hurled itself with ineffable vigour into the country dances of Edward German. Then, though the majority of residents were content with such a programme, the orchestra must also propitiate that select few who took pride in knowing 'what was going on' in London almost before Londoners themselves had found out. This section of Newborough was, apparently, satisfied that the only important happening in the capital was the advent, and subsequent failure or success, of the latest musical comedy. Nothing else counted. For the Winter Garden band to be a fortnight late in their first reproduction of the strains which accompanied it – if it had proved a 'hit' in London – would be, one understood, a local disaster of the first magnitude. Thus, for the benefit and edification of the select, the orchestra must rehearse feverishly, and perform quite soon, such forgotten favourites as *The Belle of New York*, *The Geisha*, *San Toy*, *The Country Girl*, *The Messenger Boy*, and innumerable other and equally popular variants of these masterpieces.

Distributed round the centre of music was a mathematical arrangement of seats; while beyond, on the deaf side of the bandstand – for it was glazed toward the sea – stretched a long terrace, its farther wall dropping, according to the tides, straight down on to sand or sea, rising out of them shaded toward the bottom, with dark, tough seaweed and well-plastered with limpets and barnacles. This final and most important promenade, from the whole length of which the steps above are visible, was crowded with young women of a provincial smartness, wearing dresses in such a height of fashion that they would have been unrecognized in Paris or London; light-coloured young women from Leeds or Halifax, with turquoise or false-pearl ear-rings jangling down hardly on diminutive gold chains or screwed tight into the unpierced ear. With them would stroll laughing young men in white-flannel trousers, crowned with straw hats, or, more imposingly, with panamas. The latter were a sign of grace and distinction but recently come into favour, entering hand in hand with ping-pong and the Boer War on a short but strenuous conquest of England. Cecil Rhodes had patronised them; and a good one, it is murmured, cost £100! Then there were the residents. Old military gentlemen, rather red and puffing, with long white mustachios, and heavy walking-sticks, are pacing up and down, their elbows out-turned, the two joints of the arm forming a right angle; they are continually pulling at their cuffs – stiff, white cuffs with coloured lines on them – as if on the point of conjuring, the verge of exhibiting, an alive but miraculous white rabbit. All the summer days they spend here, in-the-open-air-damn-it, and all the winter on the cliff above, with eyes fixed to the end of a gigantic telescope, pointed like a gun at the sea, in the bow-window of the commodious Gentlemen's Club, the exterior of which is painted a thick but appropriate magenta. Then, but sitting down more often than walking, there are groups of two or three old ladies, grey-haired, broad-based, who, if they move, sway a little from side to side like ducks on their way to the pond. There are always a few curates, thin, eager, and raven-coated, who have come down from the Ecclesiastical Rest Home on the West Cliff; while several bath-chairs are wheeled up and down or remain stationary

– bath-chairs that, so near the sea, look like the gigantic shells of ocean snails, deposited and overturned by some fierce wave, their tenacious inhabitants, sadly out-of-element, stretching out wandering tentacles and adhesive surfaces. Finally, Newborough being a health resort, there is spread among the rest a whole cohort of infirm, elfin, and imbecile. As if in some nightmare drama, these men, women and children loll and lollop about, with curious uncouth gait, blind or deaf or dumb, hunch-backed or idiot, or armless from birth. But none of these, as they move among the throng, attract much attention. It must, therefore, be taken as a tribute to the personality of the Misses Cantrell-Cooksey that they should invariably claim such a measure of public notice on their arrival.

Perhaps the best place from which to witness their triumph was from one of the seats on the upper terrace, though the spectacle was visible, actually, from nearly every chair in the gardens. The flight of steps, like all monuments of its period both mean and magnificent, looked theatrical as well, as if set for some very material but ridiculous ballet of the Second Empire, some startling and quite pointless convolution of blue muslin, yellow hair, and arms and legs of full muscular development. In place, though, of this ordered and golden whirlwind came down the steps, treading very gingerly, yet unable in their good-natured weakness to resist keeping time to the domineering rhythm of the Waldteufel that greeted them, these two little elderly ladies of the same height and dressed alike. Sisters obviously; indeed, such was the resemblance between them that they might have been taken for twins. Mild and timid in bearing, they yet boasted a singular bravery of apparel, in which, though the nineteen-hundred note was dominant, there were many recollections of past fashions. They were bedizened and a-jingle with little crinkling ornaments, ruby-bars, gold-bangles, slave-bracelets, small watches set with half-pearls hanging from enamelled brooches shaped like true-lover's knots; they were decked out with little pieces of lace, numerous ribbons and a thousand other joyous trifles. Regarded more as objects of virtu than as the covering or decoration of human beings, their dress had a certain beauty, a very intricate quality of design – design that, while outwardly unconnected, had in it a strange rhythm and logic of its own. It was as full of motifs as Burmese art, and as complicated. If the band stopped playing, if every voice in the garden sank down for an instant, the dress of the Misses Cantrell-Cooksey would, one felt, play its own accompaniment, announce the entrance of its wearers. All these small, shining ornaments, apparently meaningless, would tinkle, trill, and jingle sweetly, giving out a sound peaceful and silly as any cowbell heard in the Alps. But, alas! Waldteufel offered no such opportunity.

If their dresses were individual, so were their faces; for though the Age of Cosmetics had not yet returned to us, the cheeks of the two sisters, both of whom had surely seen sixty summers, were a blaze of Babylonish colour. The lips were of a cherry richness, and the hair, showing under the fashionable toque, was not so much golden or primrose as succulent scarlet. All this flaunting splendour was in rather quaint contrast to the gingerly tripping walk, the hair and cheek in direct contradiction to the pale but kindly timidity of their eyes – and, indeed, in the latter difference lay hidden the clue to their entire appearance. Determined to look young, they refused to wear glasses: and to insist on youth after it has passed requires sound eyesight as well as sound judgment. Resultantly, they looked like a pair of music-hall sisters, some popular variety turn of the late 'seventies, left over from that age but defiant of time – looked as though they had made up for their entertainment by the green, value-changing gaslight of mid-Victorian times, and after a Rip Van Winkle slumber, had woken to find themselves here, alone on the staircase, under the sunshine of the East Coast, in the hard dawn of a new, rather sinister, century.

Their appearance, in fact, as they descended the steps, was distinctly open to ridicule, yet so painfully lonely that it was with a feeling of relief that one saw them gain the upper terrace in safety, for the descent of these *opéra-bouffe* steps had taken a considerable time.

The numerous youths who were always to be found loitering on this platform, staring down at the people below, now turned round slowly, drew the knobs of their walking-sticks out of their mouths with a loud pop, as if a cork were being drawn, planted their backs firmly against the railings, and thus outlined against the sea, transferred the extreme vacancy of their gaze upon the two sisters, staring at them fixedly, and, after a time, smiling. The small boy selling programmes, and frilly-edged carnations of an ice-cream pink, made a ribald joke. But then, as the Misses Cantrell-Cooksey rounded the farther corner on to the steps that led below, the sensation on the first terrace began to die down. The youths once more pivoted round listlessly, their eyes following the bands of giggling young girls who strolled beneath them, staring in awe at the smartly-dressed visitors, or resting quietly beyond on the similar blue vacancy of the sea.

When the two sisters arrived on the lower terrace, where the band played, there was again a distinct sensation. As they progressed down the middle of the audience, glancing from side to side in the hope of securing adjacent chairs, with a loftiness of manner that was the disguise both for bad eyesight and an intense shyness, a small, rustling, tittering wind moved the heads of the flower-bright rows of people, and even the groups walking up and down the promenade beyond stopped to watch. On the other hand, a few elder members of the feminine section of the audience – residents, probably – far from being amused, appeared to disapprove, quite definitely to disapprove.

Pretty Mrs Sibmarsh, the wife of Dr Sibmarsh, was sitting with her back to the sea talking to her friend, Mrs

Merryweather. As the two sisters went by, her face was contracted with a spasm of absolute fury. 'I don't know how they dare come down like that; I don't really!' she said in hard, even tones. 'Perfect sights I call them! Twenty-eight, indeed! more like sixty-eight! If you'd seen them, Mabel, at the Hospital Ball at the Royal the other night, dressed like débutantes, with white feathers in their hair. I'm surprised they were let in. They've been here about fifteen years now, and know no one; and I always say that if people have no friends, it is their own fault. And odd, odd to a degree! I can't bear people who aren't like anybody else ... a little too odd for my taste!' And Mrs Sibmarsh looked severely at the band and tiers of greenery above, for it was before she had become artistic and psychic, before she had begun to cultivate originality, before the coralline stethoscope of Dr Sibmarsh, which, like a conjurer, he produced out of his top-hat, had reaped asthmatic harvest, and her house had become, as her friends said, 'a perfect museum' – a wilderness of old oak and Staffordshire pottery. No, that story belongs to the subsequent development of Newborough, which one day we hope to relate. At present, then, oddity offended Mrs Sibmarsh, and looking at them once more with an intense disgust she completed her verdict: 'Odd to a degree – and rich – very rich; and mean into the bargain! And to look at them, it wouldn't surprise me if they drugged! They've got a very queer look in their eyes.' And she sent up a shrill spiral of hard laughter into the blue air.

Owing to a fortunate concatenation of circumstances, it was some time before the Misses Cantrell-Cooksey discovered the disfavour with which they were regarded in the town. Indeed, at this period they were happy – more happy than they had ever been in their lives. Even their loneliness was not felt by them, so devoted was Miss Frederica to Miss Fanny, so devoted Miss Fanny to Miss Frederica. If they were both rather 'odd', as Mrs Sibmarsh stated, yet the accusation of being unlike everybody else was unjust. On the contrary, they were all too human. Nor did they drug, as was suggested, but found their release from a reality which at any rate was not too hard upon them in material matters, in the roseate view of life inherent in those gifted with the Romantic Temperament. In fact they still believed in the Age of Miracles. They felt young, to each other looked young, and when, however seldom, a doubt assailed them as to whether they appeared as youthful to others as to themselves, they found a refuge in cosmetics. The rouge and dye-pot they affected were only the methods through which a laudable, very respectable desire to keep up appearances found its vent. But, while growing ever more devoted, while hardly noticing their lack of friends, themselves accentuated their isolation by the extreme vividness of their exterior. Otherwise, loneliness was no such uncommon thing in Newborough as to have attracted all this attention. Through their own fault, alas! they had made themselves targets for ridicule; and the vision of the town, a vision sharp and narrow, could not pierce through this extraordinary outward aspect to the essential goodness and kindness within.

Apart from the childish vanity that prompted the extravagance of their appearance, and the simplicity which led them to believe that Newborough would accept their own conservative estimate of their age, not much oddity was evident in them. These facts would lead one to suppose that they had always led rather secluded lives. This, then, would account for their being unaware of their loneliness, for their rather painful gaiety, and the resolution with which they participated in every local function. Thus were they making up for a youth that had lacked diversions by extreme merry-making in their latter years.

The daughters of a country clergyman, whom they had worshipped, and on whose behalf both of them in their young days had made certain sacrifices – suffered certain disappointments, one understood – they had found themselves, some fifteen years before the time of which we are speaking, possessed of a considerable fortune and alone in the world. For, unlike most of his calling, old Mr Cantrell-Cooksey had been a rich man. Furthermore, the sisters were undoubtedly 'well-connected' – a fact which, owing to their disposition, afforded them a more constant and considerable pleasure than the inheritance of wealth, since, in its milder forms, snobbery is but a symptom of the Romantic Temperament.

They had been pretty, with a surface prettiness of skin and eye, golden hair and round, pale blue eye. The Rector would never, of course, for a moment have condoned the use of cosmetics, so that it was only when at his death they emerged from some forty-five years of seclusion, that they adopted such methods of beautifying themselves – methods not meant so much to attract others as to calm themselves. And one consequence of the pavonine glory into which they then blossomed was to make those valuable connections of theirs seem rather frigid in manner. The more rosy grew their skins, the more golden their hair, to that extent the less friendly grew their relatives. One season, the second summer after their father's death, they spent in London, but the neglect of their numerous cousins, the barren coldness of a great city in which they had no friends, were more than their sensitive hearts could bear for long: and sensitive their hearts undoubtedly were! It was a curious trait in their characters, pointing to some latent eccentricity in them, that while thus responsive, they should have still done nothing to tone down the intensity of their clothes and colouring. Surely they must have felt that there was some little connection between these and the coldness with which they were treated. Either their weak eyes must have prevented them from realising the full oddity of their appearance, or else their romantic disposition must have already and for ever warped their judgment.

They were well-pleased to settle in the large red-brick house overhanging the cliffs at Newborough. Their dear father had been fond of the town, and though they had not visited it for many years, they had often been taken there as children and, as a place to live in, it suited them exactly. The Red House, appropriately named, was large, and besides, what was described by the agents who disposed of it as its 'unique situation' – which consisted in the dangerous angle of the cliffs beneath – had the additional advantage of raking, enfilading indeed, the Promenade with its east-facing windows. In this new house the sisters began a life of peaceful happiness, and at the same time, contrasted with their former existence at the Rectory, of feverish excitement. They loved the house, and each one of the fifteen years they had spent in it had made it more dear to them. They liked the town – like is but a moderate term for the affection they felt for it – and were superbly unconscious of unfriendly eyes or cruel laughter. 'We like Newborough,' Misses Frederica and Fanny would say together, as if with one voice, 'because there's always something going on – and then it's so pretty! We can never look out of our windows without being reminded of the Bay of Naples. In the summer there is always the band; and London is so *noisy* nowadays.' And they loved the house. Yes, they *loved* it. It wasn't quite like anyone's else. Oh, no! Not, of course, that it was 'queer' in any way – for the sisters, curiously enough, shared Mrs Sibmarsh's horror of oddity. It was such a comfortable house, and had such a 'nice' garden, too, on the other side – quite like being in the country. It was difficult to imagine, when one was in it, that one was in a town. The garden, edged with split-oak palings, was full of speckled laurel bushes and dirty evergreens, graced in the spring by the spidery, thin mauve flowers of a few Indian lilacs, the dying fireworks of a laburnum tree with a hollow in its centre which had at some time been filled with cement, and later by a few perfectly correct but rather scentless roses. And in the autumn, chrysanthemums ('they do so well here') – beds and beds of chrysanthemums! The garden acted as clock for the seasons. Laburnum pointed to full spring, roses to full summer, chrysanthemums to rich autumn. The climate of Newborough, though situated so far to the north, was, they thought, so mild – but very bracing, of course. The east winds were, perhaps, a little trying. Then everything had its disadvantages, hadn't it? And it was a source of the greatest pride to them that in the depths of winter, between Christmas and the New Year, it was usually possible to find one unfolded and frost-bitten rosebud, brown as if it had passed through the ordeal by fire, dank and dark as a drowned man – but a rose none the less – lurking in the garden. In fact this square space was a continual delight, so admirably suited for garden party or church bazaar, just big enough but not too big, and so convenient! But no function of any sort ever took place there.

Nevertheless, the sisters were always remarking to each other that it was 'so nice for entertaining one's friends.'

In anything they did or proposed to do, this phrase was for ever on their tongues. Whatever they contemplated was considered only in the light of aid or hindrance to the entertainment of this imaginary host; an evidence of a need for friendship and of a hospitable disposition.

Beyond the garden, as far as the eye could see, rolled what in our childhood we were taught to regard as the 'German Ocean', displaying its various shrill and strident moods, lapping, singing, shouting, roaring or moaning. And this music, so romantic and strange, was always the pleasantest of sounds to the two sisters.

In the summer, as we have seen, Miss Frederica and Miss Fanny Cantrell-Cooksey would, on each fine day, walk down by the carefully-preserved cliffs, through the trim woods, on to the terrace by the sea where the band played. They were due to arrive there between 11.15 and 11.30. In the afternoon – after lunch (at 1.15) – they would walk a little or sit in the garden. There were, of course, frequent rests, for one got so tired doing all these things, and lying-down freshens one up so. Tea at 4.30 with a large silver kettle, with a flame under it, silver teapot, and silver sugar-basin. Ceylon, *not* Indian tea. The milk must, naturally, be poured *first* into the teacup. So many people fail to do this. And one must make the tea *oneself:* servants never learn to do it properly, do they? Emily, for instance, though she had been there many years, had never learnt to use boiling water. It must be *boiling* water. Miss Fanny, in person, would pour the water from the kettle into the teapot; and, in due time, Miss Frederica, the elder sister, would pour out the tea.

Tea, regarded not as a beverage but as a social function, was one of their extravagances – for though few people came, unless Archdeacon Haddocriss looked in to tell them about one of his new funds, it was always prepared for ten people. Lots of little cakes; and scones, supported on a bowl filled with hot water. There were certain days, however, when, if the ladies felt the need for some unusual excitement, they would inform Emily that they would be out for tea, and would walk to one of those artistic and half-timbered cafés, which were becoming such a feature of the town, where, beneath Gothic canopies of fumed German oak, and by simple dressers of peasant and cottage crockery, in a stifling atmosphere of English coffee and strong tea, they would partake of a cup of chocolate – very dainty – with the white of an egg frothed on top of it to represent cream. This would appeal to their feelings, reminding them, as it did, of that visit to Germany, in company with their Dear Old Father, some fifteen – or was it fourteen? – years before he passed away. Thus stimulated, they would return home.

Dinner, the crown of the day for every respectable inhabitant of Newborough, was at 7.30 p.m. The Misses Cantrell-Cooksey had always been used to dinner at this hour, so for them it was nothing unusual. But for most of the well-to-do in the town, dinner was a shibboleth, its hour dividing mankind – not so much a meal as a Declaration of the Rights of Man. A whole revolution was fixed between those who enjoyed their dinner at midday, and those who dined in the evening. Between those addicted to late dinner and those who still revelled in the primitive simplicity of high-tea was fixed such a gap in the social ranks as could never be bridged. And for the former, two things were of the utmost importance. One of these was never, in any evil hour or by any unfortunate accident, to refer to the midday meal under other title than 'luncheon' – or perhaps the more familiar, more vulgar 'lunch'. Dr Sibmarsh had, for instance, once referred to it in public as 'dinner' – and it took him long to live down. The other, and even more vital, thing to keep in mind, was the absolute necessity of 'dressing' for dinner. Invariably, inevitably, one must 'dress' for dinner – otherwise the nature of the meal might be mistaken! Once 'dressed' one was secure, since no man 'dresses' for high tea.

Thus in every red-brick villa in Newborough at 7.30 on a summer evening the dining-room would be illuminated; the electric light would show splendidly in its mounting of chased or wrought copper through shades, bell-like shades, of opalescent glass; and, though it was still daylight without, if one were lucky enough to walk down Prince of Wales's Avenue or Albemarle Road at this hour, one would see row after row of these glowing interiors, the very pageant of late Victorian and early Edwardian prosperity. Beneath the golden lustre of four lights that hung from the ceiling, seated before a white table, in the centre of which was usually a large doily composed of lace over a ground of dead-orange silk, upon which would stand four little trumpet-shaped silver vases, with frilled edges like sharks' teeth, each displaying at this season three or four yellow poppies, four or five sweet-peas, and misty bunches of that nameless though universal white blossom that is more like white muslin than a flower, the diners would be sitting, carefully dressed. The hostess, in a pretty gown of pink satin, low at the bosom and with puffy sleeves, wearing an amethyst or aquamarine brooch, would be talking amiably and sweetly – wearing that charming smile that made such a difference to her face, 'lit it up', as the phrase was – to the gentleman on her right, while at the same time directing a glance of such flaming contempt at her maid-servant for falling into those very mistakes of service about which she had warned her all day – and as for that, just a moment before dinner – striking her dead with a look of such awful, such diabolical hatred that any other mortal, except this girl accustomed to it, would on the spot have perished and sunk down. The earth itself might well open beneath such vehement passion – so well disguised..

The rules-of-the-game, too, were very strict. It was not, even, an easy affair to get into the dining-room; for again in this it was necessary to disprove the possible if unspoken allegation of transcendentalised high tea. If there were more than four or five guests, a regular and courtly procession would walk across the small space from drawing-room to dining-room: arm-in-arm: lady on right, gentleman on left: polite, but easy, conversation. If, however, there were but a few people, three or four, the same effect could be produced by saying in a careless Bohemian way: 'Oh, don't let's bother. Can't we go in as we are?'

Fortunately Emily was seldom forgetful, and unfortunately, it was seldom that Miss Frederica or Miss Fanny Cantrell-Cooksey was able to sweep in to dinner on the arm of a cavalier. If, though, one was alone for dinner – and had not got a headache – one could go down to hear the band again.

When the evenings were cool, the orchestra, escaped from their glass-case, were sure to be playing 'inside'. 'Inside' indicated an enormous hall near the bandstand, built to look as if it were part of the Louvre – Newborough architecture was both informed and cosmopolitan – and tastefully decorated within, in a Second Empire scheme of chocolate, turquoise-blue, and gold – all by now very faded and dry-looking, like an old sugared biscuit. Round the frieze, high up, were inscribed on scrolls the names of composers at the height of their fame when this hall was constructed. A queer medley it was, and one that would be an interesting footnote to that *History of Taste* which is now waiting to be written – for these names, considered then of equal value, represented the judgment of a generation ... MENDELSSOHN ... HANDEL ... SPÖHR ... BEETHOVEN ... GOUNOD ... VERDI ... SCHUMANN ... WEBER ... DONIZETTI ... BERLIOZ ... LISZT.

Unfortunately, though specially built for music, the acoustic properties of the hall were such that not a note could be heard properly, except from the roof, where the sound was as nearly perfect as possible, but there were no chairs! The concerts were nevertheless much appreciated. Every evening the bandsmen became suddenly transformed into individuals, escaping from a sober uniform into evening dress; became definitely recognisable as persons. This, again, affected their playing, making it more individual, less a composite whole. The two ladies had in some mysterious way conceived a great passion for the music of Wagner; and since in the evening performances the conductor, who prided himself on being catholic and modern, was allowed more to please himself than in the mornings, they were often able to gratify this passion. Perhaps this Wagner-worship was one of the oddities to which Mrs Sibmarsh had alluded: it was a curious phenomenon certainly, for otherwise they were devoid of any musical appreciation. But there is no doubt that, as much as anything in Newborough, they enjoyed sitting here in the evenings, and wallowing in the sensual melodies of that master, as in a hot bath.

In addition to these concerts there were, in the season, other entertainments. Touring companies would come down for six nights to the two theatres, the 'Royal' and the 'Ghoolingham'. Our two heroines did not often visit these, except during the annual appearance of the D'Oyly Carte Gilbert and Sullivan Opera Company. For this event, to which all the year they looked forward, it was their habit to book a box on the opening night, and a stall for each subsequent performance. Such pretty music, and oh! how witty and amusing. And nothing in bad taste, nothing that anybody need be offended at! Even the Rector, who had not much cared for festivities, had thoroughly enjoyed *The Gondoliers*. Otherwise they did not go much to the theatre unless it was something special. Then, out of curiosity, they would book seats. Once, for instance, they had been to hear Sousa's Band, which paid a flying visit to the Ghoolingham. What an extraordinary man! how extraordinary it all was, so noisy and vulgar! Still, the marches were most inspiring, one must say, and so patriotic! He had, had he not, a true gift of melody?

Then there were the occasional appearances at a special performance of famous but ageing actresses – Lady Bancroft and Mrs Kendal – or of indomitable but ageless beauties such as Mrs Langtry. It would be a pity to miss such a treat. Thus there was always something going on.

This continual round of diversion was broken every seventh day by church-going, the event of the week. Now that the Rector was no longer with them they went to church only *once* on a Sunday (churches are so badly ventilated); in the morning. After church ensued church-parade. This took place on the promenade overlooked by the Red House, and lasted until the luncheon hour.

Clasping a black-bound Prayer Book, divided by a vivid

blue or purple watered-silk marker, in a well-gloved hand, and gorgeous as the Queen of Sheba, Miss Frederica and Miss Fanny Cantrell-Cooksey would walk – though 'walk' hardly describes such stately progress ... march ... saunter ... up and down, as would all the other respectable inhabitants and worthy visitors. It was, consciously, one of the 'prettiest' sights of the town, and, what was of more importance, an observance that helped to keep up appearances.

Innumerable people walked up and down, up and down – individuals for a moment, then dovetailing into the crowd. Most of them were elderly – though there were a few children – and looked incongruous in clothes of such elaboration, as must all people of over middle-age who adopt a minutely decorated style. For a surfeit of decoration is no more suitable to the elderly than a surfeit of food. Up and down they paced, under the hard northern sunlight, anthropoids that having massacred a diverse regiment of beasts-of-the-field now masquerade in their pitiable skins; to the latter they have added the feathers raped from the osprey, and now look as though decorated for some primitive, some awful, rite. Up and down they progress, past cream-painted houses, roofed with damp-blue slates; on each sill is a box of red geraniums, before each house a stretch of green, prim grass. Far below, constant companion to their march, rolls the steely northern sea: the prospect on the other side varies. The cream-painted houses give way to golden lawns, the colour of which is enhanced by an artistic green-painted cab-shelter covered in by red tiles, a recent inspiration of the municipal architect: then, again, follow Gothic stone drinking troughs for beasts, and portentous stone houses for men. Not all the people walk. A few drive in large, open cabs, that rumble slowly; while others, ladies of fabulous age, with trembling blue lips and palely purple faces, with hairy growths on the chin, and black bonnets nodding on the top of their helpless heads, are being drawn along in bath-chairs that are so many black insects. As they are rolled past, in a flutter of bugles, heliotrope-velvet ribbons, and black kid gloves, there is a trilling of jet-like petrified laughter. Each venerable image, thus trundled, would be accompanied by a niece or daughter, pale, flat-looking women with vague but crucified expressions, like the female saints whose tortures are depicted by German Primitives. The aunts and mothers in their bath-chairs look happy though grim ('poor old things', the Misses Cantrell-Cooksey would say, rather nervously) as they clasp a Prayer Book tightly in their gloved hands, as if it were a passport for that equally tedious Heaven which they had prepared for themselves. Already there sounded from them the characteristic music of their Heaven, asthmatic and wheezy; so old were they that when through blue lips they murmured, their voices sounded like harmoniums played at a distance; and when their faces were in repose, the bones would show under the sagging parchment, for the skull was already asserting its lordship over the flesh.

In this setting our heroines showed almost to advantage. Yet as they went by, while other promenaders would be continually stopped by friends, and would stand talking together in little groups, they would never be greeted. The old ladies would stretch out tentacles from their shells in welcome to others; but our two friends would never be hailed by them. Indeed, the old ladies would be galvanised into life by the sight of them, looking at them as sourly as any younger members of the community. The burden of their complaint was the same as that uttered by Mrs Sibmarsh. 'Perfect sights! How can they get themselves up like that I can't think! And they were properly brought up too. Twenty-eight, indeed! they'll never see sixty-eight again, I should say! Real Aunt Sallies!' And after some such declamatory effort their voices would ooze back to a whisper.

In among the promenaders and listening groups Mrs

Sibmarsh herself was continually imparting information. 'Have you heard the latest, Mrs Spirechurch? What do you think those two old bundles have done now?' And many a macabre march was halted for an instant in order to hear a recital of the latest Cantrell-Cooksey folly. About three years before, the two ladies had undoubtedly given their age in the census return as twenty-eight and twenty-six respectively. By 7.30 the next night every dining-room in the town was discussing this lamentably absurd lapse from verity. It became, this topic, another thing that divided dinner from high tea. It lightened the life of Newborough; and, ever since, each movement or saying of the sisters had become an object of mingled interest and contempt.

On wet Sundays – which were almost as enjoyable as fine ones – Miss Frederica and Miss Fanny would drive to and from church in their heraldic 'Lonsdale Wagonette'. This vehicle, of which they were intensely proud, was regarded by others almost as the symptom of original sin. It was, in truth, an odd conveyance: a large, long, polished, black, roomy affair, lined with railway-carriage-blue material; indeed the interior was not unlike a railway carriage, except that the windows were above the seats, one narrow end turned toward the horses. Whichever seat one occupied, one's back shut out the view, while the view opposite was likewise obscured by some person. When the door shut, the step shut with it; when the door opened, the step precipitated one upon the pavement. How either of the two ladies ever got in or out of their conveyance, with their weak eyes and faltering footsteps, remains one of the mysteries of the past! The coachman, smartly dressed in a buff coat, sat – immense – on the box, while the door had emblazoned on it the very rampant arms of Cantrell-Cooksey. The wagonette was, really, an extraordinary creation; one of the last, most imbecile inventions of equine traffic, originally intended to aid the more rapid and complete incarceration of guests in various country houses. Its owners, however, were very content, regarding it as the supreme achievement of civilisation. It was neater and more unusual-looking than a brougham or victoria; not so 'fast' – in any sense – as a tandem; and how much nicer than those horrible, snorting motor-cars that were coming in! Not that they would ever be seen in one of those things; so trippery. And then the 'Lonsdale', most important quality, was so hospitable. There was room in it for one's friends. It would hold at least eight people, where a brougham would hold three, and it would be so useful for picnics in the Sherbourn Woods. In fact this lumbering conveyance made a special appeal to the Romantic Temperament.

Sunday afternoons in the season were also very pleasant, for there were concerts in the Winter Gardens at 3.30. The band, discarding its uniform, would adopt frock-coats, while the conductor would walk round the corner into his glass-case, curling a waxed military moustache, and sporting a top-hat. When securely within the shelter, the bandsmen would stand up to greet him; he would take off his hat, turn round, and bow. *God Save the King* – for it was Sunday – would then be played. Usually a *vocalist* would come down from London for these concerts (a vocalist is a very different thing from a singer – more sabbatical). The vocalist, running to extremes, was generally a very young girl or very old man. The programmes of these concerts were, of course, composed of sacred music, and were regarded by the town as being 'very classical'. Some, even, took objection to them on this score, for not all Newborough enjoyed 'classical' music. The adjective had a special significance. For the town divided all sounds made by piano, orchestra, or human voice into two categories: 'classical' music and – just music! Music meant *The Country Girl*, *The Belle of New York*, Offenbach, Waldteufel and, generally, anything that had 'a tune in it'; Sullivan – except for *The Lost Chord*, acknowledged as sacred – was an exception, belonging to both worlds, pagan and 'classical', but universally popular. Then came the 'classical' division, comprising any composers who had comprehended and used the rules of counterpoint, the laws of harmony, and at the same time any mid-Victorian composer, who, neglecting both, had written anthems or oratorios. For sacred music was the inner and spiritual core of 'classical' music. Furthermore, it was understood that any music played on an organ became transmuted in some mysterious fashion into sacred music. And, by virtue of this, Wagner had crept into the Sunday Afternoon Concerts, as a sort of Honorary Sacred Composer; for it was well known that the organist at Holy Trinity – the best organist in all Newborough – played Wagner at his recitals. Thus our two ladies were privileged to bathe in those luscious strains each Sunday.

After music, came tea again, at five o'clock, half-an-hour later than usual. It was always nice to have a cup of tea.

This routine continued through their fifteen years of prosperity, from about May 24th till September 27th. About this latter date, every year, it would occur simultaneously to many that the evenings were drawing in. Chrysanthemums would strike a rich note of gloom and warning in many gardens, and through the windows of the Red House, especially, would be borne-in their peculiarly muffled and musty smell, mildewed and damp as the air of the tomb. Poor old Miss Waddington – whom they saw from time to time – would inaugurate the winter season with one of those cyclone colds that were her unique gift. Bath-chairs would disappear from the Promenade and Winter Gardens. The band would be dispersed, its members drifting away to London or to various theatre-orchestras elsewhere, and soon the whole town would be echoing with the more wintry music of howling gale, roaring sea, and their domestic equivalents, wheezing, sneezing, snoring, and coughing.

Blinds would be drawn down for tea. There would be comfortable fires; the yellow wallpaper of the drawing-room would take on a warmer tone, the large oil-picture of 'Sunset Egypt' of which old Mr Cantrell-Cooksey had been so fond, a richer glow; and all would burn more brightly again in the various items of the silver equipment on the tea table. Christmas, it would be felt – in the Red House, and universally – will soon be here again. Already the shops would be getting ready for it, with an ever-increasing number of imbecile 'novelties' and a great display of red-flannel and cotton-wool snow.

The winter festivities would start in mid-November. Every five weeks there would a hospital ball, a hunt ball even – so picturesque with all the red coats and bits of foxes and things – or perhaps a concert in aid of the local lifeboat, or the performance of the Newborough Philharmonic Society which took place every six months; these concerts were also very picturesque – quite a sight indeed – with all the girls in white dresses, and all the men in black and white evening clothes. In every one of these gaieties Miss Frederica and Miss Fanny Cantrell-Cooksey would, for a varying payment, participate. Yet at the most spirited and exhilarating of these functions it may be surmised that though clad in a low-cut glory unequalled by any other ladies present, though boasting diamond constellations fixed in their hair like those stars that twinkle so brightly above the head of the Queen of the Fairies in a pantomime, the two ladies were more lonely even than in their unfrequented house. Not, one imagines, that they realised quite what it was they felt; for as the only form of human companionship to which they were accustomed was to be together but otherwise alone, or else to be together in a crowd but equally alone, since few spoke to them or acknowledged their presence, they were not so much aware of the separation from their kind as to let it altogether spoil their pleasure. In order fully to appreciate the honour of being sent to Coventry, it is necessary to have experience of other country-sides and towns. Such had never been the lot of our heroines. Nevertheless, as they left concert or ball, as wrapped in filmy, feathery cloaks they waited outside on the doorstep for the arrival of their Lonsdale – which, in spite of their constant generosity to the commissionaire, was always the last to be ushered up to the door – an inexplicable and terrible feeling of depression would assail them. Perhaps, they thought, it was only the reaction that follows on intense enjoyment. It was curious, though, for in the Rectory they had experienced no such feelings. But then life at the Rectory had not been so full of pleasure and excitement, had it, dear?

When the Carnival Ball (Costumes Voluntary) took place in February, in aid of the Children's Convalescent Home, a riot was very nearly provoked in fashionable circles by the two sisters. Few people wore fancy dress. The arrival, therefore, of Miss Frederica as a Dresden Shepherdess and Miss Fanny as Carmen was all the more noticeable. Miss Frederica wore a white-powdered wig, a sprigged-muslin dress, carried a crook, and had one very captivating black patch near the chin; while Miss Fanny, particularly alluring in a bright red gown in which sequins sparkled like a rainbow, and with an orange Spanish shawl flung jauntily round her shoulders, cast sparkling glances over her fan from those weak, pale eyes. It was rather an appalling spectacle, this *danse macabre*, though they enjoyed it thoroughly, quite unaware of the sensation caused. They stood among the waiting groups of young girls at the ballroom door, or sat together by one of the walls. But Newborough never forgot: it ranked as an event, as a topic, with that census return.

In the winter, too, there were countless bazaars in aid of various charities – not so important as the ones that took place in the summer, but more of them, and, in a sense, more exciting, more personal. The great lady of the district, Lady Ghoolingham, let it be understood that though willing to open an infinity of bazaars and sales of work in July or August, nothing and no one would, or ever should, induce her to face the harsh winter winds of Newborough, the cold of the railway carriage that would take her there from London, or the overheated atmosphere of the restaurant car, full of that mysterious and emetic scent of cabbage that haunts it always in the winter. It became necessary, then, for the organisers of good works to find continual substitutes for Lady Ghoolingham. And the Misses Cantrell-Cooksey would often remark to each other that they could not – no, they could not – think what they would do if Archdeacon Haddocriss should ask them to perform some such ceremony on his behalf. You see, it must be quite twenty years since Miss Frederica had opened that one for her father at Hubbard Stanton, and that was only a jumble sale! But Miss Fanny had seen the Archdeacon out that morning, and thought he had looked rather as if he wanted to ask something. No, she wouldn't be at all surprised; and if Frederica was asked, it would hardly be graceful to refuse. ... Alas! the venerable gentleman knew that if out of respect for their wealth and generosity he invited one of 'those two gaudy old scarecrows' – as he had heard them termed in his presence – to open any function, or even so much as to appear on the platform, the parish would be rent in twain. There would be civil war. If he wanted trouble of that sort, he might just as well introduce ritualism at once.

We have noticed, in passing, some of the minor eccentricities of the two sisters, which might possibly justify the charge brought against them of 'oddness,' but now we come to other, more marked, peculiarities. Every fine morning or afternoon in the winter they would, like most other respectable inhabitants of the town, call at the lending library to exchange their novels. There was nothing very unusual in this, except that little Mr Garrett, behind the counter, founder of the establishment, had become almost a friend. He was more friendly to them than were most of the towns-folk. Like other habituals of the library, they would demand a new novel every day – something 'amusing' and 'light' – an E. F. Benson, for example – and, unlike them, would actually get it. Mr Garrett was such a nice polite little man. A pity he was so untidy! They would then leave the library, exchanging its warm smell of cloves, sealing-wax and thumbed volumes, for the salt air outside. Coming out into the air was, indeed, like being hit in the face, at this time of year. And now they would turn their steps towards the sea-front! This was considered an extraordinary thing to do. Of all the wealthier members of the community, they were the only two who did not conspire to regard the sea as non-existent except in the summer months. All the rest of them forgot the ocean till the first spring day, and preferred to walk in the streets, among the shops, away from the fierce white wings of spray that fluttered and flapped up over the stout stone walls below. Every day in the winter, when it was not actually raining, our heroines, with that love of extremes – great light and great shadow, sun and black cloud – which is the portion of those afflicted with the Romantic Temperament, would walk by the cold, tumbling brown cliffs along the tawny sands, away, even, from the humanised sea-front. Especially after a storm would they enjoy walking along the lonely white sands. Their scarlet hair, their faces so badly made-up that the expression of each side would vary as if one half of the mask were tragic, the other comic, their absurd and complicated dresses, looked all the more fantastic for this submarine setting; and such it seemed after a storm, some strange undersea view. The sloping, pebbly border of sand and sea would be littered with a wild disarray of broken glass, worn down to round gleaming jewels by the constant fret and foaming of the breakers, of starfish, sea-urchins and queer-shaped monstrosities, heaped up with seaweed like small brown palm-trees or the long black matted hair of mermaids. There were so few people about, and the few there were would haunt the sands each day. There was always a tramp, keeping-in to the shelter of the rocks, a little bent man with a thin red beard, a battered bowler hat and a torn frock-coat, a queer parody of prosperity. Then there were the gatherers of limpets and winkles, who would pile up their salt harvest in scaly baskets. One of these men, especially, they noticed – a broad bacchanalian character, with huge northern physique, who ought to have found work harder and more remunerative than this. Him they would see bent nearly double over the flat rocks that were covered by the sea at high tide, as with a knife he removed the molluscs and threw them into the deep basket at his side.

And, most interesting of all, after a storm there would gather together those men who make a living by combing the golden sands. What profession they followed in between the gales, or where they came from, it was impossible to find out. The bacchanalian character would join them, deserting his limpets and winkles for this more profitable and entertaining employment. They would rake over the slope of pebbles and the sands beneath, just at the point where the high tide deposited its hostages. It was a gentle but fascinating exercise, and one requiring very competent eyesight and a certain agility of mind. The sisters would stand there for many minutes watching the alternately romantic and prosaic treasury which the storm had precipitated on these bleak sands. As the men combed, they would find silver pennies of the Plantagenets, old biscuit tins full of sea-biscuits, gold coins from Spain, a piece of rusty armour that had been gnawed by the waves for centuries, coppers that had been thrown to the pierrots in the summer, a glass bottle with a faded message in it – the family to which this agonised scrawl was addressed had been dead these ten years! – a bit of a weighing-machine that had stood on the sands in the summer, a Dutch cheese still round and fresh and cherry-coloured, a long clasp-knife with a curious tortoise-shell handle – all the trifles that time and the cruel tides had left over. Really Miss Frederica and Miss Fanny felt that they could stand here for hours watching, if it was not for the cold. Even when they had walked away a little, they would return for a last glimpse. Gradually a bond grew up between them and these strange diggers for treasure. To the latter there was such a break in the surface of the world between themselves and the dwellers on the West Cliff, that these two queerly-caparisoned elderly women, with their dyed hair and painted faces, seemed no further removed from everyday experience than any others of their class. They were a funny lot, ladies and gentlemen! But these two, though they asked constantly to which parish the treasure-seekers belonged, also distributed shillings. Suspicion was allayed. 'It was meant kindly,' the men thought, and in the presence of Miss Fanny and Miss Frederica the very living language of the fish-market was stifled by unexpected better feelings.

In short, to watch these men at their work was, to the two sisters, like looking-on at gambling. And here we have the second secret. This was the spark of passion that burned in them. In spite of the quiet orderlinesss of home and upbringing, these two ladies were, by nature, born gamblers. But for many years timidity, not of the possible consequences – for these held no terrors for them – but of the means and methods by which gambling could respectably be effected, had deterred them from rash action. They must not do anything 'fast.' Horse-racing was out of the question, since their father would never have countenanced the smallest bet. It must be very absorbing, though, they thought. Monte Carlo, too, was a dreadful place, full of *queer* people:

never a morning went by – the Rector had told them – except a revolver shot rang out a life. One did not always see these tragedies reported in the Press, because the Casino authorities hushed them up. It was disgraceful – a blot on Europe; but then, of course, queer people *would* do queer things. And foreigners were so queer, what with Monte Carlo and bull fighting and things like that!

Their own method of gambling would not be gambling, so much as speculation; quite a different matter. And for them an unfortunate sequel to their actions was incredible. Security had ever stood by them. Their world was not subject to these chances, these accidents, but was a solid affair of Law-and-Order, Church-and-State, governed for sixty years by Queen Victoria and now inherited by her worthy and popular son ('God Save the Queen' ... somehow they felt they would never get used to 'God Save the King' ... it sounded so funny, didn't it? ...) Investments were not like gambling at Monte Carlo, but part of an ordered and stately society. 'The very life-blood of commerce' they had read in a *Times* leading article, not long ago. No ill would befall them, for they, too, were part of an ordering of the world. It had pleased God to call them to their position. And things were going on as well as could be expected, considering that the Queen was dead. The Income Tax, though deprecated by all Newborough, was negligible; and the pale spectres of disaster and revolution were still stalking the outer confines of the world, to which they had been banished by the general prosperity, unable as yet to make a sufficiently imposing reappearance on the modern stage after such long exile. The Boer War was dreadful, but apart from the revelation of human brutality and degradation offered by the obstinate desire to fight on behalf of their country shown by those brutal, bearded farmers, there had never been really much reason for worry. After all, we were an island, and brute force had never won yet! And we had the Navy, and our generals too. Of course it was true that there were 'cranks' at large in London, 'Fabians' who wished to overturn the whole system of civilised society. But one did not hear much of them now at Newborough. And since the ordering of the world had been ordained by God, it could hardly be upset except by the Devil himself; and even he would not prevail for long.

If they gambled, being part of the ordering of this world, they would win. Of course they would win! Their temperament assured them of success, and urged them to find the means. Ever since the death of their father they had been able to gratify every desire within a limited circle – that wagonette, for example! If they could find some method of gambling which – since success was inevitable – meant if they could double or treble their income, two birds would be killed by one stone. For, while it would satisfy their need for excitement, the extra wealth accruing to them would thus enable them to buy more 'Lonsdales' – taking 'Lonsdales' as the symbol of worldly ambition. It never occurred to them that there was a penalty attached to possible failure. They had not the nervousness of the very rich. Yet the absence to them of danger did not make the game any less exciting.

Some years before the time of which we are writing, Miss Frederica had, after a period of study, found the way. Her conclusion was that herself and her sister should sell out of Consols, which now only brought in 2½ per cent., part with their other gilt-edged securities, and invest in one of her own discoveries. Miss Fanny, implicit believer in Frederica's genius, at once concurred.

The elder lady, like many of her generation, had been greatly impressed by the towering genius of Cecil Rhodes – a millionaire was then regarded as a being of high romance, a Napoleon of Finance, a Cæsar of Commerce – and by his roseate views of the future in store for South Africa. With utter faith in his views, and in the solidity of wealth, Miss Frederica invested most of their joint fortunes in South

African Mines and other speculative concerns. Their trustees, in this case powerless to forbid, implored them not to alter their old investments. But Miss Frederica knew better. She knew – for the newspapers had told her – that one must Think Imperially. What were those lines of Kipling's?

She wrote a severe, identical letter to trustees and lawyer, in which she pointed out that one must cease 'thinking in a *narrow* little way,' adjured them to put away notions inherited from the past, and to realise that we were, all of us, treading (and how true were her words) on the path that would lead us to an Imperial To-morrow.

Not one single word of these unusual developments reached Newborough, and for some time the ladies prospered almost as much as they had anticipated. Soon, though, the first cracks appeared in the ice upon which they were skating; but warnings held no meaning for them, and were not heeded. Another year passed. Nothing exceptional transpired. The summer passed, and they were a little behindhand with their accounts. The winter began, and the storms raged.

One afternoon they had been down to the sands, as was their custom, to watch the disentangling of that irrelevant treasure accumulated by the northern waves. As they walked along the Promenade they noticed that the storm was dying down. The lamp-lighter was pursuing his magic calling, and as he touched the lamps with his tall wand there was no flicker of wind and light. The blinds were already down at home. But a rich glow showed through them. It looked so comfortable. The postman had been, too. And a letter was waiting for them. Their to-morrow had come, and they were ruined.

*

So rooted were they in material prosperity, so protected had been every thought in all their lives from any frosty breath of reality, that at first they were not so much worried, as excited. But then, suddenly, the world began to take on the most unexpected and unpleasant contours. Action, for the first time, came into touch with them. Their loss unlocked the gate, and all the aversion and contempt in which they were held came pouring out, overwhelming them in a filthy, muddy torrent. Little pity showed in any face. Even those who had greatly prospered by the worldly possessions of the Misses Cantrell-Cooksey, tradesmen and their like, could not now see any further reason to disguise their feelings, however carefully they had concealed them before. People became offhand, and so rude. Some had always disliked them for their 'oddness' (they had never been like other ladies), while the rest were jealous, feeling that to be ruined was a luxury of the rich. Miss Frederica and Miss Fanny felt that they could stand anything but rudeness, for even yet our two heroines could not envisage the full consequences. Their instinct was to keep up appearances; and this was their courage. Not one word of reproach passed between them, not by one syllable would either admit that the world had changed. Everything now depended on keeping up appearances, on seeming not to mind. The fear was there, buried and smothered, but the material pinch was as yet absent.

They were perhaps a little more excitable now in their manner – on the verge of a breakdown, I thought. Miss Fanny, the injured one, had nothing but soothing and heartfelt compassion for her sister, who, though she would not discuss their calamities, would sit alone, silent, and trembling. Before Miss Fanny she was different, more talkative, more uneasy, for in truth she felt too ashamed and remorseful in front of her handiwork to utter, but she must keep up appearances.

In every shuttered red-brick villa, in every avenue and terrace in the town, the Cantrell-Cooksey affair was discussed at 7.30 each night. Folly of this sort was felt, generally to be equal to villainy. It was, Mrs Sibmarsh opined, more than a personal disgrace on the two painted old hags; it was a blot on the fair name of the town. What would tradesmen think that Newborough was coming to? Running up bills with no intention of paying them. An absolute disgrace! But then one only had to look at their eyes ...

Other people were kind but rather inquisitive. Old Miss Waddington, who happened to be laid-up with a bronchial cold that was bad enough to prevent her leaving the house, even on such a visit of commiseration as this one would be, sent her niece across to them at once. The latter returned to her aunt in a marvellously short time with a full budget of information, and Miss Waddington seemed really to be 'more herself' that evening, and had a glass of port after dinner, which she seldom did – invalid port, of course. The Archdeacon, too, was kind, very kind. Directly he heard of the affair he came round to the Red House (the sisters were still in it) and offered to say a prayer with them. Afterwards he addressed a few solemn words to them on secret vices, and, arising out of this, on the particular iniquity of avarice and gambling. But his words served no purpose, because, even if the Misses Cantrell-Cooksey had wished to continue such a career, they had now nothing with which to feed their passion. Avarice would be henceforth a difficult vice for them to practise.

The house was sold. The horses were sold. Everything went, and was lost to them beneath the ghastly sound of the hammer. The Lonsdale fetched but seven pounds. Even the silver teapot, kettle and equipment were taken from them. Nothing remained except a few of their old clothes – which did not prove very attractive items at the sale – and some photographs. The servants had left, two by two, as if leaving the ark on an excursion, laughing, happy, and without leave-taking, a few days before the Public Examination.

This event was the wonder of all Newborough, and the charge of 'oddness,' so often brought against the sisters, was fully borne out by their demeanour in court. The suggestion that they drugged – for drink was too trite an explanation of such behaviour – was widely accepted by that more temporal section of the community, which, although it existed in a seaside town, was alive to all that was going on in London, knew every musical-comedy success, had visited all the large hotels there for dinner on Sunday night, and had thus acquired a thorough knowledge of the greater and more wicked world. No secret vice could for long be hidden from them.

Rouged, dyed, and a-rattle with little ornaments, Miss Frederica and Miss Fanny arrived in court. Their answers were mostly inaudible, except that when Miss Frederica was asked where she was born, she replied that she did not know, and, in answer to the next question, gave her age as twenty-eight; and then broke down.

The total outcome of the affair was that the Misses Cantrell-Cooksey of the Red House were now left homeless, with twenty-six pounds a year between them. With unexpected generosity a few distant but notable relatives, to whom the Archdeacon sent a written appeal, came forward and made up the sum to fifty-two pounds a year – on the condition that the extra twenty-six pounds per annum should be divided into a fortnightly allowance of one pound, and given to them personally, every other Saturday, by a responsible individual. For the relatives were determined that there should be no more extravagance, no more gambling. Finally, dear old Miss Waddington, in spite of growing infirmity and advancing age, volunteered for the office of bursar. She was fond of good works.

The relatives considered that the two sisters should now find some work to do, and perhaps in time relinquish their allowance. They ought to make an EFFORT, they ought to

DO SOMETHING. People must learn to support themselves. However, even Archdeacon Haddocriss, sensible man as he was, had to admit to himself that it was difficult to know for what exact profession the two ladies were fitted.

Now, indeed, the pinch had come and the excitement had gone. But the two sisters kept up appearances to each other – for no one else was taken in! 'The worst of it is,' they would say, 'that we shall never be able to entertain our friends again.' Though the physical deprivations, to which they were condemned from this time forward, became gradually manifest, and must, after such a comfortable life, have seemed more cruel, neither of them ever mentioned these. Cold and hunger, even less than mental torture, should be allowed by respectable members of society. Once their presence was admitted, even tacitly admitted, self-respect would go out of the window.

*

At any rate it looked very clean. That was a comfort! Their room was right at the top.

The tall boarding-house, fronted with that particular white brick which is only to be encountered at seaside resorts, rose like a tower of ice, with blue shadows, from beside a suspension-bridge. The Gothic doorway, carved with cast-iron ivy leaves, had a crooked notice, 'Apartments,' stuck against the glass above the door, like a rakish patch over a very Wesleyan eye. The white side of the house, fronting the street which was a continuation of the bridge, was only five stories high; but the back of the house went down another two stories: here the brown brick of which it was built showed undisguised, and rising among tall, green trees and slopes of grass – for the back looked out on the Dale – a public pleasure-ground – it lost some of its horror, becoming merely a high brown tower. The Misses Cantrell-Cooksey's room was the top one on the street side, under the tall gable covered with rain-blue slates. The window, from the street, looked like a sinister eye. Inside, the bottom of the window was on a level with the floor, while the top of it was so low down that it was necessary to bend in order to get the view from it. The vista it disclosed was made up of a large asphalt playground flanked by a red school-building, with lines of cinder-coloured brick inset in the facade. Away on the right, rose the stone clock-tower of the railway station, modelled on eighteenth-century Dresden architecture, for the architect of the railway company had been a man of wide knowledge and appreciation. On the left was the bridge, with a few tree-tops showing above it. In the day time, especially in the summer, it was quite lively. The sound of traffic, the vibration of the bridge, the clanging of trams, cawing of rooks, and cries of the children as they tumbled round their playground, came in at the high window. For some reason or other Miss Frederica and Miss Fanny found the noise made by the children very irritating – upsetting indeed. In the winter the days were quieter; but the evenings were so long – and the nights!

It had been March when they had moved in: very cold, but the warmer weather would come soon. At first the change was so abrupt, the contrast to their past life so fantastic, as to be equally unreal. It was like playing a game, a childish game of house-keeping or Red-Indians. It must, surely, be only make-believe, and at any moment they would find themselves back in the Red House, able to resume their old life. The last few days there had been – though they would never admit it – very bitter. Everyone on the West Cliff knew them; and if they moved out of their home, people stared so. Here they had not been so well known in the days of their prosperity.

They missed their bedroom more than anything else. In this house they occupied just one room, sleeping in one hard bed. There were a few rickety pieces of yellow furniture, an empty fireplace, a tin basin to wash in. Of course, in the summer, the house was full of visitors, and it was not dark till nine. But the winter evenings were very long. They had no novels to read, and it was very cold – no fire, and nothing to do except go to bed – not even a hot-water bottle. They thought they could not be very well – so chilly and stiff, with a funny sinking feeling inside. It might, Miss Fanny thought, it might be the food. It was not quite what they were used to. Meat, for instance, only twice a week. Still, some people thought meat-eating bad for one, and in the end one might feel all the better for the absence of it ... when one had got used to it. And no dinner at all seemed strange, didn't it? And then, that horrid Indian tea. She was sure she would never get to like that!

Yes, the nights were long, especially the winter nights, and so cold, but they had never before moved in a real world; and if now it had become painfully real, it should yet be kept at a distance! Never would they admit to each other their fear of the winter. They might complain themselves of small things – of the tea, for instance – but they must never voice to each other any mortal dread. Yet though they never mentioned it, each knew that the other did not sleep for long through those interminable winter nights. It was too cold, so near the roof. Outside the bare branches would be swaying and creaking in the wind. The bridge would surely be blown away one night. At about ten a cab would rumble over it in a leisurely manner. And then for hours there would be no sound except that of the striking clocks – it would be too quiet, except for that icy sound. The sound was so cold, it was like touching iron rails in a frost. It almost froze the ears, and the brain within. Certainly it gave them a head-ache. The station clock would start first: the four quarters, and then the hour; but a fairly cheerful, business-like sound. Then would toll out the others in a sequence, each following at an interval of a few seconds. Each one would strike the four quarters and then the hour; and for all the clocks audible in the town to strike midnight took up a full quarter of an hour. St Catherine's would knell eastward with its deep bell; Christchurch would sound near by, scolding and shrewish. St Thomas would be angry and foreboding, Holy Trinity surprised. The hour was tolled out as if in sorrow: perhaps a worse one was coming in. Sleep was at an infinite distance, beyond the sound of bells and the touch of cold iron bars. Their minds were waking. They were living, and it was cold.

Then the winter days, though actually so short, seemed both long and cold; and the landlady was not at all a nice woman, very impolite. In time they grew to avoid Mrs Snaggs whenever it was possible. When they passed-by they would hear her laughing and giggling. She was not respectful. 'Goodness, what sights!' they would hear her say.

No longer could they go to concerts or bazaars, nor were they ever asked to knit anything for the Christchurch sale-of-work. It was too tiring to go out for a long walk, and too cold to stay in. They had been forced to give up the lending-library: thus that stroll, which would have given them something to do, was barred to them; and if they stayed at home, they had no books to read. Except that Mrs Snaggs had once lent them a copy of *The Family Herald.* And Mr Garrett was very kind and had offered to continue their subscription until better times came. But they could not accept his offer; it would not be the right thing to do. And then Mr Garrett was altering; his waxed moustache was very untidy, his hair dishevelled, he had a vacant eye. Things were going badly with him, too. Newborough was altering. The new big chemist's at the corner had started a lending-library; and things were not prospering with the smaller shops. Drink was a dreadful thing, but they could understand it. Poor little man! He had always been so kind and respectful. No, it was no good staying-in unless the weather forced them to do so. A little walk in the streets, but not in the main streets. People stared so.

Alas! there was some excuse for the staring. Now that there was no one to look after their clothes, hats, and boots, the two sisters presented a more than ever extraordinary spectacle. The dresses, getting daily more antiquated in their design, were yet as gorgeous in colour, and were still fluttering with torn ribbons and cobweb-like lace, but draggled, torn and untidy. Their hats had acquired shapes that could only be described as grotesque; their bronze buttoned-boots were dirty and worn down; but cheek and hair still burnt with an unnatural and unsteady flame.

One day two little boys followed them right up to Miss Waddington's door, making fun of them. It was too bad! Every fortnight they paid this, their only visit in the town, to old Miss Waddington. They would arrive in time for tea. At first, going so near their old house was very painful to them. They would ring the bell, and the maid, Elsie, would open the door, leave them waiting in the small hall between the two doors for some little time, and then usher them into the drawing-room. In the winter, when the blinds were drawn, it reminded them so much of the drawing-room at the Red House. A fire burnt brightly under a solid white-marble mantelpiece, on which were several photographs in rococo silver frames and a solid white-marble clock. On each side of this were a Dresden shepherd and shepherdess. But the old lady was 'artistic,' and there were several ferns, especially little ones, in art-pots, green merging into yellow-ochre. There was usually, in the winter, a silver vase, shaped like a small trumpet with a crinkled edge, full of jonquils, so pretty and bright, like the spring; nice comfortable arm-chairs, and a sofa, full of dark green silk cushions, with large frills.

Sometimes Miss Waddington would not be well enough to come down herself, and her niece would give them tea instead – such good Ceylon tea. The niece was not exactly pretty, but bright-looking: yes, that was the word, bright-looking: people said she was 'clever.' 'Aunt Hester is not so well to-day,' she would say as she came in, 'and has asked me to entertain you for her'; and then, before they answered as if entering a preliminary defence, she would add quickly: 'How well you both look. I am sure they must make you very comfortable in your lodgings. I saw Mrs Snaggs the other day, such a clean, sensible, respectable-looking woman!' Tea would be brought in, many small cakes and scones. And finally, after a visit lasting from half-an-hour to three-quarters, they would get up to go, and would be handed an envelope containing a cheque for one pound. No other visitors ever disturbed these tea-parties.

As a rule, though, Miss Waddington would make a special effort to be there herself to talk to them. She thought that she really must be getting quite fond of the two Misses Cantrell-Cooksey; at any rate she enjoyed their visits. Perhaps they were nicer since their misfortunes – but they were certainly rather odd. She was, therefore, not 'at-home' to other friends. No, Emily.

There would be a preliminary coughing and wheezing upstairs and in the hall. The door would open, and the dear old lady, with a white shawl round her shoulders, would totter in, shivering as if it were very cold. Miss Frederica and Miss Fanny found it rather difficult to talk to her. Indeed, the former lady seldom spoke now, even to her younger sister. Besides, what was there to talk about! They had seen so little and done so little. There remained in the summer the weather and the visitors, in the winter the weather. Or Miss Waddington would try to impart a little religious consolation to them, endeavour to make them go to church again, for latterly they had given up going to Christchurch. Certainly, Miss Waddington reflected, as they left the house with their envelope, they were getting very odd, very odd indeed. But after they left she felt better than she had done all day. Kindly and charitable; and at the same time the room had grown brighter, the fire warmer. It was a terrible thing, to gamble!

And the two Misses Cantrell-Cooksey would be walking, under cover of the winter darkness, back across the suspension-bridge to their high back window in the tall white house.

Apart from their fortnightly call, the chief thing they looked forward to in the winter was their walk on the sands, away from the town. They grew to look forward to this event of the day with more and more pleasure. Even when the north-east wind blew straight from the top of Norway, they would sit on a rock, impervious to any chill, and converse with their friends, who would, if there had not been a storm, be gathering their winkles and limpets. If there had been a gale, on the other hand, they would be engaged in the more exciting task of combing the gold sands. Excitement would flare up again in the eyes of the two old ladies as they watched the sea-hoard being uncovered. And, though they were now no longer able to distribute shillings, the men who lived by this strange employment were, even when a little the worse for drink, so kind and respectful. They treated these two poor old bundles of bones, decked out in their torn fine feathers, as if they still lived on the West Cliff. They even appeared to regard them as human beings. And, to the men's great credit, they never allowed their pity to obtrude itself.

The summer was not so difficult. The town was full of visitors and cheerful sounds; while, at low tide, they could walk under the wall of the terrace where the band played, and hear it quite well. And if they kept close to the wall they could not be recognised from above by people leaning over – though once Mrs Sibmarsh caught a glimpse of them from one of the gaps – like the intervals between battlements – in the wall. It gave her quite a turn. Still pretending to be young – and to be rich, she supposed – dressed up like that. They didn't behave like poor people; so stuck up; and one ought to cut one's cloth ... oughtn't one? Their eyes were worse than ever. There could be no doubt about it. They must drug ... morphia ... cocaine ... though how they could get it without money, she didn't know. It was positively disgraceful.

The sands themselves were so crowded with mothers and children, nurses and children, donkeys and pierrots and ice-cream carts, so vibrating under the reflected lights of sea and pool and sky, that the presence of the two sisters attracted but little attention there, except once; when, advancing near a group waiting round an empty platform, they were asked what time the performance began. After that they began to avoid the sands, until the winter brought loneliness back to them. Yet curiously enough, they made no effort to quieten their clothes, or to subdue the colouring of hair and cheek. Though cosmetics were costly, they clung to them. For, once they let these pretences die, with them would perish the last vestige of self-respect. Their eccentricity had turned into this extreme patience, and into the final agonising pretence that all was as it should be.

They had almost lost count of time. How many years was it? The most definite fact in their lives was a continual dread of the coming winter, the cold, the cold! The long winter nights closed round them. And there was nothing to do but lie awake, for they had no books, and they must save the cost of lighting.

And this November Miss Fanny began, suddenly, to notice a change in Frederica, something vague in her manner. All one night she muttered to herself, and the next day, coming up from downstairs, Miss Fanny found her crying. She did not feel very well, that was all. Appearances were a heavy burden, a difficult load. How was she to keep it up?

It was an extravagance, she knew, but would Fanny mind fetching her a small bottle of sal-volatile from the chemist? Yes, it was only a headache, but a rather severe one. It would be gone by dinner. Miss Fanny walked out with the money to Hoare & Blunt, the chemists. Mrs Snaggs, downstairs in the empty house – for in the winter there were no guests – heard Miss Frederica calling her. It was really too bad! One might be a slave, running up and downstairs with nothing to do except look after those two. Miss Fanny, indeed! For Miss Cantrell-Cooksey had asked Mrs Snaggs to tell Miss Fanny, when she returned, not to worry. She was just going out for a walk, and might not be back for a little time. She was fully decorated, a-jingle with ribbons and ornaments, while a hat, gorgeous but flattened and out of shape, crowned it all. Under her arm was a brown-paper parcel. Mrs Snaggs looked at her in amazement, and then went back to the kitchen. She did not actually hear her go out, but, though angry, gave Miss Fanny the message when the latter came in muttering, and making the most of the two flights of stairs she had been forced to come up by panting in a hollow, owl-like way. Miss Fanny stood with her back to the door, talking to Mrs Snaggs for a few seconds. Just then there was the sound of a gathering crowd outside on the bridge, and looking back out of the door Miss Fanny saw a murmuring circle of black-coated men and a few women backing away toward the other side of the road, with white, mask-like faces. Within the circle Miss Frederica's clothes were lying in a heap. She had gone out for her last walk. She had stepped, fully-dressed, with a brown-paper parcel under her arm, straight out of that high window on to the stone pavement below. She must have had to bend down to get out of it. In the parcel were a black-bound Prayer Book and the few old photographs that belonged to her. But she had kept up appearances.

*

Miss Fanny did not really feel it much. There was the inquest, and then the funeral; a great deal of activity! Mrs Snaggs had given her the message. And she often sits up quite late expecting Frederica to return, till the light in her eyes equals the flame of cheek and hair.

I last saw her at low tide, one winter morning, dressed in a white-flannel costume (a new departure for her) and very much made-up. She must really be old by now. There had been a storm, and she was sitting on a rock talking to the men who were raking over the pebbly edges of the sands and watching them capture their strange treasure. They found that morning a William-and-Mary gold piece; a small chest covered with rusty iron nails and green with age, with nothing in it; a small box, hermetically sealed, of China tea; a straw ship in a glass bottle, and two George IV four-shilling pieces.

FRIENDSHIP'S DUE

Some have for wits, and then for poets passed,
Turned critic next, and proved plain-fool at last.
ALEXANDER POPE

To Muriel Draper

IT was on a particularly crystalline morning in the early spring, after street and square had been cleansed for a while of their flowing smoke-draperies by the splashing and tintinnabulation of a hundred country-scented showers, that I was first enabled – compelled even – to observe the hero of this story. The omnibus, empty save for myself, glided smoothly on its way, and from the level of the middle branches flung out by the fine old trees that still linger in the lower part of King's Road, Chelsea – old trees, though edged now with fresh green lacings, on which the distilled moisture glistened like so many fragments of crystals, echoing back the various hard lights refracted by the wall-topping of broken glass – I could watch the antics of my kind.

Suddenly there sounded a muddled hurricane of hurrying, rather clumsy, feet; but to my surprise only one person, to whom, as to Jove, these thunder-bolts must have belonged, was precipitated on to the seat opposite as the omnibus sailed, red and proud as a turkey-cock, round the corner. Thus were we isolated on our noisy moving trestle, set halfway between the tree-tops and the ant-like world below. My fellow passenger enjoyed the fresh air, obviously; yet it seemed somehow as if he regretted the absence of the larger, more appreciative audience which, at this time of the morning, he had the right to expect. Was he, then, with his obvious love of public notice, an actor? In any case he did not look like a prosperous one, but undoubtedly there lurked in his eyes the expectation that he would be recognised. In a sense he resembled an old-fashioned player. He possessed, superlatively, that air of dominion by which it is possible to single out the stage favourite – and even more, perhaps, the stage failure. Yet though his appearance was highly accentuated, it was hardly sufficiently so for an actor; he was like an old 'But-me-no-buts' ranter, seen through the minimising glass of a *Punch* drawing. Still, if he belonged to the stage, he was a ranter, and not a naturalistic-whimsical-charm-schooler.

His face was heavy; not fat, but heavily boned. Yellowish in colour, it seemed to be supported on the two sharp points of a high white collar – higher in front than at the back – round which was twice wound a large black tie. This apparatus helped to define the prominent nose and protuberant mouth which, when open, displayed strong bony teeth that suggested a Scottish origin. His hair, black and lank, flowed a little over the back of his worn fur-collar, while in the buttonhole of the stylised but anciently-cut blue-cloth coat he affected, sprouted that small bunch of faded violets that was, in truth, the freshest thing about him. A dandified cane was held in one hand, and with the ochreous black-tipped fingers of the other he was continually rattling and scratching the dull-gilt interior of a large silver cigarette case, which lay open on his knees, taking out a cigarette, lighting it, and then throwing it away. These convolutions, obviously, were intended either to draw attention to himself, or by their familiarity to secure his recognition from others better informed than myself as to the genius of the day. Could it be, he hoped I was thinking, could it be the famous man-of-letters – the poet? ... But, unfortunately, my mind had wandered along the wrong track, and I was busily scanning my memory for the faces of actors in the old Lyceum dramas.

How, in any case, could he have expected me to think of him, in these days and without a knowledge of his identity, as a poet? It would have been a survival almost too interesting and absorbing ... for though I have known many poets (and already wish that such had not been my privilege) I have never encountered one by whose face could be distinguished his calling. Well-shaven, clean, and short-haired, the poet of to-day resembles a prosperous business man; but, and I ought to have recognised it, here was that unique Victorian survival, 'the poet's brow'! Under the grey felt hat, black-banded, bony ridges and angular wrinkles dwindled down from beneath the greasy locks to an almost horse-like nose. Perhaps, if my mind had not been otherwise occupied, I might, on the strength of nose, teeth, and hair, have diagnosed a critic – but never should I have dared to hope for a poet – for I have seen many decorative critics with curly hair, pince-nez, and an earnest look. But, as I afterwards discovered, this was Ferdinand H. McCulloch, a former writer of verse, and a critic who is still allowed to thunder denunciations of modern poetry in various twopenny-weekly or halfpenny-daily papers.

Now because the hero of this tragi-comedy is a critic (but remember that he is a poet as well), and even though I have been so old-fashioned as to head my sermon with a text (an instinct dormant in the right hand of every author of our Puritan race), it must not be concluded that I am so antiquated as to indulge in any attempt at throwing the slightest shadow of ridicule upon the critical calling. That I leave to the poets who have gone before me; for such an attempt at it on my part would be ungenteel, unnecessary and injudicious, insomuch as I am here on my trial, and to throw a boot at the jury, however unbiased they may wish to appear, would be an act little calculated to prejudice them in my favour. Nor, perhaps, is the quotation that precedes this story altogether apposite, for in this serious age of coordination and psycho-analysis no wit would ever be taken for a poet, while the link between humour and criticism appears to be even more frail – only to be found, in fact, in the eye of the watching poet. For, as our text shows, and this is my excuse for embroidering such a theme, it has long been the custom of poets to watch with interest the critical hoop-revolving of their span – a span which this hoop-revolving has so often helped to shorten.

When an epigram becomes a platitude (the Hell to which all epigrams are eventually condemned) the truth is no longer in it; and that critics are but disappointed poets has long been a platitude. In these days, on the contrary, they are the only satisfied ones, able both to confer the cake and then, subsequently, eat it themselves. Curiously enough, too, though the critic is popularly supposed to have a more logical mind, to wield a more consistent pen than the poet's, it is a fact that while critical opinion is still divided as to the comparative merits of our more famous English bards, the judgment of the latter as to the critical opinion of their day appears to have been nearly identical. Could a written testimonial be obtained from the shades of, let us say, Dryden, Pope, Coleridge, Gray, Keats, Wordsworth, Shelley, Byron, Swinburne, and from their heirs, the worst-sellers of to-day, it is probable that though the words would differ with the individual, the purport which this varying language would serve to illumine, or perhaps for the sake of decency to obscure, would be found on examination to be remarkably alike in every case. Some poets have even gone so far as to pretend that there must be more than a casual connection between the decay of poetry, which criticism has from its birth detected, and that rise of the professional critic which was apparently coincident with this disintegration. But, for myself, I prefer to think that this gradual falling-away of the English muse is due to the fact that the better, nobler, more serious minds among us are tempted from the profession of poetry alone toward the higher, more lucrative one of journalism; for, as many critics have themselves informed us lately and in print, their contribution to literature is, in reality, one of more importance than that of the creative mind, whether poet's or prose-writer's – the shadow more lasting than the substance, the parasite more interesting and enduring than the victim on which it thrives! Then, too, one has to live ... Reviewing, compared with the profession of poetry, is a well-paid one; and, as for that, the wielding of a critical pen need not prevent an occasional 'banging of the tins' (i.e. TREES – BREEZE; WOOD – GOOD – GOD; LARK–HARK; WIND – SPIN'D – BLIND), provided that it is a simple one, and may, indeed, procure for that music a more favourable reception than it would otherwise be awarded.

No one then, it is established, has a greater respect for the professional critic than the writer of this homily – because for a man to surrender the unravelling of his own mind and soul (unless these be tedious ones) in order to tear off the draperies concealing those of other people must be an act of noble altruism and Christian abnegation. And to make a personal confession let it be recorded that it is impossible to admire more than I do the weekly pursuit of Dostoieffsky and Tchekhoff through the Fourth Dimension conducted by the Ariel-like mind of Mr Muddleton Moral; while after Mr Jack Daw's revelation of the dormant beauties in the verse of Mrs Hemans, I, too, can only cry 'Excelsior!' and am the more prepared for the perception of these same qualities in his own – at first sight – strangely different subject-poems, *Soccer* and *The Slaughter-House*. Excelsior, indeed! For when these distinguished critics, very busy men, find time to use the antiquated medium of verse, yet never fail in a twice-weekly-and-once-on-Sunday donative of buns and ginger-beer to their protégés, or even an occasional laurel for the fallen (from whom no rivalry need be feared), my admiration knows no bounds.

If, then, this story is headed with a text, it is because that unpleasant and needlessly spiteful couplet, though no doubt useless as a generalisation, helps to explain something in this particular instance. For though the suicide of a minor poet would, as being an example of cause-and-effect, excite little interest, to poets the suicide of a critic – even his attempted self-destruction – would be a matter for wonder. The critic, in the exercise of his calling, commits a thousand attempts, successful or unsuccessful, at literary murder, and goes unpunished; yet if he were to attempt his own death – and fail – he would be tried; and possibly punished, for endeavouring to take his own life. And how curious is the law's accusation of a man for attempting suicide, when obviously his crime (except in cases of incurable disease) must be, not his failure to die but the confession of his failure to live, which is what attempted suicide amounts to! But of this a man is never accused, for this never punished.

*

Even as late as the year 1907 the name of Ferdinand H. McCulloch was one to conjure with in the more serious salons of West Hampstead. His reign had then lasted about ten years. For it was in the late 'nineties, only a few years before the armed might of the Great Transvaal Republic threw down its gauntlet to the people of these little islands, that our hero, already and always his own impresario, made his bow to the London public. He was then about thirty years of age, and but recently escaped from – though this was a secret hidden even from his appointed biographer – Ulster! There he had received a very Orange upbringing at the hands of three gaunt, rigorous maiden aunts, for his father, a clergyman, had died before Ferdinand could remember him, and his mother had married again. For this sin against the Victorian moral code the Misses McCulloch had never forgiven her; and devoted to the memory of their late brother, they succeeded in wresting the infant from her (she did not, in reality, seem very unwilling to part with him), and then brought him up in the same stern family tradition that had made themselves and their brother what they were. But Ferdinand, and this was in his favour, proved a difficult child. Nothing could be done with him. The Church, even, was out of the question. But he must earn his own living; so, as a very young man, a boy even, he scraped together a few pounds by writing what, we believe, are technically known as "fashionable pars' for the Belfast papers. It cannot be said that the Misses McCulloch approved of this; but it brought in a little money and kept him out of mischief. Ferdinand, for his part, was thoroughly frightened of his aunts, and would have welcomed anything that took him out of their clutches. Soon the glamour of London and of the escape it meant cast its spell on him, and he began to dream of the city he had never seen. Latterly he had been reading the lives of great men – an interesting study, no doubt, but one perilous for youth, and still more fraught with danger for the elders of the house. The life of Michelangelo, for example, is responsible for more trouble between budding artists and – if such a person still exists – art-patron than is imaginable. In that school it is that the Slade student learns with surprising ease the importance, not of being an artist, which is, after all, the fact that really matters about Michelangelo, but of being disagreeable, grasping and rude. Similarly, lives of Napoleon and Lord Byron have unforeseen and deplorable consequences; while we are told that every dirty and uncouth versifier at the universities, should he occasionally get a little drunk, excuses it by announcing that he is the reincarnation of Verlaine – or (even at this date!) of Dowson! Luckily Ferdinand had got no further than the Borgias, Michelangelo, Napoleon and Byron. Still, he was determined to be a great man, perhaps more of a Byron than a Bonaparte; and for the accomplishment of this design he must be daring and a little wicked.

How, then, was he to do it? For though it is easy to be unpleasant anywhere, it is difficult to be a Borgia in Belfast. What is more, the gaunt and triple headed spectre of the Misses McCulloch guarded, like Cerberus, the mouth of any possible Hell, ferociously barking. There was, of course, only one thing to be done – to escape to London as soon as he found a chance of doing so. After that it would be easy. Only one obstacle would then interpose between Ferdinand and Lord Byron – the writing of verse, and this was an impediment he was determined to overcome.

It must be five years before we meet Ferdinand again; five years must elapse between his escape and his transfiguration.

In those days two traditions strove and clashed together in the drawing-rooms of artistic ladies, for the shadow of the Celtic twilight, destined later to attain the density of a London fog, already lay heavy on the suburbs, and the Voice of Cuchulain was uplifted in Liberty's Drapery Department, or wailed through Soho; while older, but competing with it, although perhaps already a little losing ground, was the influence of Ernest Dowson. In many gatherings of 'modern young people' the mist wafted from the Land of Heart's Desire would be rent in twain, as an even then slightly old-fashioned 'advanced' young woman would rise to thunder 'Cynara,' or a romantic-looking young undergraduate from Oxford would proclaim, and reiterate, that he had been faithful to the lady in his own fashion. Alas! these things are altered: the daughter of the 'advanced' young woman, her hair cut short like a pony's mane, now plays the more intricate game of complex-and-inhibition with the romantic young man's son (who, like all the young men of to-day, has a post on the *League of Nations*), and the leaden weight of *The London Mercury* now rests on those slender tables upon which had once been laid the grotesque beauty of Beardsley's drawings.

Into this mingled atmosphere of a wet-Sunday-afternoon

on the Irish Lakes and Greek Passion, which we have attempted to outline, out of the harder, more material light that beats upon the city-ways of Belfast, stepped Mr Ferdinand McCulloch. But it was a Ferdinand transfigured, for like a chameleon he had absorbed both the colour and tone of his new surroundings – and had already composed numerous sets of verses! The clean, callow, tweed-clad, large-boned, Ulster-mouthed boy had flowered into what in those days was known as a 'Real Bohemian,' a dashing yet dreamy-eyed figure, full of psychic qualities and the charm of the Southern-Irish people. He sported now, for the first time, that bunch of violets to which he still clings; his black hair became lank and matted, his finger-nails were allowed to grow longer, while his formerly harsh voice became almost too soft and dove-like, for he had developed what he yet considers to be a very attractive brogue. Ulster, with its business-habits, worldly outlook, and stern Puritanism, he placed behind him, becoming – or rather pretending that he had always been – Catholic, Celtic, and sometimes, we regret to say, a little Twilight. For in the very advanced taverns, like caves, which he frequented, it was necessary occasionally, for the sake of his reputation, to plunge through the purple mists of wine. After midnight he could sometimes be seen stumbling out of his cave, like Caliban, his hair tousled, his feet a little uncertain. Once too (and it made him a memorable figure) McCulloch met Dowson in a cab-shelter. It is true that the latter poet did not pay much attention to him, hardly, indeed, appeared to see him; but it gave our hero an aura, created a legend that clung, so that years afterwards, as with head held up, and a winsome smile hung across the protuberant cavity of his mouth, he entered a room, there would be a rustling whisper of, 'You know ... the friend of Dowson's!'

Though McCulloch was not a clever man – in the sense that few ideas visited him – yet his hold on one, when once he had grasped it, was singularly tenacious. Quite early in his career he managed to pin down one principle of success – that lesson about which we heard so much, twenty years later, from the weekly preachers in Sunday papers – the VALUE of CO-OPERATION and UNITY. It will be remembered by those who succeeded in living through the 'Great War,' that our Best Minds, in the course of 'giving one furiously to think,' founding bond-clubs, or 'exploring avenues,' announced constantly that the war had not been fought in vain if we learnt the 'Value of Co-operation' – a lesson, it appeared, well worth the losing of a few hundred thousand lives. There would be no more strikes or disturbances; the workman, in the sacred cause of unity, would always give way; and a maypole and morris dance would flourish once more in the congenial atmosphere of Sheffield, Birmingham, Manchester. Well, McCulloch realised the value of co-operation and unity at an early date; and it was his own discovery. In fact, he formed what would now be known – according to whether you liked or disliked its members – as 'an interesting little group of thinkers,' or a 'clique.' There is, by the way, I believe, supposed to be something peculiarly disgraceful about a 'clique' – and if a book by someone you dislike happens to be well-received, you should invariably describe its success as being the work of a 'little clique.' Ferdinand's 'clique' was a small one, consisting, as it did, of three members. For the other two he chose, wisely, Arthur Savage Beardsall, an amiable minor poet, of rather bad health, a little real talent, and a certain slapdash facility combined with an admirable aptitude for posing, and T. W. Frendly, a poor but intensely energetic little Cockney journalist. In appearance Beardsall was slight, short, and bearded – the dark beard disguising his want of chin and look of ill-health – and Frendly, with his beady little eyes, was dapper, small and sharp as a sparrow, while his voice would trail off unexpectedly into a high Cockney accent.

His simple mind was intensely impressed with the genius of his two companions, and he reserved all his energy for the preaching of their gospel. In this association of three friends his was the humble part; he would listen admiringly, collect their epigrams and sayings, repeat them on every occasion, learn their poems by heart, recite them, and generally do an immense amount of clique and claque work. He might be described, indeed, as their boom-companion.

Beardsall, McCulloch and Frendly became inseparable; they would lunch together, dine together, and toward the end of an evening get a little drunk together. They would write, even when seeing each other every day, 'Posterity-letters'* to the other members of their clique – or rather Beardsall or McCulloch would write them to Frendly, whom they had tacitly appointed as their biographer.

Each of the three would quote, praise, imitate, caricature the two others, and finally write articles about their work, though to get either the former or the latter writings printed, it was first necessary for a review – expensive but short lived – to be started by the richer members of their as yet limited circle of admirers. For gradually there formed round this nucleus an outer circle of Admirers of the Misunderstood. The leaders of it, who lent a little feminine grace to the gatherings, were Mrs Stilpepper and Miss Ellen Durban. Juliet Stilpepper, small, dark, and rather pretty, known among her friends for the charm of her speaking voice and laughter, was the wife of that well-known artist, whose problem picture at the Academy in 1897, depicting

* Letters written by minor poets for posthumous publication to friends whom they can trust to print them. For this purpose should be chosen a rather old, distinguished critic, who will at once understand what is wanted and whose position guarantees that after his death (which, with any luck, cannot be far distant) all the letters he has put away will be published by a literary executor, or a still younger minor poet, who can be depended upon to treasure the letters, and publish them subsequently for the sake of his own importance.

a woman in leg-of-mutton sleeves and a straw hat, kneeling down on a sandy beach, her face wet with tears, with one hand pointing to an enormous orang-outang, the other to a whale spouting water – the whole composition entitled *The Mother of the Gracchi* – caused such a sensation. Her salon was famous throughout Hampstead. Within the hospitable red-brick house one would meet prominent exponents of Woman's Rights (not yet become notorious as Suffragettes), a few Fabians, many Irish and neo-Greek poets, a few lesser stage celebrities, and, later on, numerous hysterical admirers of Mr Stephen Phillips. Between the latter and McCulloch's group there was an incessant, deadly warfare. But in these battles their hostess always gave her valuable aid to the three friends; for if they prospered, how much the greater would be her credit for discovering them. It was a gamble – an outside chance; but she meant to win. This, then, was the chief platform upon which our three characters disported themselves before an appreciative audience of young ladies shod in sandals, and crowned with dusty golden hair, whose curving necks still showed a trace of the gradually disappearing Pre-Raphaelite goitre. To this latter class belonged their other chief supporter, Ellen Durban, whose sandals betrayed her as one of the first, last – and alas! least successful – of classical dancers.

Juliet Stilpepper and Ellen Durban, the earliest and most fervent disciples of the three friends, soon began to feel that their faith had been justified; for the clique began to arrive at a certain importance. Beardsall's small, easy, meretricious talent was winning him a wider recognition – shedding even on the other two a certain lustre, which at the time could not be distinguished as a borrowed radiance, but appeared to emanate from themselves. This recognition was just enough to make the clique a matter of wonder, but not sufficient to deprive its members of their prerogative of feeling ill-used, neglected, and misunderstood; while it seldom occurred to them that, had they really been good poets, they would be objects, not of interest, but of ridicule. Their lives, and carefully-prepared little eccentricities, helped them too, with their special public. From the taverns and clubs where they spent their evenings the rumour of their Tiberian but really very innocent orgies would spread excitement through Hampstead, or flicker like marsh-fire through Chelsea. By this time they had all bought brown velvet jackets, with a sash round the waist, and large romantic black hats. Beardsall had in his room a skull out of which he pretended to drink (this must have been a recollection of some life of Byron which he, too, had read as a boy), while McCulloch had, hung round one of the brass knobs of his bed, a long necklace, made of vertebræ torn from the skeleton of a man, stained purple, and looking in reality rather like the free-wheel chain of a bicycle after an accident. Much of their time, when not occupied in praising one another or laughing in a hollow Homeric manner, was spent in contemplation of suicide. Only after death – they felt – would their genius be fully recognised, while the more sudden and violent their end, the more effective for their posthumous glory. Cups of poison, a fall to the crowd below from the Nelson Monument, the lily-green death-look of Chatterton, the decline of Keats, a cloaked figure found floating on the Thames, a revolver-shot in Piccadilly followed by a dramatic collapse, or the quieter, less sensational, but sudden 'Strange Death of a Literary Recluse' – all these passed through their minds, were mentioned in low tones or lay hidden, for all to read, in the intentionally gloomy fire of their eyes. But the chorus of sandal-footed and golden-crowned young ladies implored them constantly to remember their families – not to do anything rash – though perhaps these same young women found that the thought of it gave them, too, no less than the three protagonists, a little tremor of wonder, excitement, and importance. In their less exalted moments, however, the chance of getting this thrill in real life seemed ever so remote – merely a dream of fair women.

But, to return to our hero, Ferdinand was by now turning out stanza after stanza, poem after poem, and in these masterpieces very cleverly backed both popular favourites at the same time, for while in feeling they were fervently pagan, full of wine and roses, full of the free-life of the Greeks as seen through the dusty spectacles of the 'nineties, they were yet addressed to a dreamy deity, implored by the poet as 'Dark Rosaleen' – or when it became necessary to find a rhyme for 'Thee,' as 'Rosalee'; later, he was even clever enough to mingle with these other ingredients, neo-classic or Irish, a little of the epic touch conveyed by Mr Stephen Phillips. Very poignant were these odes, and the Belfast accent made manifest in them was audible only to Hibernian ears. 'Oh, Mr McCulloch,' they would importune in the salons set on the hills, 'do recite that one ... you know ... ' At first he would refuse, gracefully refuse, offering instead to read them a short lyric by Beardsall, but in the end he would always yield and recite to them his favourite poems, which, as with many other poets, luckily happened to be his own. Sometimes he would refuse to declaim without a harp accompaniment from Mrs Stilpepper. 'It reminds me of Erin,' he would say, and while Juliet's slender fingers would draw out the syrupy music from the strings, he would wail scarcely recognisable words in a gloomy, pathetic, almost frightening way, or sing on one note in a winsome, tenderly caressing manner. 'Doesn't it make you understand *them*?' the earnest, enthusiastic band of young women would remark rather vaguely.

As he stood in the centre of the room, with eyes half closed, his face, framed in by its dark hair, and balanced over the two points of his high white – still white - collar, seemed to have little connection with the short, thick-set body below. Hanging there, among dusty green velvet curtains and the spreading host of little pieces of pseudo-Oriental china, that surged in blue-and-white foam over the walls, tables, and piano, it seemed but a large mask for his voice. Through the mouth, with its too prominent lips and teeth, came the warm high tones and winning pronunciation – tricks which, as he intended them to do, prejudiced many women in his favour, and secured him a few life-long friends: friends who would have remained faithful to the end – if only there had been one! Thus Ferdinand, his boots planted uneasily in the Celtic twilight, his head bathed in the sunshine of the growing garden cities, spent many pleasurable years, passing through the long level plateau of early manhood with his two friends beside him.

*

When the suicide of one of these three did occur, it came with the greatest shock of all, the shock of the long-discussed and half-expected; for when something long talked-about, and even long prepared, happens – as was the case with the European War – then surprise overwhelms one. Beardsall, on a short holiday from his journalistic duties, and possibly from his friends, was found shot dead in the bedroom of a small, shabby hotel in Paris. Ferdinand, Frendly, and his group of admirers were overwhelmed with sorrowing astonishment. His death was, perhaps, a greater tragedy than any of them imagined, since the end of this poor, tired, ill, little man may have been due, not so much to poverty, weariness, or ill-health, *or* to the feeling that he was an unappreciated genius, as to his recognition of the fact that he possessed very little real talent, and that his reputation was already out of proportion to it. For a long time he must have felt the strain of being forced to carry more than he could bear. It was in August that his death took place, and one hardly likes to think of him wandering about in the city with its holiday air. To the English, accustomed to London, there must be always something heartless and too logical about Paris, a quality that must make even death more hard to bear. The streets, set out for the pageant of a vulgar imperialism that has long been swept away, are like a plutocratic feast prepared years ago for some swindling financier, a feast that still remains dusty and untouched. The architecture, always hard, logical, and equal, is nowhere as good as London's best, nowhere as bad as London's worst. The large stony gardens, set with hundreds of statues that lack the wistful, unconscious humour of our togaed senators, or Achilles Monument, are emptier than usual, and the sun beats fiercely down upon them, while the idyllic, rich tranquillity and falling green shadows of the Bois only mock the lives of the poor, reminding them of the hateful contrast between farmhouse and city-slum, garden and tenement, rich and poor. In this smooth-faced, very luxurious city, the poor little poet's fate overcame him; he was in his room for some two hours before he died. We know nothing of his thoughts during those two long hours that preceded him into eternity, as he walked about in that small, hot, gloomy bedroom.

After the first shock had passed for the two survivors of the clique and their friends, a period of intense activity set in. First of all there were obituary notices to be penned, articles on Beardsall's life, accounts of his death to be written, then his literary remains to be edited, and many poems and letters to be published. How well, and with what kindness, the dead man had played his part, for in all the letters, and even in most of the poems, were affectionate references or glorious tributes to Ferdinand and Frendly. Finally came the great work, *The Life and Letters of Arthur Savage Beardsall*, by T. W. Frendly and Ferdinand H. McCulloch, profusely illustrated, and issued by a famous publishing house at a guinea net.

This book was a masterpiece of judicious booming. Frendly did the hard work, McCulloch embellished it; and as far as the latter was concerned it was a truer form of autobiography than many to which we have lately been treated. Affectionate references to him appeared in nearly every letter, while not only did our hero-editor include in the volume, poems, letters, jokes, epigrams, and denunciations of his own, but there were almost as many photographs of him as of Beardsall, and whenever the latter appeared in group or caricature, there, at his side, was the very easily recognisable face of Ferdinand! After the publication of this *Life*, the dead poet's work received a wider recognition than he had ever hoped or deserved, so that in country-houses, when conversation had ebbed, the artistic member of the house-party would say, 'I suppose you knew Arthur Beardsall?' and point to a book lying uncut on the table. But, oddly enough, Ferdinand McCulloch's fame did not appear to grow similarly, or to the extent expected of it.

During the two or three years taken up by this juggling of life, letters, and poems, there were, of course, many meetings between the two survivors of the group and their old friends. At first our hero was seen – if anything more often than formerly – in Juliet Stilpepper's drawing-room, or in the salons of the other artistic ladies; though, whereas at one time he had always been asked to recite his own poems, he was now invariably requested, instead, to declaim those of his dead friend. Even Ellen Durban, formerly the most fervent admirer of his Muse, now only asked him to recite Beardsall's work. The truth of the matter was that their friendship with a temporarily rather famous poet – and still more with one who had perished by his own hand – shed an unearthly radiance not only on Ferdinand (which halo cancelled out his own) but on all the friends, and especially on Mrs Stilpepper and Miss Durban. This was not at all what our hero had expected. Gradually he began to shun these parties, and would more frequently meet the ladies at some club or restaurant, pleading as excuse a growing absorption in literary criticism and journalism. But the truth is that he did not care much for gatherings at which he was no longer the chief personage, ousted always by the spectre of his dead friend. Frendly, or 'T.W.' as he called him, was still in constant attendance, doing as much propaganda as ever. Ferdinand's verses were yet to be met with in the pages of journals, but his signature seemed an omen of little prosperity, insomuch as his name printed – if only in the list of possible contributors – was a sure indication that this new review would live for one number only. By this time the world of the late 'nineties had pased with the Boer War, and we soon find ourselves in Mid-Edwardian days. The neo-classic form of verse, though still surviving – like everything else – at the universities, was dead elsewhere; the Irish twilight was beginning to deepen into night; and signs began to appear of a modern movement in English poetry, similar to that which had blossomed in France through the last few decades of the old century. And this new poetry attracted to itself all those who like – or liked to like – things modern, so that many of our hero's former admirers forsook him, and even neglected to read Beardsall. Ferdinand's verses appeared less and less often, and, instead, he wrote critical articles devoted to the iniquity of the new verse, and signed, impressively, 'Ferdinand H. McCulloch.' And what thunder of the Gods against modern decadence was contained in these prophetic messages, though he always attacked the less well-received, and therefore probably better, poets. For he would never attack popular idols, hoping always to obtain their favour. His abuse of those he dared to abuse only equalled his fulsome praise of those he dared not attack, whom he would describe as 'Standard-bearers' or 'Knights-of-the-Grail'! But what roused his ire especially was that quality described as 'obscurity' (the latter being anything he could not understand), and one could only conclude that to be an 'obscure' poet was somehow worse than to be an obscure journalist.

It must be admitted that, with the passage of time, Ferdinand's manner lost none of its jauntiness. On the contrary, he developed more and more that air of dominion we have noted, remaining faithful to all the developments of his personality. His long fingernails, the fingers stained orange with nicotine, still feverishly scratched the inside of his cigarette-case as he drew out a cigarette, lit it, threw it away. His long hair, bunch of violets, Irish brogue, high collar, and serpent-like tie were all in their pristine splendour. Constant he remained, as well, to his Lares and Penates; however often he changed his apartments, there you would find that necklace of purple-stained vertebræ, which had been hung round the end of how many lodging-house beds, and the skull-loving-cup which he had inherited from Arthur Beardsall. Only two alterations, apart from those which Time made for him, could be detected in his appearance. The collar was less white – had now more the tone and texture of vellum – while the velvet jacket and large black hat had been discarded for more sober garments, better befitting a critic and solid man-of-letters! The rest of his detail sufficiently proclaimed him a poet. Whatever the development of his personality or circumstances, our hero could be trusted to dramatise them for his friends.

Lately Frendly appeared to have been doing more propaganda for himself than for Ferdinand, and was in consequence prospering, for he was a sharp, active little man. This unexpected turn of events – or of the worm – annoyed McCulloch considerably, and, consequently, he saw less and less of 'T.W.' Other admirers, such as Juliet Stilpepper and Ellen Durban, clung to him; for now that the boom in Beardsall was beginning to decline, they remembered the second string to their bow. They cherished him, still expected something of him ... But what was it? – what could it be?

Ferdinand would never enter the salon now. He was determined never more to risk being asked to recite the poetry of another, and Mrs Stilpepper's harp lay there dim and golden as Ellen Durban's hair, its strings silent and untouched. Instead, then, of his going to these gatherings, the two ladies would meet him each week for luncheon in a little restaurant at the side of a narrow alley off Fleet Street. The meal was fixed, always, for the unusual, almost exciting, hour of 2.15. Ferdinand's office was round the corner, and though he occupied a rather subordinate position there, at each step away from it his importance grew visibly.

In the midsummer of which we are writing the sunlight falling through the leaves of the few scraggy trees in the court outside made a pattern of wavering golden disks, flat and round, on floor and pavement. It played, too, with rather terrifying effect on the faces of those eating, bringing out again the more dusty, less golden, tone of Ellen's hair, exaggerating her high cheek-bones, revealing her large bony feet shod in sandals, and contrived a whole set of tricks for poor Mrs Stilpepper's too sweet countenance. It magnified the pores and wrinkles, intensified the romantic lines, of Ferdinand's head, till one was reminded of Gulliver's horror when, lifted up to the level of the Brobdingnagian faces, he observed the pits, hollows, and furrows that graced them. In the room, too, the sunlight seemed to draw out the smell of stale food, to unmuffle the incessant noise. But not one of those present talked louder or more often than Ferdinand, though it was, in reality, quite unnecessary, as this little table of three people was in any case very noticeable; even Juliet, the most ordinary of the group, won public attention by her speaking voice, which, noted among her friends for its dulcet tones, was now almost too musical in its utterance. As for Ellen, her appearance could be trusted to gain attention anywhere, since with her large sandalled feet, big bones, general untidiness, and that cloudy crown of golden hair which had been – and still was – her pride, she now more resembled an animated haystack than a human being.

At the end of luncheon, when our hero leant back to light a cigarette, taking one with difficulty from that voluminous and dented silver case, drinking a cup of coffee – which, like the coffee in most English establishments, tasted alternately of meat-extract and iron dumb-bells – it was an experience to see his manner, as of a conqueror, at whose slightest word the journalistic world, here assembled, would quake. The ingratiating brogue slid on its oiled passage round the room, winging its easy way from table to table, so that all could hear; while invariably, at the end of the meal, would come the familiar menace of suicide. Year by year, month by month, these threats increased. But it almost seemed, as he continued to talk in this way, as if the expression on the faces of the two ladies brightened a little, for an instant became animated, as though instead of threatening them he had promised them something ... Ferdinand was too immersed in his own grievances, in the perpetual recitation of his troubles and ill-treatment, to notice any of these subtle, very slight, changes of expression. Perhaps it may have been due to some alteration in the falling lights and shadows dripping through the small branches of the trees outside. Yes, he was sick of it! he said ... absolutely sick of it! ... (and he would laugh in that hollow way) ... sick of it! Ellen and Juliet were, naturally, very upset. It would be too, too, dreadful – appalling – after all that had happened ... Still, of course, he was right in a way, in what he said, and they agreed with him that he would probably never be properly appreciated in his lifetime. After his death, undoubtedly, his reputation would stand higher, much higher. One couldn't doubt it. Look, for instance, at the posthumous appreciation of Beardsall, a friend of all of us, a good poet, certainly, Ferdinand, but no better than you are! But McCulloch, though looking rather pleased at this declaration of faith, would point out that such was the deterioration of the public taste that even Beardsall's fame stood less high than it did ten years ago, just after his death. 'I'm sick of it!' he would reiterate; 'I've nearly made up my mind to do it – sick of it all' ...

But, 'Oh, no,' they cried, 'he couldn't, he mustn't do it! He must think, not only of himself, but of his friends ... think how they would miss him, reminded at every turn by letters, poems, photographs ... might even be blamed.' ... (As they talked the colour came back a little to their faces.) After all, they might say it, mightn't they? Wasn't there something ... something due to friendship? Something? And as they continued to plead they experienced again that little thrill of wonder, expectation, and importance which had visited them after Beardsall's death. 'But promise us, swear to us, that you will never DO IT!' they cried.

'I won't promise now,' Ferdinand answered, 'but I will give you m' definite decision on Monday at this table, after luncheon. But in your turn y' must promise NOT to mention the subject to me till after the meal is over, for if it must be m' last, at least let it be a jolly one;" and soon after this the two ladies fluttered out into the open air, while Ferdinand, a grim look on his face, his chin upheld by the apparatus of tie and collar, slowly swaggered out after them.

Now it happened that on the Monday I witnessed the final scene of the drama; but, alas! the final scene was laid not at the end but in the middle of the tragedy, which may continue for another three decades after it should have finished.

Rather later than the usual luncheon-hour I went to the restaurant to meet a friend. The room was very full and noisy; there, at a table set for three persons, were seated two rather queer-looking middle-aged women. They were very quiet, hardly speaking to each other at all, but on their faces could be detected a slight flush of expectation, while in their eyes gleamed a fire which I had seen before in other eyes, but when? Then I recalled the faces of the older women-gamblers at Monte Carlo.

Presently there was borne in on us the sound of important footsteps outside, and a little man entered, with a large bony face and a high, not necessarily white, collar, round which was coiled twice a large black tie, like the Delphic serpent. In the buttonhole of his coat was a bunch of violets – or rather violas, for the former could not be obtained at this season; and I remembered, suddenly, my former meeting with him on the top of a motor-bus a year or two previously.

He wished his two friends, whose excitement had, in the meantime, obviously increased, a good-morning in his succulent Irish voice, ordered luncheon, and sat down with the air of a monarch, who sits down so that others need not stand. But, in spite of his importance, he seemed depressed. His two companions said little and ate less, but fever shone in eye and cheek. It was a rather gloomy affair, the luncheon, though it lasted long. The conversation was confined to politics and a certain amount of heartfelt condemnation of modern poetry. Only once, too, sounded out that hollow laugh. But it seemed to me, watching, that the excitement of his two companions was steadily increasing.

And, after the coffee, the little dark woman said, in a voice musical as a xylophone or a set of musical glasses: 'Well, have you decided ... Ferdinand? Tell us as quickly as you can; remember Our Suspense.' And, with a solemn expression, came the answer, in that rich tone, 'I have' (and after a long pause) 'I have decided ... NOT TO ... ! I give you m' word.'

The light faded out of their faces as they thanked him; and for the first time in all these long years of association they found they had to hurry away quickly, after paying the bill. Ellen Durban had to take her class in classical dancing earlier than usual that afternoon; Mrs Stilpepper had her family (and all that) to look after ... So he wasn't going to, after all ... and the two women stepped into the bright sunshine outside and quickly parted.

In the dining-room I was asking my friend, 'Who is that little man just going out?' and he replied: 'Oh! that's an Irish journalist, McCulloch. I believe he used to write verse; he's always here with those two women ... he was a great friend of that poet, the fellow who committed suicide ... what was his name?'

Many times in the years that followed we saw him there lunching alone, for the other actors in the small drama would no longer play their parts.

THE GREETING

FROM outside the long, large windows fires could be seen flickering in many wide grates, while the comforting sense, more than smell, of warm food oozed out of the whole house, subduing the sharper scent of frosty air. The dining-room table, she noticed as she passed by, was laid for three persons, and decorated with four small silver vases, from which a few very rigid flowers drew themselves up into the light of the windows. The sideboard showed beyond, bearing various drab meats and some pieces of plate, its cold glitter tempered by the flames with patches of warm orange.

As soon as Nurse Gooch was shown into the drawing-room, almost, indeed, before she had shaken hands or remarked how nice it was to see a fire, they went into luncheon. But seated before this white expanse, these three people could not succeed in materialising any conversation, that, as talk should, drawing its strength from the group but stronger than any individual member of it, would continue almost automatically, reproducing itself or taking on a fresh form from time to time. In the same way in which spiritualists claim that the presence of one sceptic at a séance is sufficient to prevent any manifestation, however hoped for and credited by the majority, here it was difficult for the talk to glow or prosper, when one of this small party was continually exerting her will to the utmost in order to produce a lasting and uncomfortable silence. The stagnant quiet of the room was seldom broken, then, except by the rather horse-like stepping of the footmen, or by the thin, stringy voice of the invalid projected through the mute air in querulous inquiry. And, in the very act of speaking herself, both by the purpose and calculated tone of her question, she enforced a silence on the others. Colonel Tonge tried to make conversation to the new-comer, placed between him and his sick wife, but his abrupt, pompous little sentences soon withered, frozen on the air by his wife's disapproval. Mrs Tonge, however, as we have said, permitted herself to ask a question occasionally – a question which, though it appeared innocent, was designed to convey to her new nurse the impression that she was an injured, ill-used woman. 'When, Humphrey,' she would ask, 'do you intend to put electric light into the house? I have asked you to do it for so many years now. I am sure I should sleep better, and should not be such a worry to you or to nurse,' or 'What about that summer-house, Humphrey? Will it be ready for me in the spring? If I am still with you, I intend going there every day when the weather is warmer. Perhaps I shall find a little peace there in the woods. But I fear it hasn't been touched yet.' To these questions the Colonel returned smooth, soothing answers, but ones which did not commit him in any way; but these, rather than conciliating the invalid, seemed only to vex her the more. But at this early period, before she understood her nurse, before she knew that anything she said would soon be pardoned, she did not actually as yet accuse her husband of doing all in his power to make and to keep her ill, but was content to let this accusation remain implicate in her questions, and in the sound of her voice. Still, Nurse Gooch felt instinctively that Mrs Tonge did not want to hurt her, that she was not in reality ill-natured, but that this calculated putting-out of the social fire was the outcome of a thousand little injuries inflicted by an imagination warped by constant illness and want of sleep. But whether it was due to the atmosphere created by this friction between husband and wife, or to something in the surroundings – in the house itself – she did most certainly, at this first moment of her arrival, experience an uneasy feeling, a slight repulsion from the Grove, which passed as soon as she became better acquainted with it.

Tonge's Grove, a square house, lies like a box thrown down among hanging woods and open commons – a charming residence in many ways. Like a doll's house it seems, each room giving the correct proportion to the rather under-life-size figures it displays. A curiously inappropriate setting, certainly, for any drama, the protagonists of which must find themselves cramped in their action by the wealth of detail imposed. The very comfort and well-being of the place would give a grotesque air to any but an accustomed or trivial event. For here, long habit appears so much more important than the occasion or fact it originally enshrined, inanimate objects so much more actual, more active, than human beings, that it is upon the house, and not upon its owners, that our attention is first focused. It is this superfluity of things, combined with a rigorous pruning of reality, that gives a certain significance to any fact of life should it be strong enough to enter these gates, yet remain quick. For reality, which is usually unpleasant, seldom touches lives such as these except at birth, of which, fortunately, we are all ignorant, or at death, a latent, lurking fear (an ogre at the end of every passage), but one which it is our very human convention to ignore.

The Grove is not really a small house; the rooms in it are large and numerous; but, like a square toy thrown in among garden beds and stables, crinoline-shaped lime-trees and red-walled angular orchards, among, in fact, all the long-settled paraphernalia annexed to a prosperous, well-ordered way-of-life, it was endowed with a perfection such as at first to make it seem miniature, like some exquisite model seen through a glass-case.

Certainly there is beauty about an estate of this kind: that tamed country sentiment, so English in quality, clings to it, till even the bird-song that trickles down through the dripping blue shadows thrown by tall trees seems arranged, punctual, and correct as the mechanical chirping of one of those clock-work birds that lifts enamelled wings out of a square black box; and even the cuckoo, who makes so ominous a sound from the cool green fortifications of wood or hedgerow, here changes his note till it rings hollow and pure as a church bell. No sense of mystery broods in the green and open spaces bathed in yellow summer sunlight; here are no caves, grottos, or tumbling torrents: everything is neat, shallow as the clear, slightly-running streams that border the wood; yet surely such beauty is, in a way, more fantastic than any of Leonardo's piled-up rocks or those worlds of ogres and giants to which we are carried off by some of the primitive painters.

In the winter it is, that all these country places are seen in their best, their most typical, phase. Stout built for cold weather, these houses take on a new quality, upstanding among hoar-frost, glowing warmly through the crisp, grey air. The first impression of the Grove would be, we think, a childlike memory of potting-shed smells, full of the scents of hidden growth; an odour of bulbs, stoves, rich fibrous mould, and bass, mingles with the sharp aromatic smell of the bonfire that crackles outside. On the walls of the shed the bass is hung up like so many beards of old men – ritual beards, like those of Pharaoh or Egyptian priest, which, perhaps, the gardener will don for the great occasions of his year. This one he would put on for the opening of the first spring flower, coming up glazed and shrill, its petals folded as if in prayer, out of the cold brown earth, beneath the laced shadows woven by the bare branches of the trees; this he will wear for the brazen trumpet-like blowing of the tulip-tree; while that one he reserves for the virginal unfolding of the magnolia, or the gathering up of petals let drop by the last rose. But the gardener himself soon dispels these tender imaginings, as you see his burly form bent over various cruel tasks – the trapping of the soft mole, or in aiming at the fawn-coloured fluffy arcs of the rabbits, as they crouch in their green cradles, their ears well back, nibbling the tender white shoots that he had so carefully nurtured.

Outside the shed in many glass frames large violets, ranging in tone from a deep purple through magenta to an almost brick-red, their petals scintillating damply, glisten like crystallised fruit seen through a glass window, sweet but unapproachable. The ground of the kitchen garden is hard and shiny, starched with frost; trees, shrubs, and the very grass are stiff and brittle, sweeping down under the slight wind with a shrill, steely sound. But the orchard walls still glow as if stained with the juice of the ripe fruits that press against them in summer and autumn, red, purple, and bloomy, while the house beyond shows warmly through the tree whose topmost twigs pattern themselves about it, like cobwebs against the sky; soft it is, as if cut from red velvet. Out of its doors and windows sounds the monotonous, dry-throated rattle of pet dogs, setting up a comfortable yet irritating competition with the noises of stable and farmyard, where rosy-faced men bustle about, lumbering in heavy boots; or, leaning to one side, the right arm lifted and at an angle, blow loudly and whistle, as they polish still more the varnished horses, their breathing lingering on after the in them sharp air like dragon's-breath. Through the windows of the house each fireplace shows up, while the red flowers blaze in it, or die down to a yellow flicker, fighting ineffectually against the thin silver rapiers of the winter sun. But more than all these things would you notice here the bitter cackle of a green parrot, falling through the drawn-out air with a horrid clatter, tumbling all lesser sounds down like a pack of cards. Certainly that menacing silly sound of a parrot's laughter would be your most abiding memory.

On such a noon as this it was that Nurse Gooch had first driven up to the Grove; so that, even if her first impression was a rather uneasy one, she had at any rate seen it wearing its most pleasant, most comfortable, aspect; for at night the character of every house changes – and this one alters more than most. The smiling comfort of the surroundings is lost, fades out into utter blackness, and a curious sub-flavour, unnoticed in the day, manifests itself. There are places and moments when the assumptions, the lean conventions on which our lives are based, become transparent, while, for an instant, the world we have made rocks with them. It is, for example, usually assumed that there are no such creatures as sea-serpents, yet there are certain places in Europe, on our own placid coasts even, of such marvellous formation that we feel, suddenly, that the existence of these monsters is a certainty – that it would surprise us less to see a vast beast, such as those painted by Piero di Cosimo, with flame-forked tongue, gigantic head, and long writhing body, coming up out of the fathomless green depths, than to see a passing country cart, a clergyman, or anything to which our experience has accustomed us. There are moments, too, when death, which, as we have said, it is usually our custom to hide away in a dusty corner of our minds, peeps round at us, grimacing – and we realise it as one of the universal and most awful conditions upon which we are permitted to take up life. So it was with the Grove, when darkness coffined it round. The dwarf perfection, which we have attempted to describe, would gradually disappear; for the very dimensions of the house seemed to alter as the rooms became swollen with darkness, full of inexplicable sound. Dead people walk here with more certain step than the living, their existence seems more substantial, their breathing more audible. The boarding of the floor yields under an invisible step, as if some strange memory stirs in it, and the panelling of the walls, the very furniture, make themselves heard with a hard, wooden creaking, which is magnified in these rooms now grown to the new proportions with which night endows them. And, in the darkness outside, everything moves, stirs, rustles.

It was therefore not to be wondered at that the Grove should have acquired the reputation of being haunted, though, really, the unhappy restless air that pervaded it at night may have been due more to its long association with a family of sad, unfortunate temperament – amounting in certain cases to something worse – than to the actual walking presence of any ghost. For ever since the present house was built, late in the seventeenth century, it had been in the possession of the Tonges and, until recently, until in fact the present owner had inherited the estate, there had been a long history connected with it of brooding melancholy, that must have been nearly allied to madness.

But Colonel Tonge, as we have seen, presented an ordinary enough character, with nerves unaffected, betraying no sign of hereditary disorder. Among the properties we have described – house, lawn, garden, farm, and stable – this not altogether unattractive figure emerges, strutting like a bantam. A proud little man, with a fairly distinguished military career, fond of hunting and shooting, he was much engaged in the business of an estate, the extent and importance of which he was apt to magnify in his own mind. In addition to these interests, he was involved in the affairs of every district committee, and, as became him in his dual capacity of squire and military man, was much to the fore in all those local philanthropic schemes which had for their object the welfare of the ex-soldier, or the helping of widow and children.

Yet in spite of this inherited make-up of country gentleman and the acquired one of soldier, there was about the Colonel on closer acquaintance some quality that removed him ever so little from the usual specimen of his class, just as there was something about the Grove that differentiated it from the run of English country houses. In what, then, did this difference consist? Partly, perhaps, in the stress that he laid upon the importance of his belongings, and therefore of himself; but more, surely, in the extraordinary calm that marked his demeanour – a quiet unruffled calm, not quite in accord with his bristling appearance and apparent character. One never saw him lose his temper, never even about trivialities, such as is the way of most military commanders; yet this restraint did not seem to arise so much from good nature as from the fear of losing his self-control even for a moment – suggesting that he was suppressing some instinct or emotion which must be very strong within him, if it was necessary continually to exert such an iron self-discipline. This contrast between nature and manner showed itself, too, in the difference between his uneasy, wandering eyes and the tightly-drawn mouth. But if Nurse Gooch had, with more than her normal sensitiveness, felt at first that there was a rather queer atmosphere about the house, she had at any rate detected nothing unusual in the look or manner of this amiable, rather pompous, little man, and, indeed, the only person who appreciated thoroughly these various subtle distinctions was Mrs Tonge. This poor lady had married her first cousin, and appeared to have inherited or acquired his, as well as her own, share of the peculiarly nervous temperament of this family. Thin, tall, and of that ash-grey colour which betokens constant sleeplessness, her rather sweet expression, while it was in direct contradiction to her restless, irritable soul, was the only remnant of a former prettiness. For, when first she married, she had been a good-looking, high-spirited girl, but had suddenly, swiftly, sunk into this state of perpetual and somewhat nagging melancholy. She was in reality a stupid woman, but her frayed nerves bestowed upon her an understanding of, and insight into, the unpleasant side of life that were alarming in the sureness of their judgment, and must have made of her a trying companion. She added to these heightened perceptions a sense of grievance, aggravated by an absolute lack of any interest or occupation, and by the fact that she was childless. She complained constantly, her chief lament being that there were only three creatures in the world that cared for her, two dogs – a Pomeranian and a Pekinese – and her beloved green parrot! Often she would add a remark to the effect that her husband would like – was, in fact, only waiting for – Polly to die. His triumph would then, apparently, be complete. And it must truthfully be said that the only thing which ever seemed to disturb the Colonel's calm was the idiot-laughter which the parrot would let fall through the darkened air of the sick woman's room. But though the slightest noise at any other time would strain Mrs Tonge's taut nerves almost to breaking-point, she appeared actually to enjoy her bird's head-splitting mirth; while the parrot, in return, seemed to acknowledge some bond of affection between his mistress and himself, for, were she more than usually ill, he would be ever so quiet, not venturing to exercise his marked mimetic gifts, even repressing his habitual laughter.

This love for her parrot and her pet dogs, together with a certain trust in, more than affection for, her young nurse – a trust which developed as the months passed – were all the assets of which Mrs Tonge was conscious in this life. For the rest she was lonely and frightened ... very frightened. Her whole existence was spent in a continual state of fear – one of the worst symptoms, though quite a common one, of neurasthenia; she was afraid of her neighbours, her husband, her house, terrified by everything and everybody alike. But, while frightened of everything, she was as consistently opposed to any plan for the alleviation of these imagined terrors.

Afraid, though seemingly without reason, of her husband, she was yet never able to refrain from making the fullest use of any opportunity to irritate, hurt, or annoy him. But he was very patient with her. She would taunt him with things big and little; she would attack him about his self-importance, or goad him before the nurse about his fondness for giving good advice to others, in a manner that must have made him feel the sting of truth. She would even accuse him of wishing to be rid of her – a poor invalid and one who was in his way – an accusation which, however, she could never really have believed for a moment. She would tell him that he had a cruel soul, and in her sick mind seemed to have fashioned a grotesque, caricatured little image of her husband, which, to her, had at last come to be the reality – an image, unlike yet in a way recognisable, of a queer, patient, cruel, rather wolf-like creature, hiding his true self beneath the usual qualities attached to the various very ordinary interests and pursuits in which his life was spent.

In spite of this extraordinary conception of him, Mrs Tonge was always calling for her husband. Her plaintiff voice echoing through the square, lofty rooms would be answered by his gruff, military tones so often that one of the parrot's most ingenious tricks was a perfect rendering of 'Humphrey, come here a minute!' and the answering call 'Yes, Mary, I'm coming,' followed by the sound of hurrying footsteps. Thus, though frightened of him, though almost hating him, the invalid would hardly allow her husband to leave her, if only for a day.

Still more was Mrs Tonge frightened of her house – that home which she knew so intimately. But, in the same perverse manner, she would never quit it, even for a night. While suffering terribly from insomnia, and from that fear of darkness which, though it usually leaves us when our childhood is past, had never wholly left her, she was steadfast in her refusal to allow Nurse Gooch to sleep in the same room, thus lessening these nocturnal terrors by human companionship. On the contrary, the sick woman not only insisted on being alone, but was resolute in locking both the doors of her room, one of which led into her husband's bedroom, the other into the passage outside, so that had she been seized with sudden illness, which was not altogether unlikely, no help could have reached her. Thus, bolted securely within those four walls, she would indulge her broken spirit in an orgy of sleepless terror. The dogs slept downstairs: her only companion was Polly, noiseless now, but faithful as ever, sitting hunched up on his perch, his dome-like cage enveloped in a pall of grey felt; and, even had he sounded his bitter, head-splitting laughter, it would have seemed more sweet than the music of any southern nightingales to the poor invalid, tossing about on her bed. For the parrot, alone of the animal-world, could give his mistress some feeling of momentary security.

Day would come at last, to bring with it an hour or two of grey, unrefreshing sleep. The afternoon she would spend knitting, seated in a large arm-chair in front of the fire, in her overheated boudoir, crowded with strong-smelling flowers. Photographs of friends – friends whom she had not seen for years and had perhaps never really cared for – littered all the furniture, and clambered up the walls, over the fire-place, in an endless formation, imbuing the room with that peculiar morbid tone of old photographs, yellow and glazed as death itself. Bustles, bonnets, then straw hats and leg-of-mutton sleeves, showed grotesquely in these little squares of faded, polished cardboard, set off by a palm tree in an art-pot, a balustraded terrace, a mountainous yet flat back-ground, or one of those other queer properties of the old photographic world. The wistful smiles on these pretty faces were now gone like her own, the smoothness of the skin was now replaced by hundreds of ever so small wrinkles, the fruit of care, sorrow, or some seed of ill-nature or bad temper that, undreamt of then, had now blossomed. The rest of open space on table, piano, or writing desk was taken up by diminutive unconnected vases of violets, freesias or jonquils, their heavy breath weighing on the air like a cloud, seeming among these photographs so many floral tributes to dead friendship, each one marking the grave of some pretended or genuine affection. The room was overloaded with these vases; the flowers lent no grace to the room, no sweetness to the over-burdened air. The Pomeranian yapped at Mrs Tonge's feet, the Pekinese lay curled up in a basket, while at her elbow the parrot picked at a large, white grape, the stale odour of the bird's cage mingling with the already stifling atmosphere of the room, till it became almost intolerable. Here the invalid would sit for hours enjoying one of the thousand little grievances from which she was able to choose, turning it over and pecking at it like the parrot at his grape; or, perhaps, she would be gripped by one of the manifold terrors of her life. Then that supreme horror, the fear of death (which, as she grew older, claimed an ever-greater part of her attention), grimaced at her from the scented shadows, till it seemed to her as if she sat there knitting endlessly her own shroud, and the vases of flowers transformed their shapes, rearranging themselves till they became wreaths and crosses, and the hot smell they exhaled became the very odour of death. Then she would ring again, calling for Nurse Gooch, but even that familiar footfall would make her shudder for an instant.

Her only pleasures now consisted in the tormenting of her even-tempered husband, or, in a lesser degree, of the poor young nurse – to whom she had now become attached in the same sense that a dog is attached to any object, such as a doll or an indiarubber ball, which it can worry. But Gooch, good and amiable, clean-looking rather than pretty, her face fully expressing that patience and kindness which were her two great qualities, won the affections not only of the invalid but of Colonel Tonge, and even of the servants – this latter no mean conquest when it is remembered that there is a traditional feud between servants and trained nurse, almost rivalling the other hereditary vendetta between nursery and schoolroom. Nurse Gooch was really fond of her patient, in spite of the maddening irritation of her ways: nor had she been unhappy during these eighteen months that had followed her luncheon at the Grove on that first winter day. For after the hardships of her own childhood, she appreciated this solid, very comfortable, home, while it presented to her a full scope for the exercise of those protective instincts which were particularly deep-rooted in her nature. Often, in a way, she envied Mrs Tonge her kind husband and charming house, thinking how happy the invalid might have been had only her disposition been a different one. For in Colonel Tonge the young nurse could see nothing but consideration for his ill wife, and kindness indeed to everyone, till, slowly, she formed in her own mind an image of him very different from that fashioned by his wife. To Nurse Gooch he was a model of suffering chivalry; to her his stature and heart seemed great, his importance equal to his own estimate of it. In fact, he became that very appealing combination – one which always fascinates the English people – a hero in public, a martyr in private life. And it was a source of great comfort for her to reflect that by keeping Mrs Tonge in as good a mood as possible, or, to borrow a military phrase, by intentionally drawing the fire on to herself, she was able to some small extent to alleviate the trials of the husband. Then she could feel, too, in some mysterious manner, that he was grateful for it, that he began to take a pleasure in her society, in the knowledge that she understood his difficulties, applauded his moderation. Often they used to sit together, consulting with Dr Maynard, a clever doctor, but one who lacked courage, and was in the habit of giving way to his patients.

Gradually, therefore, if any new symptom showed itself, if any new problem arose regarding the invalid, it was with the nurse and not with the doctor that Colonel Tonge would first come to talk it over.

Existence at the Grove, though each day appeared to her encompassed in the span of an hour, so that she was continually finding herself landed, as if by some magic carpet of the fourth dimension, at the corresponding time of the next day, yet seemed eternal; even the state of the sick woman, though her nerves became ever more affected, appeared to be stationary. Outside there was the fat, placid life of the countryside to be watched, the punctual revolution of the seasons. First came the ice-green glitter of the snowdrops, frosting the grass of the park with their crystal constellations; then these faded, withered, turned yellow, deepened to the butter-colour of the daffodils that ousted them, flowers swaying their large heads under the spring winds, transparent, full of the very colour of the sun; and, almost before you had time to observe it, they would flush to a deep purple, would be transformed into anemones, the centre of their dusky blossoms powdered with pollen, black like charcoal dust, or would adopt the velvet softness of texture which distinguishes the rose from other flowers: and summer would be in its full flame. Then, inside the Grove, you found good food, punctual hours, a calm routine broken only by the outbursts of Mrs Tonge, or by the bitter cackle of the parrot, its feathers green with the depth of a tropical forest, its eyes wary and knowing. It looked cunning, as if in possession of some queer secret – some secret such as that of the parrot encountered in Mexico by the traveller Humboldt – a bird which alone in all the world possessed a tongue of its own, since it spoke a language now extinct. For the tribe who talked it had been killed to a man in the course of America becoming a Christian continent, while the bird had lived on for a century.

The summer was a particularly hot one, and as it burnt to its climax, Mrs Tonge's irritable nerves inflicted an increasing punishment on those around her. The Colonel, who was drawn away on various long-promised visits to old friends and taken to London several times on the business of his estate, left the Grove more than usual this July, so that the full brunt of any trouble in the house fell upon Nurse Gooch, who would often have to shut herself up in her room, and, strong-minded, well-trained woman though she was, cry like a hurt child, so intolerable was the strain imposed upon her by the invalid. The latter soon realised when she had made the tactical error of being too disagreeable – or, perhaps, one should say of concentrating a day's temper in one short hour, instead of spreading it thinly, evenly, over the whole of the sun's passage, so that, looked back upon, it should tinge the day with some unpleasant colour in the minds of her companions or servants. And being possessed of a certain charm or a false kindliness, which she could exert whenever it was necessary to her, she was soon able again to engage the nurse's pity and affection.

'Poor thing,' Gooch would think to herself. 'One can't blame her for it. Look how she suffers.' But however true was this reflection, it was the sick woman who was still the chief opponent of any plan for the mitigation of her sufferings. Though her sleeplessness became worse, though the prospect of those long, dark hours threw a shadow blacker than the night itself over each day, yet she still refused to allow Nurse Gooch to rest in the room with her; while Dr Maynard, who should have insisted on it, was, as usual, completely overborne by his patient.

It is difficult to describe, though, how much Mrs Tonge suffered, locked in her room during those sultry nights, for their darkness appeared to cover a period easily surpassing the length of any winter night. As she lay there, her limbs twitching, memories dormant in her mind for forty years would rise up to torment her. Her parents, her old nurse (all dead how many summers past!) would return to her here in the silence. All the disappointments of her life would revive their former aching. Once more she would see the gas-lit ballrooms in which she had danced as a girl, and the faces of men she had forgotten half a lifetime ago. Then, again, she would see her wedding. All these memories would link up, and coalesce in feverish waking dreams of but a moment's duration, but which would yet seem to hold all eternity in their contorted perspectives. Wide awake now, she would recall her longing for children, or ponder upon one of her thousand little grievances, which took on new and greater dimensions in these hours. Here she was ... with a parrot as her only friend ... in this everlasting blackness. The thought of death would return to her, death that was at the end of each turning, making every life into a blind hopeless cul-de-sac. Long and hard she would fight this spectre of finality, against which no religion had the power to fortify her spirit. Then, after midnight, new terrors began, as the Grove woke up to its strange nocturnal life. Footsteps would sound outside, treading stealthily, stealthily on the black, hollow air; the furniture in the room, cumbersome old cupboards and chests of drawers, would suddenly tattoo a series of little but very definite hard sounds upon the silence, as if rapping out some unknown code. But when everything was swathed in quiet once more, this new absence of noise would be worse, more frightening than were the sounds themselves. It would smother everything with its blackness; everything would be still ... waiting ... listening! The silence, from having been merely a form of muffled sound, or perhaps a negation of it, became itself positive, active – could be felt and tested by the senses. There it was again, that creaking – as if someone was listening ... someone certainly ... someone standing on a loose board, crouching down in the darkness outside, afraid to tread for fear of waking one. Then would follow a distraction. A new code would be rapped out as something tapped on the window-pane ... tap – tap – tap, like a mad thing. Only the wind with that branch of ivy, she supposed. There it was again ... tap – tap ... like a mad thing trying to get into her room ... tap – tap ... into her very head, it seemed! Outside the house a dog would bark once, menacingly, and then its rough voice would die suddenly, as if silenced. Footsteps would tread again down the long passages, footsteps more distinct than ever this time. And once or twice they lingered stealthily at the bolted door; the handle would creak, grasped very carefully, turned by an invisible hand; and was there not the sound of a smothered, animal-like breathing? The wolf-at-the-door, the wolf-at-the-door, she says to herself in that fevered mind, where it seems as if two people, two strangers, were carrying on a whispered conversation of interminable length. Then silence comes once more; an unequalled stillness pours into the room, and into the corridors outside, so that the tapping, when it returns, takes on a new quality, rippling this quiet blackness with enlarging circles of sound, as when a stone is cast into a small pool. Tap – tap – tap ... again tap. Perhaps she is only dead, being fastened into her coffin. Tap – tap ... they are nailing it down, tap – tap; and she lies dead in the silence for ever. Then far away the taps sound out again and the coffin is unnailed. But this time it is the parrot rapping upon the bars of his dome-like cage with his hard beak; and she is reassured. Grey light clutches again at the swathed windows, and the furniture of the room grows slowly into its accustomed shape; the things round her fall back again into their familiar contours, and are recognisable as themselves, for in the night they had assumed new positions, new shapes, strange attitudes ... and the poor nervous creature lying on the rumpled bed falls asleep for an hour or two.

But as the light drips stealthily in, filling the black hollows of room and corridor, the housemaids, warned by Nurse Gooch to be more than usually quiet, scratch gently in the passage outside like so many mice, scratch with a gentle feeble sound that must inevitably rouse anyone – even a person who sleeps well by habit and is at that moment deep-rooted in slumber. For this timid, rodent-like noise is more irritating to the strongest nerves, will awaken more surely, than any of that loud, sudden music to which we are accustomed – that music of blows rained accidentally but with great force upon the fragile legs and corners of old furniture or brittle carving of ancient gilded frames – blows delivered with the back of an ever so light feathery brush. Thus Mrs Tonge would open her eyes upon one more hot and calm morning.

As she lay there, in the semi-darkness, she could hear faint voices sounding in the passage. Soon after she has rung her bell, Nurse Gooch comes in with the letters, as clean and kind as is possible for a human being to be, bright as are all trained nurses in the early morning; too bright, perhaps, too wide awake, and already making the best of it. Her hair has a dark golden colour in it under the light, and gleams very brightly under the cap she is wearing, while she talks in an even, soothing voice. As she goes down the corridor toward the invalid's room the housemaids take her passing presence for a signal that they may resume that noisy bustle of cleanliness with which they salute each day. Suddenly motes of dust whirl up into the air beneath their brushes, turning under the already searching rays of the sun to columns and twisted pillars of sparkling glass that support this heavy firmament, pillars prism-like in the radiant array of their colour. As the housemaids, bent nearly double in their long white print dresses, move slowly over the carpet, brush in one hand, dustpan in the other, their movements break up these columns, so that the atoms that compose them fall through the air like so many sequins, and are violently agitated; then these take on new shapes, and from pillars are converted into obelisks, pyramids, rectangles, and all the variety of glittering forms that, bound by the angles of straight lines, can be imposed upon this dull air and earth by the lance-like rays of the morning sun.

In the room she still lies in bed, turning over the unopened envelopes of her letters. Gooch goes to the window and talks to the parrot. As she uncovers the cage the bird breaks into its metallic laughter, that rattles down through the open window into the shrubbery, like so many brassy rings thrown down by a juggler, for they curve in again at the pantry-window, where John the footman is standing in an apron, cleaning the silver with a dirty-looking piece of old yellow leather and some gritty rose-pink paste. As he polishes the convex mirror formed by the flanks of the silver bowl, while his face reflected in one side assumes a grotesque appearance, the contorted trees and twisted perspective of lawn and garden show in the other. The second housemaid peeps in. 'Oh, you do look a sight!' she cries, bridling with laughter, pointing to the bowl in his hand. 'I may be a sight,' he says, 'or I may not, but I'm not a blarsted slave, am I?' 'Well, you needn't answer so nasty,' she said. 'It's not that, it's that parrot – 'ark at it now. I shall be glad when 'e comes back; one can't do no right in this place. Everything is wrong. First it's one dam thing, then another. Nurse sticks it like a soldier,' he says, 'but I stand up for my rights! I'm not a slave, I'm not, that I should stand there letting that blarsted parrot screech at me like a sergeant-major on a parade ground, and her talking a lot of nonsense. I'd like to wring its bloody neck, I would – they're a pair of them, they are!'

And certainly – Nurse Gooch herself had to admit it – the invalid was this summer more than ever exacting. For many months past she had worried her husband about a summer-house, for which she had formed one of those queer, urgent longings that sick people consider themselves free to indulge. The hut had stood there in the woods, year after year, unnoticed, falling to damp decay, when, as if given new eyes, Mrs Tonge saw it for the first time, and determined to make it her own. Here, she felt, it would be possible to sit quietly, rest peacefully, in an atmosphere different from that of the Grove, and perhaps find that sleep denied her in any other place. As the summer-house was in a very dilapidated condition, she asked her husband to have it repaired for her, but met with a very unexpected opposition. The Colonel, used as he was to furthering every plan of his sick wife, absolutely ignored this new entreaty. Which fact, unfortunately, only strengthened her determination, and made her persist in her caprice.

There was, in reality, some danger in letting Mrs Tonge remain alone for a long period in a spot so remote from the house – she refused, again, to allow anyone to wait with her in this solitude – for though, as is the habit of permanent invalids, she might live for many years, yet she was a nervous, delicate woman, very liable to a sudden attack of illness, and here no help could reach her. But Dr Maynard, with his customary inability to say 'No' to a patient – or, perhaps, because he felt that the rest she hoped to obtain here would be more valuable to her than any unexpected attack of illness would be dangerous – gave his sanction to the new scheme. Colonel Tonge, however, still urged the doctor to forbid it, making a strong protest against what he considered this folly, and himself steadfastly refused to have the place touched up in any way, or even swept out. The invalid changed her tactics: from anger she passed to a mood of plaintive injury. 'I know, Humphrey,' she moaned at him, 'that you only go on like that because you hate to think that I am having a peaceful moment. What harm *can* there be in going to the summer-house? It doesn't hurt you, does it?'

The Colonel, patient as ever, would show no sign of ill-temper, putting the case as reasonably as he could. 'Mary, my dear, it is really very unwise and foolish of you. I know how much unemployment there is, how unsettled is the countryside. You should see some of the tramps that are brought up before me on the Bench. That summer-house may seem deep in the woods, but it is very near the high-road. You can never tell who will come into the park. Anyone can get in. There's no lodge near that gate, I tell you, my dear, it isn't safe. I can't think how you can be so silly. It's folly, sheer folly!'

Mrs Tonge cried a little: 'I'm not afraid of tramps or motor-cars, or of anything on a road. But I know you'd do anything to prevent my getting any rest, Humphrey. I believe you'd like me to go without any sleep at all, as long as it didn't worry you. I know you're only waiting for me to die.' ... And the poor little man, discomfited, walked away. He was always so patient ... like that ... and kind, it made Nurse Gooch feel a great pity for him. But she thought he was wrong in this particular instance – wrong ever to oppose the invalid's wishes, however seldom he did so; and knowing her influence with him, she persuaded the Colonel to say no more about it, though he still seemed a little uneasy. Yet so great had become his reliance on the young nurse's judgment, that she easily induced him to pretend to his wife that he now thought his opposition had been mistaken.

But Mrs Tonge could not be deceived. She knew perfectly well that he did not really approve, and it therefore gave her an increased pleasure to rest in the summer-house. Getting up later than ever in these hot months of the year, she would go there every afternoon. She forbade her two pets to be with her, so that a piteous, plaintive yapping filled the Grove each day after luncheon; only Polly, devoted Polly, was privileged to share this new solitude. Curiously enough, she did not feel frightened here. The rather ominous silence of the woods held no menace for her, she was happier among these dank shadows than in her own bedroom or placid flowering garden; and, whether from perversity or from some form of auto-suggestion, it was a fact that when the nurse walked out to the hut to bring the sick woman back to the house for tea, she often found her in a slumber more peaceful than any she had enjoyed for years.

Between two and three o'clock each fine afternoon a queer procession could be seen walking over the lawn between the beds of flowers that lay like embossed embroidery among the sleek grass. First of all came Mrs Tonge, never glancing aside at flower or tree, her upright carriage and slow-moving walk bestowing an almost ritual air on the proceedings; then followed the uniform-clad figure of the nurse, holding newpapers and a small cluster of three or four grapes for the parrot in one hand, while from the other dangled the sacred dome. The grapes transparent, jewel-like, catching the prevailing colour, which was that of the penetrating glow of sunlight through green leaves, focused the eye as they moved along, till they seemed like some mystic regalia, even drawing the eye away from the more metallic colouring of the parrot, who, as he was borne along, shrieked continually, taking an obvious pleasure in scaring the poor timid birds of the English countryside by a display of flaming plumage and alien, rather acrid, laughter. Slowly they passed over the shrill, water-smooth lawns, where single high trees stood up fleecy against the sky, or, over-burdened by the full weight of summer, trailed their branches right down upon the fragrant ground, into the dark woods cloudy with foliage and rank with the smell of tall nettles, elder-trees, bracken, and all those things that grow in unkept places. No bird-song sounded now in this ultimate unfolding of the seasons, and the little path that led winding through this wilderness lay like a curling green ribbon, of a brighter hue than the surrounding shrubs and velvety with moss, from which weeds sprouted up at the corners like small tufts of feathers. This untidy ribbon, lying without purpose across the woodland ground, led to the rustic hut which the caprice of some former mistress of the Grove had caused to be built here, rather pointlessly, some ninety years ago. Under a round roof, sloping down from its centre, and covered with the rough bark of trees, it lay mouldering beneath the structure of branches which hung motionless, as if cut from cardboard, on the heavy air. Sponge-like, it seemed, in its dampness, like some fungus lying about at the foot of a tree. Great knots of ivy clung to the upper part of the door, while, where the peeling bark had fallen away,were revealed arrangements of rusty nails, geometrical, but growing like thorns out of the wood. No view was framed in the pointed spaces of the two windows, except the light which trellised itself with the shadow of green leaves along the ground, or, flooding a stretch of bracken, played first on one leaf, then on another, bringing out unexpected patterns, making each bent-back leaf, as it was touched, the centre of some shifting arabesque design such as is woven in Eastern carpets.

The parrot would be placed on the dingy, bark-covered table; a grape would be half-peeled, and pressed, like a melting jewel, between the bars of the cage. The wire dome would then be draped ceremoniously with grey felt; the invalid would lie back in her long chair, a rug over her knees, the countless newspapers which it was her habit to read placed at her side; and Nurse Gooch would walk back briskly through the dark stillness of the wood out again into the droning odorous languor of the garden.

As Mrs Tonge rested in her long chair, she found, certainly, a peace otherwise denied to her in the grim world of a sick woman's fancy. No argument, she determined, should ever persuade her to give up this siesta. Day followed day, each warm and bright-coloured as the other; only the leaves became a little ranker in their scent, the woods yet more silent. But sometimes, as she was on the border of sleep, already seeing the queer avenues of that land which she could so seldom reach, while through its landscape she could still distinguish the more rational, familiar features of her real surroundings, a sound like a rushing wind, or as if gigantic wings were beating on the taut drum-like fabric of the air, would startle her for a moment, and, looking round, she would see the tall stiff trees lift up their canvas branches, caught by a false breeze, as a motor-car passed between the two high hedges that concealed the road. Above this hidden white scar a high whirling column of dust would dance for a few seconds, as if it were some jinn of the air made visible for the moment; or, again, she would be lulled by the kindly, cooing voices of the country people, which floated over to her, for, as her husband had pointed out, the road was in reality very near the summer-house. But these things did not appear unpleasant to her; and, in any case, how much better were these explicable sounds than that state of suspended animation, alternating with a sudden show of life, which she had grown to dread so much at night in her own room!

The hot weather continued, and with it the life of the Grove. Colonel Tonge, as we have remarked, was away this summer more than was his wont, but the routine of the invalid, the nurse, and the servants repeated itself almost automatically. Every afternoon Nurse Gooch would walk out with the patient to the hut and would leave her there, only returning in time to fetch her back to the house for tea. One afternoon, when the Colonel was expected home from a short visit to Major Morley, an old friend and brother-officer whom, though a near neighbour, he saw very seldom, Mrs Tonge suddenly made up her mind to stay out in the summer-house for tea, telling the nurse to bring it out to her at five o'clock. Now, though there was nothing very original or startling in this idea, Gooch, who in matters relating to an invalid did not lack a certain subtlety, at once expostulated – not, indeed, from any feeling of disapproval, but because she well knew that the sick woman would in reality be deeply disappointed if her nurse seemed pleased, or even satisfied, with this new break away from the normal programme. The nurse, therefore, succeeded in putting up a show of anxiety, saying such things as that the patient ought not to be too long alone, or that the Colonel would be hurt and annoyed at finding his wife absent on his return. Finally, pretending to be persuaded against her better judgment, she agreed to bring tea out to the summer-house at five o'clock; then, placing the parrot's cage on the table, she covered it up, completed her ritual, and walked back to the house through the hot, strangely sultry, afternoon.

Mrs Tonge felt an unaccustomed luxurious ease steal over her as she lay stretched out on her couch reading her papers, though perhaps perusing them less carefully to-day than was her custom. As a rule, she read them from cover to cover – births, deaths, marriages, sales, advertisements of all kinds; and, while these journals represented every shade of political opinion, she was quite unmoved by their varying propaganda. She regarded them, in fact, as her one form of relaxation. This afternoon, however, she could not fix her attention on them. She peeled an amber, honey-scented grape for Polly, who mumbled back lovingly but softly. What a difference even an hour's sleep makes! She wondered when Humphrey was coming back, feeling that she had been rather hard with him lately – in fact, for some time past. With a sudden impulse of affection the image she had formed of him in her own mind was broken, and he became to her again the young man whom she had loved. She determined that she would be nicer to him; and certainly she felt a little better to-day. The afternoon in the summer-house seemed just warm enough ... and quiet ... nicely quiet she thought. Slowly, almost contentedly, and for the first time for many years without any fear, any nervous feeling, she stretched her limbs until every nerve in her body became quiet, and sighing gently, let sleep wash over her tired limbs, her worn-out mind, in soft delicious little waves.

But, though the dampness of the hut may have tempered that afternoon heat for Mrs Tonge, it seemed very breathless outside. Even Nurse Gooch, as she sat sewing in her usually cool room, felt rather overcome. Oh, how hot it was! And the house was very still. As a rule you heard the servants chattering, moving through the passages; the jingling of silver or the rattling of plates would reach you from pantry or kitchen. But to-day there was no noise – not a sound, except the hot insect-like droning of the sewing-machine, as she bent over it, running the needle along the white edge of the new linen, which filled the room with a rather stifling scent. But directly she stopped, even for an instant, silence flooded the room. Well, one can't look after a case like this for eighteen months without feeling odd oneself sometimes, she supposed! Yet there was something queer about the stillness. There must be going to be a storm, she thought.

No sound came in from farm or stable at this high-up, open window, on a level with the motionless green cradles of the birds; but down below on the lawn a single leaf would suddenly burst out into a mad fluttering, as if trying to indicate the secret of this general alarm, and then be still, too still, as if it feared to be caught in an act of rebellion ... In the flower beds, then, a single violent coloured blossom would wave out wildly, flicker for an instant like a tongue of flame, then float once more stiffly upon the glazed heat. She was quite glad to finish her sewing, get the tea ready, and leave the house. But the air outside was even hotter than within – suffocating – so that one could not breathe, and as she passed out into the furtive silence of the woods she seemed separated from the world she knew. If I go on like this, she said to herself, I shall soon be the next invalid! Yet the walk seemed longer than it ought to be, so that she was continually being confronted with little twistings in it which she did not remember, though she had trodden this path at least four times a day for several months past. Still she knew, of course, that it must be the right one. But somehow or other, she was startled this afternoon by things that usually she would not notice – the ordinary, rather inexplicable rustlings of the woodlands, for instance. Doubtless these were audible yesterday as to-day, but as a rule she did not heed them; and once or twice, certainly, it seemed to her that she heard a peculiar scampering, as of a hurrying through thickets, or the dragging crackle of twigs and brambles as they released their clinging hold on invisible garments. It was with a distinct feeling of relief, then, that after quite a long walk, she caught sight of the summer-house round the next turning. It had a very human, friendly look to her this afternoon; yet it belonged so much to these woods, this soil, that it was like a large mushroom growing out of a taller green tangle. The invalid did not call out to her, even the parrot was silent – an indication, usually, that its mistress was asleep. (How queer it is the way she can sleep here, and nowhere else!) Nurse Gooch cried out cheerfully, 'Wake up, wake up! I've brought you your tea!' Still there was no answer, and, skirting the blind corner of the hut, carrying the tray in front of her, she was already standing in the low doorway before she had even cast a glance at its dark interior. Thrown suddenly into the quiet smallness of the summer-house, where she was at such close quarters with everything, almost within an arm's span of each wall, she was unable to breathe for a moment. An overwhelming sensation of nausea took possession of her, so that she felt that she, too, would fall upon that terrible floor. Yet, though the whole universe swung round, her trained eye observed the slaughter-house details. There lay the murdered woman, her head on one side, her skull crushed by some ferocious blow, her face twisted to a mask of terror – that queer unreasoning terror which had never left her. Dumb, blinking in its overturned cage, the parrot was hunched up, its feathers clotted together with blood. Clutching the bird's cage as if to save it from some fresh disaster, Nurse Gooch rushed wildly out of the summer-house into the motionless woods.

*

As she approached the Grove, her own sense of discipline asserted itself, forcing her to slow down her pace, to set her mind a little more in order. But now it was, actually, that the full shock came to her, for in that sudden blind moment of fear, when her limbs had melted one into the other, when her heart had bounded to her very lips, she had been unable to think, had experienced no feeling except an endless surprise, pity and disgust. Afterward curiosity, as well, intervened, and she began to wonder who had done this thing, and why such a brutal fate had engulfed the poor, timid, elderly woman. And then she was forced to steel her soul for the next ordeal: she would have need of every particle of strength in mind and body, since it devolved upon her to break the news. Through the library window she could see Colonel Tonge standing by the empty fireplace, and even while she was still labouring under the blow that had befallen her, she dreaded telling him of it as the not least awful incident in this terrible adventure – nearly as overwhelming, indeed, as had been the actual moment of discovery. Her respect, and fondness, even, for him, her knowledge that his had not been a happy marriage, only made the task a more difficult one to face and endure.

With an unexpected nervous susceptibility the Colonel seemed to feel the burning, panting breath of tragedy almost before she had spoken. Perhaps something out of her control manifested itself in her face, in her air; but as she entered, he looked at her with eyes as fearful as her own, and it seemed as if he, too, were mastering his emotions to confront something that he dreaded. 'Go on, go on,' he said, 'what is it?'

*

Month followed month, and he still shut himself up in his room, till he became so changed in looks, in manner, as hardly to appear the same man. All pride, all self-importance had left him. The spring had gone out of his walk, the jauntiness out of dress and carriage. Every hour of the day he loaded himself with reproaches – for not having been firmer, for not having absolutely refused to allow his wife to stay out there alone – for having been away at the time of the tragedy. Gooch would hear him, unable to sleep at night, walking about the passages, pacing up and down, up and down, till the first grey light crept in at the corners of blind and curtain. It was as if the spirit of sleepless terror that had haunted his wife had now transferred its temple to his body. Incapable of attending to the business of his estate, to which formerly he had devoted so much consideration, he now seldom left the house in the daytime, and, if he did, in whatever direction he might set out, his feet always led him sooner or later to the same place, and he would be startled, aghast to find himself in the woods again.

Anything that reminded him of his dead wife had to be hidden away. The two poor little dogs were removed by his married sister when she went home, after a quite unsuccessful attempt to cheer her brother and give him comfort. The parrot, now never laughing, never speaking, languished in an attic, attended only by Emily, the housemaid. The other servants, too, were kind to the bird since it had for them a fatal attraction: not only was it connected with death, having about it the very odour of the cemetery, but was in itself the witness and only relic of a brutal crime, so that it possessed the charm popularly associated with a portion of hangman's rope, and, in addition, was a living thing possessed of a dreadful secret. But the parrot would never utter, and downstairs – where the conversation, however wide the circle of its origin, always in the end drew in on to one topic – they had to admit that Polly had never been the-same-like-since. Occasionally Emily would leave the door of the cage open, hoping that he would walk out or fly round as he used to do. But nothing could tempt him out of his battered dome. As for Colonel Tonge, he had never liked the bird, hating its harsh laughter, and this solitary, now silent, witness of his wife's end filled him at present with an unconquerable aversion.

Great sympathy was evinced everywhere for the poor widower, crushed under a catastrophe so unexpected and mysterious. But the public sympathy could do little to help him ; and though some solution of the mystery might temporarily have distracted his mind, even if it could not have rallied his spirits, none was forthcoming. He went through all the sordid business associated with murder – inquest and interview; the crime remained odd as ever in its total absence of warning, intention, or clue. Who, indeed, could have plotted to murder this invalid lady, possessed of few friends and no enemies? And what purpose was served by this intolerable brutality? It is true that, after a time, the police found a stained, blunt-headed club, obviously the weapon with which the fatal wound had been inflicted, buried deep in the bracken; but, in a sense, this discovery only removed the murder further from the public experience, in that the possible motive of theft was at the same time disposed of – for with this weapon were found the few rings, the gold watch, and small amount of money that the dead woman had about her, as she had lain asleep in the summer-house on that sultry August afternoon. The police, thinking it possible that these articles had been hidden from an impulse of fear, that the original motive had indeed been the ordinary one, arrested a tramp found wandering in the district, hiding himself at night under hedges and in the shelter of empty barns; but though he could not give a very detailed or convincing account of his doings on the day of the 'Hut Murder' – as it was called – the evidence that connected him with the crime was not enough to secure his conviction. It remained, however, the impression of many people, among them of both Dr Maynard and Nurse Gooch, that he was in reality guilty of the foul act of which he had been suspected. Colonel Tonge, though he followed every detail of the trial with a painful interest, could never be induced to discuss the possible guilt of the tramp, but it was noticeable that after the man's release his nervous condition became more than ever marked, which led them to conclude that, in his opinion too, the person accused should never have been acquitted.

The bereaved husband's insomnia troubled him sorely; he had no peace, no rest by day or night. The only person able to bring him relief, to lighten his burden even for a moment, was Nurse Gooch; so that Dr Maynard felt it his duty, for once, to insist on her remaining at the Grove until the Colonel should display some sign of returning health and a reviving spirit. The nurse, for her part, had always liked, pitied, and admired him, while, by one of those curious human instincts, all the compassion, all the affection even, which she had given so freely to the dead woman, was now made over to her new patient. And then she, too, felt remorse, had things on her mind with which to reproach herself. How well she could understand and sympathise with his self-accusation! Why, conscious as she had been of her influence over him, had she not supported the Colonel's wise protest against his wife's use of the summer-house, instead of urging, as she had done, that it was a reasonable plan, and finally persuading him to withdraw his objection to it? Terribly she felt now the responsibility so foolishly incurred, that perhaps she was in part to blame for the tragedy, even in the matter of allowing the invalid to wait out in the summer-house for tea on that dreadful afternoon; and in the months that followed the murder it was one of the few pleasant things in her life to reflect that she could, by her presence and sympathetic understanding, lessen his misery ever so little, giving him for a little while a passing sense of comfort.

When, after many long, lonely months, he made her an offer of marriage, saying that life without her support would be to him an intolerable burden, she accepted his proposal, realising that the interest she felt in him, the overwhelming pity that sometimes clutched at her heart, was but a disguise for love. Regardless of any difference in age or outlook, she hoped, by becoming his wife, to help and ease the remainder of a life, the unhappy tenour of which had now deepened into a more dreadful tone.

*

The honeymoon was spent in France, in order to make for them both a complete break from the background of their lives. But even among the lush meadows and rich trees of Normandy, away from any sting of association, Humphrey did not recover at once, as she had hoped, his old buoyancy. Listless, uneasy, restless, he would for hours be silent, wrapped in a melancholy that did not ordinarily belong to his temperament, while, in his broken slumber and sudden awakenings, his wife could detect the existence of a great well of sorrow that even her anxious affection could not plumb, a grief her love could not solace. The discovery of the extent of his affliction caused her further worry, made her dread their return to the scene of his past life. But as time passed it was obvious that his spirits were returning; and when he told her that during their absence the Grove had been entirely repainted and redecorated, she began to feel happier, hoping that it would seem to him like the beginning of a new life.

Almost two years to a day after the crime, they returned from their honeymoon, but Colonel Tonge did not seem conscious of any sense of anniversary, while she, naturally, would not mention it to him. But it made her feel a little uneasy.

As they drove back from the station, the new chauffeur quite by chance, by one of those dreadful inspirations which are only given to stupid people, drove the newly-married couple down the concealed road near the summer-house, instead of taking them in by the near lodge. Colonel Tonge obviously experienced no emotion, but his wife felt for the moment as if she would be stifled between these two high hedges. How like was this afternoon to that other one! No leaf moved on any tree, no bird let its song trickle through the cloudy, too-dark leafage; the air was hot, motionless and still, though through it ran those same secret tremors, inexplicable tremblings. For the new Mrs Tonge the whole atmosphere was stained with memories.

Yet she soon forgot the uneasy promptings of her heart and mind in the pleasure she felt at the reception which awaited them. She had always been a favourite with the servants, and the latter could never forget the poor Colonel's sufferings, so that they had taken an especial care to give the newly-wedded pair an inspiriting welcome. The Colonel stopped to talk to them, while Mrs Tonge, eager to see what alterations had been made, stepped into the house alone. It looked charming, she thought, with the new smooth paint on the old walls; and, unable to repress a slight thrill of pleasure, which she felt to be wrong, though she could not quite exorcise it, at being for the first time mistress of a house – and such a lovely house – she walked on through the empty, gleaming rooms that led one into the other. The last room was the boudoir. She entered it softly, closing the door behind her, wishing to explore its impression to the full, for she wondered whether it would make her feel an usurper, a stranger in someone else's place. But no! it was a new room to her: gone was the feverish atmosphere of the sick-room, with its dead air, over-heated and scented with innumerable flowers: gone was that dead look imparted by the yellow glaze of countless old photographs and by the spreading litter of trivial little objects. And while she bore toward the dead woman no feelings but those of pity and affection, yet, being of a practical nature, she was glad that nothing remained of the old mistress – nothing that could call up painful memories. The room was quiet and restful; the long windows stood wide open on to the pleasant water-cool spaces of the lawn, that unfolded up to the borders of the wood where stood tall fleecy green trees, while under their blue shadows ran the murmur of shallow streams. The healthy scents of tree and grass, the peaceful watery sounds, and honey-gathering, contented drone of the bees as they hung over the flowers, drifted into the house, diffusing an air of ease and comfort. This was *her* house, *her* garden, *her* home, and she now had a husband to whom she was devoted. Why, then, should she ever allow her mind to dwell on the tragedies of the past? Was it not better to forget utterly, to obliterate the memory in her husband, by offering him all her love, till gradually these possessions to which he had been so attached became dear to him again? ... but just then, behind her, she heard the thin voice of the dead woman crying out – a voice, grey with fear and breaking. 'Humphrey,' it sighed, 'what is it? Oh, my God!' ... And then the sound of a heavy dumb blow and low moaning, followed by burst after burst of idiot laughter, as with a fluttering whirl of flaming green feathers the parrot flew up again to its empty attic.

HIS SHIP COMES HOME

ARTHUR BERTRAM, or not to deprive his personality of its full efflorescence we should perhaps record in their entirety the names Arthur Otho Augustus, had for many years enjoyed that distinction implied in being what is sometimes referred to in the obituary notices of fashionable journals as 'a familiar figure about London'; and, for his proper appreciation, it is necessary to consider what this to him so particularly appropriate journalistic phrase is intended to convey. Surely not merely that he spent his life wandering through the various streets, metropolitan or suburban, of our island-capital? Nor, to the initiate, would it suggest for a moment that his demeanour was marked by any peculiarity that would make him the centre of a vulgar attention prompting children to cry out or point a finger, as, to give an instance, was noticeable in the behaviour of that retired General whose wont it was for many years to stroll down Piccadilly neighing like a horse. Idiosyncrasies of this kind are apt to make their owners too conspicuous, and the rather unconventional conduct of this latter gentleman did focus a part of the public attention upon him – so much, in fact, that when finally he attacked a hay-cart passing down the street in front of his military club, in order, as he said, to find forage for himself, he was, as we think, erroneously deprived of his personal liberty. Injustice is sometimes more visible to children than to those better able to express their feelings, and, even at that early age, it seemed to us that the poor General, as a soldier, a cavalryman even, who had mixed more with horses than with men, and indeed always made a point of neighing himself rather than speaking, had in reality some claim to that distinction which he boasted; while, for the rest, there can be no doubt that he set a fine example to his fellow-clubmen, on whose part a gradual awakening to the fact that they, too, had practically become horses, could but add to the amenities of our social life. But no obsession, such as this, separated Arthur Bertram from his kind. He was much more human than horse-like. His behaviour, on the contrary, was noticeable for its extreme correctness; so that the phrase we are discussing must be taken not to mean that he paraded any of the many streets in the town, but as indicative of the fact that he knew in what streets to walk, there to be observed by fellow-readers of the fashionable journal. Summed up, then, it implies the possession of enough leisure to display in the correctly chosen place characteristics, sufficiently, but not too, personal to be noticed by others of equal leisure but less individuality. Thus a seemingly hollow little phrase can, like a cipher, convey an exterior, an outlook, a way of life almost, to those for whom it is intended.

Yet it was only as a middle-aged man that Bertram's ugliness, enhanced by a highly stylised manner of dressing, became so intense as to shed upon him a certain lustre When he was young, it was his companion whose smile crowned him with a reflected glory, like the Aurora Borealis that plays round the Northern skies, giving him more interest even that that possessed by the original. From the beginning of his life as a man of fashion, he made it his rule always to be seen in the company of the Woman-of-the-Moment, and, if possible, to be in love with her. He had one remarkable gift in that he could foretell the advent of fame six months before it blazed up. This gave him time to make friends. His instinct in this matter was really unusual. He was seen, first with the leading professional beauty of Marlborough House days, then with the wife of the rising playwright, the most famous actress of the year, or the sister of an artist whose renown had at this moment reached its zenith. The discrimination he showed in, so to speak, 'spotting the winner,' gave a flattering quality to his attentions, which no doubt helped him to other conquests. His affection became the equivalent of a bestowal of a public laurel-wreath upon the lady, or upon her brother, or husband – a halo of which Arthur kept just a chip, sufficient to illumine himself, as commission. It helped him, too, with other women to be seen in the company of some famous person: to those who did not know him he seemed a distinguished, almost a brilliant, figure.

But the world hinted that Bertram occasionally reaped other, baser, more material rewards than the acquisition of fame, or requited love, from those connections – or should one write transactions? – that the laurels turned to gold within the hands of this alchemist; that he was not above writing to the 'Woman-of-the-moment,' informing her, rather needlessly, of his poverty, in letters which she would be unwilling for her relatives to read, hinting, as they did, at some association between them, which had, in fact, never really existed; and if his hints, his demands, were not satisfied, would always refer to her in public with a tender leer of implication. Combined with these tastes and recreations Arthur was a fervent Catholic, and an arbiter of good form, though, as the public suspicion of him gained ground, he cleverly cultivated the style and manner of a successful brigand.

Scandalous rumours, such as these we have mentioned, are often the fruit of the imagination, the invention of enemies; yet if, as was apparently the case, Mr Bertram had no fortune of his own, it must be admitted that he enjoyed an unexampled run for other people's money. A younger son of a younger son, his natural advantages were limited to a magnificent air, an amount of self-possession, certain aristocratic relatives, and an ugliness that in its ultimate blossoming was to attain a real significance. To these was added a talent for dress, into which he threw all the energy usually absorbed in, and the imaginative qualities often killed by, the practice of cricket or golf. Also he was generous, undoubtedly generous. The bouquets which he was in the habit of presenting to his favourites would have filled the Crystal Palace, the fruit would have won first-prize at any show; however poor he was, however short of money the recipient of these soft tributes, he never failed in their offering. But, afterwards, would come a day of reckoning.

Arthur must have first assumed his rôle as a very young man, in the early seventies of the last century, a period that offered to any adventurer of aristocratic connection an unrivalled opportunity for polite plunder. 'Society' – the word was one of bounded application never then used to indicate any community including brain or manual worker – was undergoing those changes that would, in the space of another thirty years, put an end to it in this sense. It was, though seemingly stagnant, already in a state of corruption that would make it a perfect Golconda for any adventurer with the right attributes. For, being a world much talked of, but unknown except to a few who never spoke of it, it possessed a certain glamour, like that appertaining to some superlatively secret form of freemasonry – a glamour which, with its gradual expansion, it was to lose for ever. As in those days large hotels and restaurants were nearly unknown, it follows that the habit of eating in public was not much indulged in by any class. It was not even easy, therefore, to see the world unless you were of it. This cloak of invisibility was very valuable, giving to it the attraction of the unseen, as well as of the unknown: here was some influence in the midst of us, some veiled mysterious power, the respect for which was like that felt for the Dalai Lama – a feeling which, were he to show himself, would swiftly diminish. Yet the process of invisibility had already begun, so that at this particular stage 'society' was like a partially-materialised spirit at a séance, something that might appear in your own house if you encouraged it sufficiently with baked meats or human sacrifice, employed the right medium, had enough superstitious belief in its existence, and would swear not to turn the light on suddenly or ask an unexpected question. Mr Bertram might, if suitably rewarded, attempt to materialise it for you in your own rooms, though possibly he promised more than he could achieve.

Arthur Bertram was related to more than one peer; and all through the first three-quarters of the nineteenth century members of the English nobility were regarded with the reverence due to an almost supernatural order of beings. Illustrative of this is the following quotation from the second volume of a trilogy which we found recently:–

'"Oh, Lady Arvon," said Hester, in a scared kind of voice, "will Mr Brown, I mean Martin, ever become a peer? I did not think of that." ...

'"Certainly he will, little Hester, if IN THE NATURAL COURSE of things HE should outlive HIS FATHER," answered Lady Arvon, as she lovingly kissed the flushed cheeks.' ...

One would diagnose the years 1860 to 1870 from the descriptive passages in the book; for in its sentimental pages the ladies recline on circular settees – ottomans, as they were called – from which their skirts billow out in front at the angle of falling water, while the gentlemen, with dark whiskers still clinging to their cheeks, lean over them in positions of polite but easy elegance. But, actually, this book, perhaps the last of a long tradition, was written in the year 1888 and dedicated to William Ewart Gladstone!

This respect, this reverence, for the invisible world of which the peerage formed a sacred inner core, deepened with the wealth of the person who felt it. To bathe in this radiance, to share this true light, was the ambition of many.

Thus, though 'society' was still dominated by the great territorial magnates, and yet enjoyed a certain political power which was the legacy of the eighteenth century, the great outcrop of rich people created automatically by the diversion of trade to this country from France and Germany during the war of 1870 was already knocking at the door with a golden nugget. Their method was at the same time to propitiate and outbid the world, by the magnificence of their entertainment; and Arthur Bertram, trading on his advantages, was often a guest at the intensely respectable but otherwise rather Trimalchio-like banquets of Sir Gorgious Midas.

Though his ugliness was yet in its raw stage, Arthur had already shown the sureness of his instinct, not by any attempt to improve those qualities of heart or head in which he may have been slightly deficient, but, on the other hand, by a resolute insistence on his bad ones. This gave him what was taken by many for an easy, aristocratic air. Through these gilded saloons, full of tall palm-trees, that soared up into the hard gas-light of mid-Victorian nights like so many giraffes, their glazed and withered leaves spreading out bone-like structures till they seemed like the skeletons of some extinct monster, through smaller rooms full of roses, orchids, and carnations, the exquisite colours of which threw into a more hideous contrast the suffocating draperies of that dusty age, through corridors full of huge plants, their leaves blotched with corrupt colours like those of decaying flesh, he would strut to the bobbing tune of some now obsolete polka, talking in a loud insolent voice about the rarity in these places of 'really well-bred people.' He would stare long and impertinently at those not fulfilling his standard in this respect; nor would he spare his host or hostess, for, whereas others laughed at them fitfully and behind doors, Bertram had the courage to do it constantly and in the open. His calculated drawl, a dry creaking sound as of some box with rusty hinges slowly opening, alternated with slow important clearings of the throat, and was accompanied by a complete set of facial grimaces, regular as Swedish exercises. There would be that fascinating twitch of the mouth, or that lifting of the skin from the forehead; an enchanting shutting of one eye, opening of the other, such as were introduced as the symbols of Upper and Lower Egypt into the ceremonial mummification of dead Pharaohs. All these little touches were added to his appearance in order to combine a quality of dignity with natural fascination. The open eye, however, was alert and twinkling, the skin, sallow and rather lined, had about it something of the texture of crocodile-skin. If any woman, particularly one of his famous companions, was mentioned, he would smile in, as he thought, a pleasing way; the rusty hinges would creak open and eject some phrase such as 'poor little woman,' or 'divine little creature,' by which you were intended to assume that the lady referred to had loved and lost; for he based his policy as a professional on the axiom that nothing succeeds like success; and it was his arrangement with the world, an understood thing, that in his rôle of Don Juan he was irresistible.

Thus, past those same circular settees that we have mentioned, now burdened with no crinolines, where men, moustached and not whiskered, talked, with perhaps less easy elegance, to ladies with bunchy little skirts, sitting demurely upright under palms mangy as tropical beasts in an English climate, by plants that seemed to harbour cruel insects of the burning forests, Arthur Bertram would lounge, strut, and swagger. While, from the near distance, the sound of a string band, like the humming drone that comes up from jungles, would reach you with warm gusts of air. Against this background his dry voice would be heard, alternately insulting the rich and deploring his own poverty; but always he hinted, in his own phraseology, that one day his Ship would Come Home. But in what that frail barque consisted, Corsair, Indian treasure ship, or the floating shuttered barge of Elaine, was never to be discovered.

Thus his life passed easily enough, except for periodic financial crises, which always seem to be the worst of troubles. He lived in two small rooms, dark as Caliban's cave, in Ebury Street. But one could not think of him in that setting; for out of his dingy retreat, dirty and uncomfortable, he would appear resplendent, bearing his daily tribute of flowers, a gardenia in his own buttonhole, glorious as any peacock leaving its nest, and mouthing such phrases as 'well-bred,' 'distinguished-looking,' 'Soi-disant, of Our Class.'

For a brief interval of three years the regular course of his life was interrupted by marriage. It soon resumed its normal trend when, true to his reputation as a gallant man, he allowed himself to be divorced. Much sympathy was felt for Arthur. On the one side was to be considered a certain financial gain, on the other his reputation as a man of the world, a modern censor of morals (for such he had now become), his profession of the true faith, which does not allow of divorce, and his rôle of gentleman. It was a struggle for him; but in the end Arthur was relieved of his religious scruples, and Mrs Bertram of a share of her small fortune and her husband's bullying manner. Let it be understood, however, that his wife regarded it as a bargain.

She had, in any case, been too poor for her husband. A pretty, rather silly woman of provincial upbringing, she had been caught by his amazing manner, by the reflected glory of his friends, the distinction of his relatives. He was so well-bred too. While Arthur, for his part, imagining her to be richer than she was, felt a longing for a quieter, less transient way of living. Perhaps, too, owing to difficulties, he had been forced to realise his assets rather suddenly. Then, though of bourgeois origin on her father's side, Ina's mother came of Russian princely stock. This gave Arthur a new opening. He would meet you in the street, and roar like an angry lion about those pretenders to Russian princely rank whose names were not even mentioned in the *Almanach de Gotha* ... 'while my wife's mother tells me' ...

Poor Mrs Bertram sank back into a welcome obscurity, and Arthur resumed a life based on the broad foundations of his small, though slightly augmented, capital and his renown as a Don Juan. In this third phase, which was but a continuation of the first, Arthur wore a double tiara; the aureole of success in affairs of the heart, of failure in those of the world; the latter, by its interest and appeal, helped him to fresh conquests. And his appearance, too, was more developed. By now he possessed a really magnificent ugliness, and one of which he made every use. It may have been due either to some form of æsthetic perception, or to quite unconscious artistry, but having always had a slim, rather elegant figure, he appeared early in life to have realised the great artistic truth that elegance of form and distinction of dress enhance the quality, whatever it may be, of the face above; that a slim figure and well-made, well-thought out, clothes can make an ugly face more hideous a thousandfold. How much more effective would Caliban be in what is known as 'faultless evening-dress,' than in those conventional clothes of the cave-man which he usually affects! Thus Arthur used his figure, his dress, his manner even, to enhance the awfulness of the face that crowned them, set like a grotesque jewel. And, indeed, in contrasts such as these, lies the whole art of the grotesque. The gargoyle aids the leaping spiritual beauty of flying buttress, Gothic arch and spire, while the cathedral in return lends its loveliness to display each individual gargoyle. A dragon makes plain the ideal and peaceful beauty of a Chinese landscape. The sad ugliness, the useless effort of a dwarf, enhance the richness of seventeenth-century costume. Thus, Arthur pressed his youthful slim figure and stylised clothes into the service of that sallow muzzle-like face that surmounted them. No woman could pay a greater attention to her toilet than did Bertram. He achieved distinctly the personal note. In London he wore an idealised version of the usual dress that belongs to the familiar figure about London: striped or check trousers, beautifully creased, a black tail coat – what used to be known as a 'fancy waistcoat' – a stock-tie with a pearl pin, the gift of his unfortunate wife, and, finally, balanced above that head as by a conjuring trick, a grey top-hat. A Malacca cane of unusual height completed the effect. while his walk was so calculated as best to display each elegance.

The background of the early nineties against which Arthur now found himself, after the rapine and triumphs of nigh twenty years, had a certain amount of character. Our hero would explain 'that things change so fast nowadays' – for the Oppoponax and White Rose of his early youth had now given way to the odours of 'Chypre' and 'New Mown Hay'; odours which were actually allowed to mingle in the drawing-rooms with the fragrant smoke of Egyptian cigarettes! What is more, certain young men did not hesitate to wear in public, in London even, shoes of brown leather, a recent discovery.

But the London background of this period had more character than the present one, was more essentially different from that of other cities; and Arthur, in his small way, had become one feature of a familiar prospect, since sadly altered. The narrow streets, full of shops engaged in a more dignified competition to attract the senses, were fresher, brighter than they are now. There was then about Bond Street and Piccadilly an almost patent-leather finish. Everything shone with paint and sparkled with varnish. Through the large sheets of glass, shelves and rows of bottles gleamed like coloured crystal. The frayed edges of Northern sunlight rehabilitated themselves in the depth of these green, silver and crimson waters, even recovering and giving out a little warmth, bringing the perfume out of the bottles as they would draw the secret breath out of country flowers, or press it out of tropical blossoms that live but a day, until a surge of scent, stronger than that of any garden or forest, poured in overwhelming torrent from the shop into the street that lay cold and hard as a canal outside. Passing on farther, behind yet more glass, we see sparkling silver, crystal, and scaly leather mirror-like with varnish – those ugly useless ornaments for which the English are still justly famous. Everything is neat and well ordered, everything is well made. Here the smell of leather, of lion and crocodile skin, of sweating African jungle and slimy Indian river bed, were strong enough to frighten the horses – arranged in pairs like those animals you see advancing into a diminutive ark in early tapestries – were they aware of anything but attentive grooms in comfortable stables, or, perhaps, of being given apples and carrots on Sunday mornings after church. Flowers, arranged skilfully yet with an unbelievable want of art, pressed their hot faces against the crystal walls that imprisoned them – the open pleasant faces of roses, orchids like battle-scarred generals, flowers of fever and blood, and carnations, looking as if they were cut from stiff, frilly paper; while little indiarubber bands held up their chins from an elderly sagging, giving a forced, fresh look of youth. Among this well-organised, rather tired, riot, a love-bird pecks at steel bars with hard metallic clatter. Then there were windows full of baskets of fruit, of the full, healthy scent of mould and autumn orchards, though in the same place were queer toys, fruit scaled like reptiles, so that no man would willingly eat of them, and oranges, round and warm as the sun. Then follow open marble shelves of cold, shiny fish that look as if they came from the Dead Sea, displaying damply white tones or circles of rainbow colour, while near by hangs a whole world of birds, hams and meat, that would please equally a housekeeper or the denizen of a jungle.

In the centre of this narrow street stands, like a granite rock, a broad figure in a large square blue coat, with boots like ships and a hat that is a blue dome. This is the guardian of 'lor-an'-awder,' straight out of the last Drury Lane pantomime harlequinade, a gruff, burly, blue figure with one white-gloved paw held up in warning. This uplifted hand holds in check, as if by magic, a line of vehicles more frail, more fantastic, than any in the world. Stranger and more unreal than any gondola that cuts the Venetian waters with knife-like prow are these angular, black scallop-shells on high, round wheels, scallop-shells like those from which Botticelli lets his golden Venus be borne in upon the foaming tides. High up above the shell, so that his weight must surely overbalance his frail equipage, sits, like a monkey, a red-faced figure with shiny top-hat, whip, and red-buttonhole. Fabulous, indeed, is the speed of them, as they roll along, jolting slightly in the fashion of a man walking a tight-rope. And, straight out of this queer, narrow perspective of houses, shops, and carriages, two figures impinge on our sight. A tall good-looking lady, in leg-of-mutton sleeves and a little hat, and – with her – a well-dressed, elegant figure, mouthing and twisting its great muzzle like some Red Indian chief in war paint. It is Arthur Bertram with the Woman-of-the-Moment; and how this background displays our hero! About him is the same ugly element, the same hideous smartness. The shape of his top-hat fits in with the perspective of the chimneys, the glaze of it echoes the paint and varnish of the shops. His patent-leather boots reflect, as in a black mirror, the huge slabs of glass in the windows, the trivial objects behind them, while they in their turn send back a watery reflection of Arthur and those glittering ornaments that distinguish him. Even the well-marked brick of the houses helps to show off the texture of his face.

But, alas! this townscape dissolves as we look at it: the strange vehicles have been dashed up like shells by the raging tides, shattered on the beach of time. Here and there are survivors, in the museums, beside a family coach. Perhaps one may lurk in the back alleys of those streets of which for so long it was the ornament, sought out and made much of, but now an outcast. The Woman-of-the-Moment is thirty years older, and Arthur – well, Arthur is just his own dear self!

In the country, or still more at foreign watering-places, Arthur could give freer rein to his personal taste. There, quite frankly, and, we think, from his point of view, wisely, he based the harmony of his clothes upon the brigand-theme: flowing blue cloak, romantic hat, long gauntlet-gloves and a cane, higher than his London one, persuaded the inhabitants that here was someone of immense renown. Used as they were to the ways of the English, yet here was something odder still. No one, surely, but a Personage Incognito would dare to attract to himself so much attention; surely that face, too, was the property of one of the European Royal Houses, a Prince in Exile, the king of ... ?

The years went by, ever more swiftly, as is their way, but Our Familiar Figure would still be seen walking down the customary streets at the correct hour, though he was more often alone than formerly. His nimbus was now his own. With head erect, balancing that grey top-hat apparently without an effort, he would straddle down the street, snuffling like a bull-dog, grimacing horribly to himself and making wry faces. The innumerable little leathery lines in his countenance were led up to by the single immaculate crease in each trouser, or thrown into bold relief by the sober patterning of his cravat. A friendly but rather unprepossessing leer would greet his friends. There would be a roar, the angry roar of an old man, rather inarticulate but ending in the well-known phrase, 'Soi-disant, of Our Class.' Then he would remain silent for a moment, and, drawing a folded handkerchief out of his pocket by its angle, would brush away invisible specks of dust from his sleeve. The friend would now be treated to a fixed stare of some duration, followed by a writhing of the facial muscles, and then, swivelling one bright-gleaming eye round the corner, he would remark with the usual drawl, the usual loud, dry-throated rasp in his voice: 'Ah! there goes that divine creature; such a well-bred woman, too, which is none too common in these days. We used to be great friends.' Or, 'Do you know who that is? If you'd known her, my boy, as I did (poor little woman) twenty years ago.' ... Then would come variations based on the same theme, and the climax would be a short sermon on the morals of the day, followed by the customary dissertation upon his own poverty, which was indeed becoming a problem for him.

By now between the ages of sixty and seventy years, Arthur may fairly be said to have reached the Awkward Age. Women with famous husbands or brothers now preferred the company of these relatives to the tiresome attentions of, as they put it all too frankly, this old bore. No more loans of fifty pounds from ladies, following upon a written account of Arthur's romantic dramatisation of their friendship, came his way. But he never lost faith, firm in the belief that one day his ship would come home – a supposition that had sustained him through many difficulties and for many years. Though the impoverishment of the whole world, as a result of the war, made existence more difficult for him, though he was now forced to spend a great part of the year in being looked up to by the English colony in cheap foreign watering-places, yet he was still always to be seen in London at the correct time, in the correct place. His manner, his air, were more in the Grand-Style than ever. He let it be seen and understood that he was a relic of a past epoch, a grand old English gentleman, damn it, such as could not flourish in this degenerate age! Still there were, undoubtedly, moments in the night when Arthur asked himself what the future held for him. It might not be a long one, but it might be extremely unpleasant. His bills became to him a maze, which he walked blindfold, and with no hope, while through the thick hedges peered the evil gleaming eyes of his enemies. And when he woke again to the still blackness of the middle night, it must have seemed to him as if the banquets of Sir Gorgious Midas were, too, but delightful, fantastic dreams. He would sigh, reflecting how his world had changed out of all recognition, but unaware of the minute part himself had played in this dissolution of the old order, as is the ant of the overthrow of a garden-bed, or the coral insect unconscious of his destructive yet creative mission.

The Midas family, though they, too, had changed with the times, were still on very good terms with Bertram, whose insolence in the house of the old merchant was transformed into obsequious praise in the grandson's ancestral hall. No one could play the old family-friend better than he could, and a long-standing connection like this was felt to be part of the Midas feudal make-up. Bertram used to tell his friends that it made him blush, absolutely blush, to think how the country had treated Lord de Normanville, old Sir Gorgious's grandson. No one had been more 'keen-on-the-war,' no one had lent more motor-cars, believed more spy-stories, or given more vegetables to the wounded than had this peer! No one had so swiftly observed – immediately before the Armistice, indeed – the danger of our falling into the enemy's trap by accepting their complete submission – by, in fact, allowing a premature end to the war; no one had denounced this folly of unheeding statesmen more energetically than had Lord de Normanville from his seat as hereditary legislator; and, finally, no one was more surprised when asked to contribute towards the cost of our glorious battles!

The family of old Sir Gorgious were now fast selling the great bulk of their inherited acres, and were content with two motor-cars, where formerly they had been forced to employ seven. In fact Lord de Normanville could cry poverty with the richest in the land. But though the stately homes were going one by one, there were consolations; and on the top of all his other sacrifices he still managed to entertain a few friends from time to time, though, of course, in a very simple manner. It was at one of these pleasant gatherings that Arthur met his second destiny, whose rôle was filled by the ample fortune and generous figure of Mrs Fullard: this lady, a fascinating widow, was possessed of much wealth and sprightliness.

These parties always had something very original about them, quite different from other people's. Lady de Normanville always liked to *mix* her guests; that was the secret of it, she confessed – though at first sight the personnel appeared to be much the same as at other 'simple gatherings' of the kind. In a curious way the talk always showed a tendency to return to finance, by which was meant the iniquities of taxation – though, of course, other subjects would be touched on. Dinner, on the first night, was most amusing. Arthur sat next to Mrs Fullard, while the eruptions of green and purple brocade and the numerous ancestral portraits on the wall threw into rich relief every detail of their appearance. Old Sir Hankey Twadham, the former Minister at Sofia, was there, too, with a new – or at any rate new to him – rather risqué story, the worst of which was that, as he confided to all the guests in turn, you had to be careful to whom you told it. His eye wandered round the table mournfully, in search of a possible victim. Then that round disc of glass behind which his eye was displayed like some precious object in a crystal *vitrine* would twinkle gleefully, and he would say: 'I shall try it on Mrs Fullard. She's all right! It will make her roar. It makes me laugh every time I think of it.' Dear old General M'Kinnan was also one of the party, and could be seen heavily crunching his red, swollen mandibles, or moving a hand like a lobster's claw in occasional explanatory gesture of some killing anecdote in connection with the Irish Rebellion. The curious part of it, too, was that the leaders were all 'clever men,' 'but they don't go far, do they?' he asked with a first suggestion of passion. 'Look at Curzon! I remember him at Eton. Could anyone call *him* a *clever* man? and look where he is now!' This peroration of the General's made an immediate appeal to the audience, who took it up and worried it in couples, carefully, in their various corners. Again he focused attention by another of his *killing* stories about the rebellion. What an extraordinary thing! Everybody screamed. But the conversation did not remain long at this frivolous level. The Prince of Wales's tour of the Empire was discussed. It was marvellous how the Boy had Smiled. The General expressed it as his opinion that once he had got over those blackguardly hurdles, or hurtals, or whatever they are called, the Royal Tour would do more good than a thousand machine-guns. Meanwhile, at the other end, Lord de Normanville held the field with some interesting reminiscences of his more recent disputes with the Inland Revenue and Super-Tax Authorities. He felt it his duty, though always unwilling to make himself conspicuous, and, indeed, always trying to pass as an ordinary citizen, to write to them pointing out that after deducting Income Tax, Super-Tax, and his annual expenditure, he was left with an income of six hundred a year. An answer had been returned to him, couched in the most insolent terms suggesting that he should cut down his expenditure. He had replied, with dignity but without loss of temper, making it clear that any curtailment of his expenditure would increase unemployment, already sufficiently prevalent, and that he was unwilling at this juncture to do anything that might in any way injure the Commonwealth. Followed a short but very interesting discussion on Bolshevism; Sir Hankey, who plunged into this discussion off the deep end, forgot the point of his story in the middle, and, instead, gave minute details of what he had heard in Sofia before the war. If, he added, he told them only half what he *knew* now ... and the pearls encircling billowing necks became a shade paler in their radiance. Several people, indeed, felt positively faint. Lady de Normanville rallied the talk by appealing to General M'Kinnan. 'General, if you had to have your portrait painted, whom would you choose?' The gallant old soldier, who considered portrait-painting as quite a different thing from any other form of painting, and always attended the opening days of the exhibitions in Bond Street, was immensely flattered by this question – much more so than if his opinion had been asked on tactics or horses. 'Why not Oswald Birley? There was a man who could paint what *he* saw, what *you* saw!' Mrs Fullard, who was very artistic, suggested M'Evoy, but Arthur thought M'Evoy's work was rather *too* weird, wasn't it? Lady de Normanville pointed out that he never seemed to finish his portraits; besides he made everyone look alike. Whereas Glyn Philpott finished them all, absolutely, and made everyone look different. 'A clever man, that !' said the General suspiciously.

Conversation split up again, drifting into sets of twos and threes, and it was now that Evelyn Fullard completely captivated Arthur Bertram by confessing, with that pretty trilling little laugh of hers, that if she had her way she would *make* the miners go down the mines and work. While people with fifteen thousand a year were paying nearly half their income in taxation, the colliers – who had nothing to keep up – were earning five pounds a week and paying no taxes at all. As for herself, she had been obliged to borrow money from the bank this year to pay her Super-Tax! It was this adorable mixture of wit, charm, and common sense, that fascinated Arthur. He proposed after three days; and they were married within three weeks of their first meeting. It was a real romance!

The honeymoon was spent on the shores of Lake Maggiore, in the Pucciniesque setting of soft air, palm-trees, and lapping waters; a neighbouring casino added interest to the natural beauty of the landscape. While there Arthur managed quite quickly to solve that Super-Tax trouble. Wherever they went, the romantic couple attracted great interest. They were an interesting pair. Arthur was triumphant; he appeared, bathed in that tender, rosy glory in which the later Venetian painters depict, on wall and ceiling of patrician palaces, the apotheosis of Procurator or Doge. And, on his return to London, he became a more familiar figure than ever. He had entered the third phase; he had conquered the Awkward Age.

It looked, in fact, as if his ship had come home at last. Alas! it was merely the Hundred Days over again, the ship but that *Bellerophon* which was to make him an exile in a foreign land. For now Mrs Bertram made manifest the devil within her; her pretty little golden laugh showed itself to be the key to a temper infinite and terrible in its variety. The plebeian origin of his wife, to which Arthur had willingly and, as he now said, foolishly blinded himself, peeped out from behind the enamel. She made it clear that she had no intention of allowing Arthur to relieve her of the necessity for borrowing from the bank to pay her Super-Tax; she even refused him a small allowance. She irritated his susceptible nerves at every turn with vulgar little tricks, and displayed a revengeful, unforgiving spirit.

How, he asked himself aloud, should he introduce such a woman to his friends? It was impossible ... Mrs Bertram, in a fury, the varnish cracking in every direction, shouted out that he had no friends now, if he'd ever had any! Finally, in an almost apoplectic temper, the fair one had him turned out of the house. An intense domestic warfare of manœuvre and counter-manœuvre, attack and counter-attack ensued. Arthur fled to Atterly, her 'place' in the country, and succeeded in enlisting the sympathy of the agent, who particularly disliked Mrs Bertram. But the agent received orders – which he could not disobey – to cut off the water and the electric light, and was thus prevented from following the dictates of his heart. Then Mrs Bertram came down in person to superintend the siege. Arthur was ejected – but with great skill commandeered his wife's motor-car, and before she could arrive back in London by train had already seized her house there. Finally, both of them felt that the position was an undignified one. The lawyers now swooped down, and by their various proposals netted in a good haul. Arthur's old religious scruples returned to him with redoubled force. His fervour was extraordinary. He became a Savonarola. Would he consider ten thousand pounds down for the selling of his soul? Certainly not! Twenty thousand? But even this did not tempt him. He became too obstinate in his desire to outwit his wife; and Mrs Bertram became thoroughly out of temper again. She made up her mind to be rid of him without any payment at all, and – being a woman used to getting her own way – by sheer brutality, ill-temper, and insult succeeded eventually in dislodging him from her home. Arthur was goaded into such a fury that he left of his own accord, to spend the remainder of a broken life declaiming against the former object of his affections, or, as he now called her, 'that scheming old woman.'

His clothes remained glorious as ever, his manner as magnificent; he still talked of his ship coming home; but gradually poverty forced him into a bitter exile. One heard of him taking his aristocratic relatives out from their camphored chests, and airing them, before old ladies, in those *pensions* of France, Germany, and Italy that had become for him a series of more comfortable but even more desolate St Helenas. The tale of his wrongs, one heard, was ever fresh in his memory. Bravely as ever, no doubt, he pursued his allotted path; but silence sank down on him, and the London that had known Arthur Bertram for so long, knew him no more.

*

The sea was smooth as a watered-silk banner, and no wind lifted the white edges. Hot and calm was the water on that summer day. The growing detail of the harbour approached us swiftly, veering in its position from time to time. Lighthouses, piers, quays, trolleys and cranes, dividing up the horizon with angular but rhythmic precision, were imprisoned in the tawdry blue, in the transparent ball, of sky and sea, as in crystal. Every sound seemed struggling to escape from the hard, material globe that contained it. Porters cried nasally, old women hawked oranges and chocolates, while small boys cried ecstatically the French versions of the names of English newspapers. All round us was the usual disorderly bustle that masks the deadly efficiency of the French people. We were discharged over small bridges into this throng and out of it – and beyond, almost automatically, into a motor-car. The streets were dull, the coast-line flat; nothing to do in all this weary waste except, we supposed, to watch the ship come home each morning from England.

And just then our attention was suddenly riveted by a familiar figure bearing toward us. Magnificent in flowing blue cloak, his long gauntlet-glove made a majestic movement with a very high walking-stick, as this straddling, snorting personage, grimacing and making wry faces, went on his way toward his ship that had already come home. He was rather late that day, and in his hurry did not notice us.

THE MACHINE BREAKS DOWN

HUGH DEARBORN was already middle-aged when I first remember him some ten years ago, but middle-aged with an unparalleled elegance, an unimpeachable style. His greying hair, his mask-like face, through which peered those witty, rather wicked eyes, his hands of carved ivory, were all made with an exquisite but rather snuff-box-like finish. This well-groomed and tailored figure, this Voltairean mask, rather too developed for the slender frame and covered with small, delicately chiselled wrinkles, formed but the very gentlemanly shell for an intense vitality out of all proportion to it – formed, in fact, the beautifully finished cabinet-gramophone case, from which sounded a wonderful but intolerable music. Not that his voice was musical, in the sense that our grandmothers used that term. It was not. His laugh never resembled a peal of church bells sounding at eventide, or a rather carelessly played xylophone, as did the elegant tremolos of various old Victorian ladies. On the contrary, his voice, touching every emotion for the necessary moment, never sunk into cloying sweetness, having, rather, that enchanting trick of putting a note in the wrong, unexpected place, and then recovering, which you find in the best modern music – find originally in Rossini's *Can-Can*, that first clear gem of modern music, and then in Debussy, Ravel and Stravinsky.

The actual manner of his conversation was perhaps less modern than its content. Artists of the spoken word vary in their methods. One, whose manner I admire most of all, talks, argues, sinks beneath the logical waters, is on the point of drowning, but as he touches the ocean bottom, finds some new pearl, and swiftly brings it to the surface: his is an absolute reliance on his own brain and tongue, never afraid to risk all on an absurd argument, never fearing to sink, knowing always that he will find a new treasure. But Hugh's system is different, formal; it is as the Garden of Versailles compared with that of Hampton Court – stiff, mathematic, well ordered; his voice a terrible instrument, his art one that dies but never surrenders.

From the first Hugh Dearborn possessed a peculiar interest for me – an interest aroused by some apparent contradictions in his character. Here was this exquisite shell, the fruit of fifty or sixty years of toil, but an instrument for an hour's conversation – conversation that like a flower blossoms and then dies – a mule-like art without hope of progeny. Usually the artist is led on by a desire for immortality or perhaps fired by a craving for money, but here was a real case of 'Art for Art's sake.' The best Hugh could hope for was an invitation to dinner, but the very perfection of his conversational technique, the very insistence and monopoly of his great art, often tended to prevent his humble end.

And this art itself, unpremeditated and yet such a technical achievement, surely could not flower on the barren air without any but purely physical preparation? Then again, after Hugh's performance of the new Symphony at the luncheon table, I once heard a rather unkind friend say to him: 'Really, Hugh, you ought to put it in a book!' And this made me wonder why he had never employed these gifts in some other, more permanent, form. And how much longer, in any case, could this delicate, ageing instrument stand the ceaseless wear and tear of such a vitality?

Thus, from the first, Dearborn interested me and I collected information about him. It was certainly a mysterious life. A friend of mine, I found out, had met him originally in the garden of Walter Pater. I pictured the scene. To us children of sadder and wiser days the eighties of the last century seem a halcyon but ever so distant age; Alfred

Lord Tennyson ever so much more distant than King Alfred burning the cakes; the young manhood of Mr Arthur Balfour ever so much more remote, more legendary, than the youth of King Arthur or the Quest of the Holy Grail. A halcyon time indeed, with spring always in the warm crystal-clear air; with the laburnums, the lilacs, the lobelias and copper beeches in a perpetual riot of unsubdued and unbridled colour. There was a continual movement and sparkle in the lives of the well-to-do. Poet Laureates still wrote quite successful odes to members of the reigning family, who were then of greater interest to their subjects than professional cricket or the doped death of Miss Flossie Highfly. The county families were yet safely out of the way, secure in their distant tea-bound mansions, busy killing the beasts of the field, the birds of the air. Riches were still respectable, the rise of a millionaire was yet a romance. On the other hand, you could be poor without being thought insane, and the silver epergne was gradually retiring into the lodging-house homes of Bloomsbury. Shepheard's Hotel would soon be open in Cairo (or was it already?), and we were on the verge of an optimistic young Imperialism that would grow to a climax with Kipling and Lady Butler. And, to those who liked it, there was a pleasant stir in the world of art. Painting and prose were both stretching themselves after a long sleep that had been broken only by the short Pre-Raphaelite nightmare. This was the time of the neo-Greek: white marble mantel-pieces, Alma Tadema, the prose of John Addington Symonds, the drawings of Du Maurier and Frank Miles – all were supposed, rather vaguely, to recall, to equal even, the art of Phidias. Bustles, bonnets, straight profiles and diamond myrtle-leaves were the order of the day. For the more precious there were water-lilies, almond-blossom and flowing draperies; for the very knowing, chatter about Whistler and Walter Pater.

Thus, in the garden of that old-world city, through Parnassian groves, over smooth classical lawns that glowed, as they would have said, like sad green velvet, under weeping willows which wept more gracefully than they do now, and through which there always rattled a slight fresh wind from the East, suggestive of the clattering of willow-pattern plates, wandered our young hero, in ever so clean white-flannel trousers, talented and exquisite. The old æsthete, who seldom committed himself to prophecy, leant over to my friend and said: 'That young man will go far!' ...

From those days, alas! until the early nineteen ten's I know little of Dearborn's career. He went everywhere, knew everyone – poets, painters, the first lady who wore 'bloomers,' boxers, philosophers, and Channel swimmers, wasting the perfect blossom of his art on the worthy and unworthy alike. His art developed continually. His talk became something outside himself, a disembodied spirit. From a fine art it became a devouring growth, that in the end swallowed up the author of its being. He was Frankenstein, his conversation the monster ... but a monster with charm.

To meet him was always a pleasure, to part with him the subtle torture of a thousand farewells. Perhaps Hugh himself wished to leave you, but his art forbade him. It made him linger, led you to the longed-for terminus with a hundred little anecdotes that crucified your spirit; though regarded objectively they were round, full, delicate, and smooth as a ripe peach. But his conversation, monstrous ectoplasm that he materialised, wound round you like a serpent, bound you with a thousand octopus-like tentacles, released you for a moment, like a cat with a mouse, and then grabbed you again, draining your blood like a vampire..

Dull people used to think it funny to say: 'I wonder what he does when he is alone.' Others suggested (and this was to me an interesting hypothesis) that he only existed in relation to his friends and acquaintances – his conversation but the magic rope up which clambered this fabulous spinner of words, like an Indian juggler, till, ceasing to climb it, he dissolved into the void. This perhaps might account for that lingering farewell; for when it was said, Hugh, too, would cease to exist for a while. But he was too personal, too positive for that; and, like all people of talent, as opposed to genius, he was too dated. He had little tricks, and these tricks belied his mask and proved him to be real. That manner, for instance, of wiping his eye, on entering a room, with the corner of a beautifully-folded, slightly-scented pocket-handkerchief, as one who was still laughing at some witty conversation that he had just left, did not that betray him? Was not that conversation one that he had held with Whistler, Pater, or some other already legendary figure? – was it not perhaps only a forty-year-old memory? On the other hand, it may have been a signal, like a bugle call for focusing the attention; for Hugh, a true artist, liked to have the attention of his audience, and, if slighted, if interrupted, a strange fury gleamed from those wicked little eyes.

Like all beautiful objects, Hugh never aged, only becoming a little more worn – worn with the thin wrinkled elegance of a Chinese grotesque; but his talk became always fuller and richer. He was never silly, never dull; and again, like all *objets d'art*, though mannered, he was never really affected. Yet there was about him a quality that was sometimes a little sinister, sometimes a little sad; a mystery, certainly. But from the first, being an artist myself, I guessed that his art was a hard mistress. I have said that Hugh Dearborn knew everyone – the world, the flesh, the devil, the ass and the artist. Among his greatest friends (for his art was bilingual and surmounted all obstacles) was Henri Schmidt, the famous Parisian portrait-painter, himself a master of conversation, in an age of which he and Hugh were perhaps the only two high exponents of that art. Schmidt painted his portrait, and it is a masterpiece.

Dearborn is presented to us sitting in an arm-chair with his beautifully crinkled grey hair, his mask wrinkled and wicked, and rather over life-size, looking straight out of the picture. All his attributes are here – ring, cigarette-case, tie-pin, cane and, so to speak, the rest of the artist's equipment. This, then, was Mr Dearborn when silence took him ... when he was – alone! On the exquisite mask was a smile, like that Leonardo portrayed on the face of the *Gioconda*, the smile which, we are told, was caused and maintained by the music of hidden flutes – and this wonderful smile of Hugh's is as surely caused by hidden music, by the dead music of his own young voice, by remembered passages from talks with Whistler, Pater, and Oscar Wilde. This picture ranks high as a work of art, but its sadness is unbearable.

Hugh was, however, grateful to the painter for it, and many of his preambles ran: 'As I was saying to an old friend of mine, who I know would interest you, especially with your real interest in, and love of, modern Art (but I expect you know him already?) – a man who really is, I think, one of the most interesting and (though perhaps I ought not to say it, for he is one of my greatest friends) amusing, but I mean really one of the most (*crescendo*) brilliant men, the painter, Henri Schmidt.' ...

The war came and went, rolling me over, submerging me as it did most of the younger generation, filling our souls with anger, rancour and hatred, with pity and love. Mr Dearborn, unsubmerged, began to work at other things than talk for the first time in his life. He worked hard and usefully translating various papers for the Government, being a master of languages as well as of language. The war did not break his indomitable spirit; he never grumbled, nor did he envy the younger men in the trenches, as did so many of our over-age patriots. He behaved, in fact, like what he was – a gentleman. Though there may have been little cracks in the foundation of his spirit, he appeared more elegant and gay than ever, and even took to dancing once more. After working ten arduous hours, with very little actual conversation, in a horribly improvised office, he would dine and then dance till five o'clock in the morning. His vitality was more amazing than ever. High above the coon-born music, above the vulgar, savage and sentimental strains, one could hear the floating 'dying fall' of his voice. Never was anyone so gay, so young, for his age as Hugh Dearborn, but it must have been a strain even on that giant energy. He would go to bed at three o'clock, at four o'clock, at five o'clock each morning, in the highest spirits; but who can bear to think of him, as he slept alone and old, in his charming flat? But the next day at ten o'clock he would walk to his office, gay and beautifully dressed as ever, and alas! (as journalists write about royal visits) with a word for everyone.

Soon after the war I paid a visit, in search of health, to the plaster-shores of the French Riviera; and at Monte Carlo we met. Every morning at twelve o'clock, to the droning snort of a brass band, Mr Dearborn, in white-flannel trousers (oh, how long ago was that day in the garden of Walter Pater! ...), would descend the steps on to the pink-sugar terrace. The war had altered him, and although looking no older, he was beginning to show signs of eternal youth. But under the blue skies, in this hard, trembling light, enhanced by cacti and tropic flowers, and by this sugar-icing world, his appearance took on a new quality, his voice a new tone. He became more real, his warning voice took wing, soared out to sea like the albatross in *The Ancient Mariner*, borne in, as it were, on the crest of a returning toy-wave. His essentially aristocratic finish, and even the rather tired rasp, felt more than heard, of his voice, put the population of international profiteers to shame. It would be many years before these beaked harpies could produce an article with such a finish ... I saw and heard a good deal of Mr Dearborn that spring, and grew to love his conversation. My mind would wander in it, as in a forest; I would lose my path, led away by strains of unfamiliar music, and then be pulled up suddenly by some well-known landmark – the name of Henri Schmidt, or of Durant the boxer – and in that forest I found many homely things that I little expected, and, though on the whole exotic, it was decidedly less so than the war, which at the time we conspired to consider a natural life – and much more restful.

In May I left Monte Carlo, and for nearly two years lost sight and sound of Mr Dearborn.

Two years afterward I was wandering about Italy with young William Erasmus, the writer. It was his first visit to the peninsula, and he was very much on the look-out for copy, though his calm, languid air, as of one dwelling on Olympian heights, was calculated to disguise the fact. But he was always watching, listening, and peering. He had, I suspect, written several Italian travel-sketches before leaving England. He was, however, a charming companion – a companion only too appreciative and receptive, his appreciation of anything amusing or interesting that was said being made even more obvious later, and in print, than at the time. Truly we must have livened up the landscape with the necessary grotesque touch, I with my fleshy Hanoverian face and big body, William, tall and thin as a young giraffe, with the small head of some extinct animal, some kind vegetarian creature that subsisted on the nibbled tops of young palm-trees in the oases – the Giant Sloth, for example! And how often, when I saw silly little jokes of mine appearing under the guise of musical or scientific articles in the weekly papers, did I wish that his character had been true to his appearance, that he had indeed resembled more nearly the Giant Sloth instead of possessing that vast and terrible, assimilative and possessive, energy.

After leaving South Italy we visited Rome and Florence, from there exploring some of the smaller Tuscan towns. The country was in the full efflorescence of early May, only the vines were a little backward, the leaves and tendrils still looking like golden coils about to spring out and release their stored-up energy. Little hills vibrated into the distance like rings of smoke, and the foreground was full of blossom – not the impressionist drifts of colour that you find in northern Europe, but flowers of every colour, each one separate, stiff and geometrical in design, as those in an Italian primitive, or in one of the landscapes of the Douanier Rousseau. The days grew even hotter, and any sudden little blue wind that rose among the distant hills, and played for a moment in the flowering fields, bore an unimaginable load of scent.

One morning we reached the delightful small town of Lucca, finding our rooms in the chief hotel, which had been the palace of one of the noble families in the eighteenth century, when Lucca had been a rich and independent State. The hotel was full of large, lofty rooms with golden curls and network, the prevailing tones of the old paint being light blue or pink, the whole effect being more that of the French than the Italian eighteenth century. The rickety bedstead, shabby German tablecloth, and dingy modern furniture looked very remote in these chambers built as a background for gilded beds, rich brocades, and powdered wigs. Three sounds of the street – shouting, snarling song, and shrilling bird-chatter of the market-place – were very faint at these patrician windows, lapping at them softly like small waves. Everything in the room was bright and quiet as in a coloured glass slide. In fact, the whole hotel had an indefinable atmosphere.

The town itself is a lovely one, with gardens and avenues of chestnuts, whose heavy leaves support their glowing, torch-like flowers on the thick battlemented walls that girdle it. We examined the churches, mostly Romanesque buildings of black and white marble, exotic as zebras, of a fabulous sculptural beauty, but seemingly less connected with the present town or its inhabitants than any pagoda whose blossom-like bells drip down their honey on the Chinese gardens. Yet none of the inhabitants seemed to feel the contradiction between their lives and their back-cloth. There the cathedral stood, like a zebra in the market-place, or like an elephant supporting a howdah – they paid no attention to it. In England these things are different. Any stranger stranded under the wide arches of York station for five minutes would guess instinctively the nature of the Minster, the Bishop's Palace, and even of the Archbishop himself. There is no need to explore. Anything queer will soon be tidied up, and, as they say, 'put to rights.' But in Italy civilisations crowd together: marble churches of the twelfth century, brick-built Gothic palaces, gilded rooms with bellying balconies, and finally the iron bedstead and newspaper, universal symbols of modern culture, cling to each other, each the concrete form of a different view of life.

Thus we explored the town, talking. Then followed an early luncheon, after which Erasmus, who during his four and a half weeks in Italy had already become more Italian than the Italians, even talking the language with such an exquisite *bocca Romana* that the Romans were unable to grasp his meaning, retired for that siesta which was to him the crowning proof of belonging to a cosmopolitan *intelligentsia*. He had, however, already peered into the visitors' book for copy, but found none – not even a resident or casual Englishman in the hotel, which was, as he remarked, none the worse for that; and no doubt comforting himself with thoughts of how unspoilt was this really very sophisticated small town, he retired to rest.

The afternoon passed quickly, and the day dwindled into the dinner-hour.

For a time we walked about the brightly-lit town, but the cinemas were full, and we had seen *Lucia di Lammermoor* the previous evening, so that we returned through the humming streets to our hotel. William went to bed at ten o'clock. Half-an-hour afterwards he called me excitedly into his room, high, gilded, and full of dead air that magnified each sound. His lanky pyjama-clad figure and receptive ear were pressed ecstatically against a door – one which led into the next bedroom. 'Who can it be? Who is it? Who is it?' he whispered. And then, quite clearly, each word taking on a greater significance in this room that seemed like a gilded tomb, I heard ... 'As I was saying only a few days ago to a man, a great friend of mine, who has, I think, really one of the most amusing and interesting personalities – a man who, I know, would delight you, with your knowledge and genuine appreciation of modern art – a really witty, but, I mean to say, brilliant and delightful man, Henri Schmidt.' ...

Thus the poor tired voice dragged on, trailing away into the huge silence of the palace. Hour after hour the monologue continued; sometimes the voice stumbled and there was a weak repetition. Often the stories belonged to an earlier date, the references to those long in their coffins, and through the weak tones of an old man you could catch the fresher notes of an art whose technique had not then been perfected to such a metallic pitch. His smiling, trembling voice conjured up the applauding laughter of other days, when he had possessed a more appreciative audience than latterly. This, then, was how Hugh had talked to Whistler, to Pater; this was how ... But now at three o'clock in the morning the voice sank down to a slight moan. It haunted me, the stillness of the room. What was the mystery of that beautifully-finished being, lying in that vast apartment that belonged to another age of perfected technique? Whose voices answered him in his mind, whose laughter?

Morning came to find Erasmus charmed and inquisitive, myself uneasy, not daring to break into the darkened silence of that room. No name was in the visitors' book; no one was to be seen, no voice sounded. Luncheon came, and we watched with mute inquiry.

But at about two-thirty Mr Dearborn came downstairs, elegant and gay; his mask was rather heavy, tired, and ill-at-ease, though the detail of his appearance was as fresh as ever. But there was a curious thick dragging of his speech, an occasional twitching in the muscles of his mouth. He gave me a hearty but uncertain welcome, avoiding my name. He told me he had been rather ill, and had come here to be alone until he was better able to face the world – his world.

Then it was that I understood – realised the full tragedy of that vocal practice in the small hours. He had been pleading with his art, his Muse, his cruel mistress, to return to him, but the string was broken; she had spread her wings and left the tired old mask: the shell, though still perfect, was empty. The cabinet-gramophone case was complete and beautifully finished; but it was made for only one purpose, and there came no sound of the old music. Art is a hard mistress, mysterious in her intentions. As I left him, never, alas! to see him again, there was a slight return of his powers, and, looking at me, he said: 'One spring afternoon I was in the garden of Walter Pater, walking over the lawn' ... And then I remembered the Parnassian groves, the weeping willow-pattern trees, the exquisite and talented youth in white-flannel trousers, and the words of the old æsthete: 'That young man will go far!' ...

TRIPLE FUGUE

FOREWORD

UNFORTUNATELY a story so far removed from the usual human experience demands some preliminary explanation of the scientific, political, and social facts with which it is connected.

During the course of the last twenty years much has been written, in police-court news as well as in fiction, of the occurrence of triple or quadruple personality. Instances have emerged of an individual possessing three or four distinct egos, souls, personalities, or whichever of the three terms is at the moment most in favour. Each of these entities, while unconscious of the proximity, the existence even, of the others, is yet liable, through we know not what operating cause, at any instant and without warning, to yield place to one of them. It is possible, therefore, that this rarer, more unusual narrative of three separate bodies with but one animating force between them, and each normally ignorant of the intimate tie which binds him to the other two, may be found to possess a certain psychological interest.

A theory has long been formulated as to the 'group-soul' belonging to various of the lower forms of life. Several eminent scientists and philosophers have suggested that – for example – blackbeetles, though each is physically an entity, a smaller or larger insect of dark colouring, exist spiritually (if the use of this adverb in such a connection is pardonable) solely as a group, or, perhaps, as a small number of groups. Each individual beetle forms a single link in the spiritual chain that binds them and is called the group-soul; each is a component part in a composite personality. And this supposition, too, may explain the phenomenon of enchantment. For these repulsive little insects can, like rats or snakes, be charmed, enticed, by one who has the gift or secret, out of the house. The professional usually claims to have inherited this faculty; it is difficult to get from him any explanation of it. But probably his secret is that he can practise a form of mass-hypnotism – he can hypnotise the group-soul of these creatures and lead them out into the wilderness. Thus is revealed to us the secret of the Pied Piper.

Similarly it should not surprise us to learn that one individuality is shared by several human beings; we have only to look round for it to be suggested to us that this form of economy is one that commended itself to the Creator. Indeed the possession by one person of more than one ego is increasingly, enviably rare. In genuine instances of this sort some method, surely, should be discovered of isolating the surplus ones; they should be treated as unearned increment, distributed among the many thousands in need of them – even if this filling of empty places should entail for their owners a fate like that which overwhelmed the Gadarene herd. Each individual, or perhaps one should say each unit or numeral, should possess under a democracy,[1] as adjunct to three acres and a cow, one personality – neither more nor less. But, alas! the influence of democracy, as we know it, appears to have been not so much to give each man a soul as to make the absence of one not so unusual as to be noticeable. Its trend has been, increasingly, to banish eccentricity and encourage its reverse; to make men alike in the possession of useless but pretentious knowledge, ill taught and ill digested, alike in their lack of simplicity, intelligence, and personality. All that is now needed to make the tyrannical triumph of this system complete, is some form of eugenic

[1] *N.B.*—When we refer in these pages to 'democracy' we are not considering it as an idea, but *practically*, as it has been known for the last fifty years in Europe and America.

control, which will finally banish both genius and imbecility, ill-health and unbounded vitality. And the reverse of eccentricity is, undoubtedly, that simian quality of mimicry which, inherent in man, now makes all men alike. Mimicry, indeed, is man's original sin, for when the first individualist monkey had decided to stand up for his rights and be a man (an eccentric monkey that, if ever there was one!) his fellows proceeded to mimic – or some say 'ape' – him, thus building on an insecure foundation, since, in the very act of declaring themselves to be men, they were in reality making a proclamation of essentially monkey-characteristics.

The old dynastic and aristocratic systems of government encouraged, subsidised almost, eccentricity worthy and unworthy alike; and no eccentric, not even the least estimable, would deign, except in the spirit of satire, to mimic his fellows. But with the coming of industrialised, commercialised, and capitalised democracy, every man and woman too had, under pain of ostracism, to dress, talk, and behave alike – or rather as they imagined their 'betters' would dress, talk, and behave. Previously there had been no 'betters' – only richer or poorer, stupider or cleverer, only those better or less good-looking, less or more powerful; facts were acknowledged without envy; but now, with envy, came the assumption of 'betters.' A vicious circle was established. Everyone pretended feverishly to be something or someone he was not. The workman pretended to be a small shopkeeper, the small shopkeeper to be a large one, the large shopkeeper to be that mysterious thing a 'professional man,' the professional man to be a country squire, the rich manufacturer to be a nobleman of long pedigree, dukes to be workmen, kings to be democrats and hereditary presidents. Each, by his own act, laid claim to some distinction which could never be his, and by this very claim admitted an inferiority. For if I shout in your face that I am as good as you are, at once I prove myself inferior in manners. Except for those whose struggle for life was so hard as to leave them no time or desire for self-deception, the world became a matter of acting and make-believe, giving such falsity to every value, such crooked perspective to every event, that when the greatest tragedy in human history came, every nation was equally surprised and unprepared, though each had, in reality, done nothing else except prepare for it, consciously or unconsciously, during the previous half-century. The war, certainly, was the final triumph of the system. Every man, the world over, was forced to fight to make the world Safe for Democracy, whether he believed in it or not – though the war itself was undoubtedly due to the very form of government for which he was now urged to fight, and one, in any case, peculiarly unsuited for the prosecution of a successful war. Emperors and kings, manufacturers of armaments, wealthy noblemen, humble profiteers, none of whom had previously shown much affection for his darling ideal, now advanced into the market-place to demand, to insist, that the world be made Safe for Democracy. And the Democrats of a lifetime were taken in once more. The people of every country allowed only the most brutalised or hypocritical of their countrymen to come to the top and rule them, thereby proving how much they had gained by education and the other blessings which they owed to the system they were now called upon to defend. The few democrats who really believed in the people, and saw how disastrous a war would be for them, were either hounded out of public life or thrown into jail.

Just as one man had for a century past been taught to regard himself as the equal of another, so had each nation been taught to consider itself the equal of its neighbour. Each country must have a bigger navy, bigger army, be a greater power, than those that bordered it. The result of this healthy competitive and democratic spirit was a war disastrous for all who entered it: and once the war started, since each man must be as his fellow, each country had to join in. It became 'the thing to do' – 'good form.' Every nation – except Spain, which had never been democratic, and the Scandinavian countries which were genuinely so – had to enter the arena on one side or the other. Even Oriental, lazy countries like Turkey lost their heads, or were driven into it. Each land must show that it was as great a power, that it could spend as many million pounds a day, as many million lives a year, as its neighbour. The general attitude towards a non-belligerent country was 'Yah-boo! You're not a great power. You can't afford a great war. Yah!'

The ultimate consequence for democracy of this orgy of killing and spending, was the utter revolt against it of Russia and Italy, two of the more intelligent European peoples, who seem to prefer, in the rage of the moment, any tyranny however awful as long as it is not the peculiarly smug one from which others are suffering. For years democracy had been talked of as if it were the ultimate aim of humanity, an end in itself; instead of being merely one more experiment in government, at the best one of many other methods of governing, and one obviously unsuited to certain races. But the war has broken down the tyranny of this idea in several lands.

In the meantime the same old system continues in most of Europe; for how long, no one can tell. Every man and every woman still insists on the acquisition of new rights and the abnegation of old ones. And in the middle of this whirlpool of aggressive action and abject renunciation, is still stranded, on a level surface of peaceful but quite pointless life, a society which insists on no rights and admits no duties except that of self-enjoyment – a worthy though humble aim, which it nevertheless seldom has the intelligence to maintain.

Even thirty years ago this world must have displayed character, a stupid, horsey, sporting character. But the bankruptcy of the aristocratic principle, the advent of industrialism, and, above all, the arrival of rich Jews and Jewesses, entirely altered the scene. Mimicry became more general, for of all races the Semitic is most imitative, original as are many descendants of this remarkable stock. In order to mingle with the people among whom they must live, it has been necessary for them greatly to increase their natural gift for protective colouring. Even physically they alter their characteristics, becoming paler and fairer as they move north, darker as they move south, darker yet towards Africa, yellower and more almond-eyed as they move eastward once more. Theirs is essentially a cuckoo-civilisation. As artists they prove themselves executants more than originators. They excel in dramatic art, they play the tunes that others have written better than the composers themselves. They, it is, who have, perhaps, infused into the world of pleasure a new love of millionaire-art and respect for it, a love of the theatre, of dressing-up, and creature comforts. But there is a bad side to these activities; for the Jew who cannot pass as one of a crowd has to design a rôle for himself, and many of these are engaged in a febrile but fruitless attempt to be something other than they are – Irish patriots or Spanish gypsies, French barons and Austrian noblemen, viceroys or Pre-Raphaelite painters, Celtic mythologists and American citizens, Armenian poets and Persian princes. At the same time, without being eccentric, they are apt to run to extremes – to be poorer or richer than all others, greater capitalists or greater Bolsheviks, more 'modern' or more conventional in their taste for art.

The world they have influenced for the last quarter of a century is, then, perhaps a little more intelligent, but one with far less character, than before the corruption began; more cosmopolitan, more like the world of pleasure in every other capital – in New York and Paris, Berlin and Rome. But it has become the 'right thing' again to manifest a faint interest in music, poetry, portrait-painting, above all in house-decoration; and books, even if their pages are still uncut, lie about once more on the drawing-room tables.

In this world the prevailing and unexciting vice is that of mimicry. Each man has become the shadow of his neighbour, each woman the reflection of another. A few people, a very few who have personality, who are prominent for beauty, wit, impertinence, or even for that attractive capacity for enjoyment which among these attentuated phantoms has become uncommon, are reflected a million times in their friends. A woman will see reflections of herself as many and varied as those contrived in the mirrors at a dressmaker's. Gesture, smile, colouring, clothing, even the tone of the voice, are aped by hundreds and passed on, like the sacred lamp, from one to another. In someone met casually a whole portrait gallery of friends can be discovered; while these, in their turn, will dissolve, to reveal the further, paler spectres of their ancestors. Depth after depth they stretch; a continual deepening of dimensions that becomes like the discovery and exploration of secret caverns, an exploration attended always by a quality of horror, for you may find the gigantic skeleton of an extinct animal, the remains of a dead friend; and places unlived in are apt to be haunted. To meet one of these shadows is not unlike pulling-out section after section of a telescope – only, at each prolongation of it, to be greeted by a familiar yet unexpected and indistinct feature – which had previously escaped you – of the landscape. Another section is extended and focused, in order that you may concentrate on this new landmark and see it more clearly, but in the very act a further familiar object is disclosed to the eye, always slightly distorted by the lens, until the whole process becomes a nightmare.

For at each handing on of it, the imitation, though very recognisable, becomes a little different, as if the colourless soul of the person through whom it has passed had yet contrived to alter the image ever so minutely. One line is slightly firmer, coarser, in its drawing; another more blurred. Each image has behind it other ones, the family features, its portion of the group-soul. Each image is like one of those old-fashioned Christmas cards with a view on it, which, when a tag of paper is pulled, dissolves slowly into other landscapes; and at times the two melt into a muddled whole.

Apart, then, from the few genuine persons who move among the shadows, each new arrival at party, theatre, or restaurant, exhibits a soul that is like one of those rooms of distorting mirrors that were to be met with formerly at Earl's Court, the White City, and Luna Park. Someone is reflected, reflected for ever in a thousand distorted variations, while the number of the reflections helps to disguise the emptiness and small dimensions of the place itself. In the relation of one mirroring to another, fresh designs are formed constantly, other shadows suggested, as in a kaleidoscope the same small pieces of coloured glass move ever towards fresh arrangements. Pondering every movement of these exquisitely lacquered but composite figures, new distant views are conjured up. At the end of one gesture you will see, as in a garden, a perspective of gracious but silent deities; and these again are reflected in the water that hurls them downward, head first, into the blue void of the sky. Each distant-sounding voice has an echo of other utterances; some even are echoes of voices, genuine voices, now for ever silent. The dead speak for a time as clearly as the living in these empty houses; yet are as bare and desolate, a vacuum into which no great wind will ever sweep.

It is, in fact, possible to unpack many people as if they were so many portmanteaux of stolen personal belongings; to take out of them a gesture, an expression, a tone, the palpable and familiar property of another. Let us illustrate this. Once we sat in a restaurant, at the next table to a polished and elegant lady, unknown to us, but whose every movement was recognisable; in whom, as she talked, a whole ancestry of shadows could be unravelled. That lifting of one finger like a shepherd's crook declared itself as a reflection of an early copy of Mme de Blank's rendering of a mannerism in her friend, Lady Carabas. To watch the wistful smile unfolding on those lips was equivalent to peeping through the keyhole of the garden of the Knights of Malta at Rome, where far away can be distinguished the solid, very personal dome of St. Peter's; for far away, behind this delicate echo, lies the caressing but bulky smile of Lady de Bludyer. The little dry laugh, too, lacquered as the west wind on a Chinese screen, is but a transposition in key of Mrs Kinfoot's serving up of Ethel Misborough's laughter; while that innocent, round-eyed sucking-of-the-thumb is merely an unauthorised version of Lady Ethel Cressey's almost unconscious imitation of her cousin, Lady Septuagesima Goodley, a woman of genuine, if difficult, character, who, now in late middle age, employs this trick as proof of her lamb-like and misunderstood disposition – a proof which has finally convinced her easily-gullible friends.

Thus in these varnished hollows could we isolate for the moment a hundred reflections of a few genuine personalities. Nor, altogether, do these mirrorings make the world unpleasant. The student of social life can play a detective game for his own amusement; while to the mirrors and mirrored, the constant vibration and echo, the innumerable variations on the same key, give a certain brilliancy and cold sparkle to gatherings, filling empty rooms with a scintillation of light thrown back as through crystal and deep waters. One or two colours are vibrated in every tone and shade; a note is struck out that is responded to by every shallow object, every translucent substance, in the room. Who knows but that if every shade became a person, every echo a genuine voice, there would be a riot of colour, a storm of sound too strong for us? ...

*

In order to write it, the story that follows compelled us to advance along various tracks, already noticeable, until these converged, and we found ourselves in the year 1948. This future already looming over us is more difficult to grasp than any other, just as the equidistant past is the hardest to recall. Both are so little divided from the present, so fantastically alike, so grotesquely different.

If we take a compass and, fixing the leg that is to remain steady in the present year, begin to circumscribe, as it were, a circle, the diameter of which is twenty-five years, we shall notice that the people and background of the year 1898 through which it passes seem slightly contorted, are invested with a certain air of improbability which is termed 'quaintness' – rather ugly quaintness still, for it is too near to have become focused and 'picturesque.' Similarly, if we continue the circle into the future, the people and background near that circumference have the same quality – one which would be lacking in a more remote age, so strange would it seem.

Among a myriad possibilities the immediate future holds always two highly probable alternatives. One, ever the most likely and at this moment seeming almost a certainty, is of a complete break, a tremendous reaction against the immediate past and all that it represented; the other, an exaggeration of present tendencies. From these two it has been necessary to choose the latter, to make the future age like our own, so that as if comparing two similar profiles, we notice the likeness by the slight differences, and gain a more complete knowledge of one by gazing on the other.

We move, then, in the same world of rather hysterical

shadows, the same state that somehow moves on by its own impetus. We are greeted with the familiar echoes and reflections that we have been discussing. Many of those prominent in the arts, in literature, in the State, are the same persons we know, only older and no wiser, while all are seen through the glass of time as men are seen through the medium of water. The water is unruffled and deep, so deep; and the bodies of the swimmers are near the surface; yet all are elongated and drawn out, or broadened and foreshortened, their colour subdued or accentuated by this seemingly transparent element.

PART I

The first scene of our strange drama unfolds itself in the respective bedrooms of Mr Valentine Leviathan, Lord Richard Cressey, and Mr Freddie Parkinson at the hour of 7.55 one Friday evening in the early May of 1948. In this way we are enabled to make the acquaintance of our three protagonists while they are still dressing for their parts.

Mr Valentine Leviathan, impoverished but hopeful – from his own point of view – member of the great Anglo-American mercantile house of Leviathan, is discovered, hurried, harried, and out of humour in front of a diminutive looking-glass in a hired flat off Belgrave Square. The apartment is fussily decorated, over-upholstered, yet uncomfortable in a hotel fashion. The softness and depth of the arm-chairs, the thick carpet and other properties would produce in one unused to them a feeling of asthma, hay-fever and croup. Too proud to work much, too poor to be idle, Valentine writes articles on French politics for *The Morning Star* – a newspaper, the venerable owner of which is a friend of the family. He knows no French and little politics, but by dint of a certain facility for skating over ice that no longer exists – which he was forced to acquire during several years at a large public school, where it was understood that though you need not learn anything you ought to pass the examinations – just manages to impress his readers with what he leaves unsaid.

'Clever chap, that! You can read a lot between the lines,' the old gentlemen used to say, puffing whale-like in their club windows, which seem the glass walls of some gigantic aquarium. And, indeed, reading between the lines you could distinguish almost anything which suited your mood. Regarded strictly, however, as to what they said and how they said it, Valentine's articles were sympathetic yet impressive, having the character of essays written by a sick schoolgirl and subsequently corrected by a prim but kindly nursery-governess. They were full of suggestions, suppressed enough to be convincing, of-being-very-much-in-the-know, and of what-fun-we-are-all-having. Occasionally these would be varied with distinguished compliments and authoritative warnings to our Allies. At other times this one of our three heroes turns a more honest, congenial, but secret penny by revealing the movements of friends, and interesting facts about them, to the readers of the illustrated daily papers.

While, with little corners of white lather still on his face from shaving, he hurries from one room to another looking for a towel, we are privileged to read the latest of these ramblings. 'Hats off to President Trotsky' we shall read to-morrow glancing through the pages, 'Salute Denmark,' and then, sandwiched between these commands, come to Valentine's gossipy page, typical development of his time. At present these social jottings are lying in a scrawling handwriting on an untidy desk, while near to them is their envelope, ready, and addressed to the editor.

'A friend tells me,' they run:

The Pecksniff Prize

'Pamela tells me that Lord Richard Cressey has been asked to present this year's Pecksniff Prize for English Literature; an event which will take place in late July at the Skimpole Hall. Lord Richard is, of course, the third son of the fourth Duke of Kirkcudbright and brother of the present Duke. He is also known as a promising diplomat (he is said to have been responsible for that *thrilling* Yugo-Slovak Jingo-Slav crisis last year) and is already quite a figure in literary and artistic circles. His novel of Balkan life, *In a Yashmak Garden*, created quite a stir, and, it is rumoured, was mentioned in private conversation by Professor Criscross to the venerable Earl of Chiswick, that last of the Great Victorians. He has also published latterly a slim volume of powerful nature-poems, under the title of *The Buzzard's Bastard*, in which he makes a strong plea for the feeding of young cuckoos. This, too, has been very favourably received by the critics, and has already gone into a fifth edition. Lord Richard's many friends hope that as well as being asked to present the prize, he will also be allowed to receive it.' ...

A Notable Wedding

'Dearest, the Cressy wedding was quite the event of the 1946 season, wasn't it? How strange it seems that it is already two years ago! Both the bride and bridegroom, who are very artistic, were related to numerous important families, and such lovely clothes! The six bridesmaids were all dressed in sheath-gowns of ruby tinsel, and a note of originality was struck by the bride's wreath, which was made of silver paper and worn upside down. The orange flowers were made of mother-of-pearl, with gilded-tin stalks, and sewn on to the bandeau. So chic! Lady Richard – or Goo-Goo as she is known to her friends – is petite, piquante, and pimpante, and was, of course, niece to Baroness d'Arenheimer, the well-known French philanthropist, and daughter of Mrs Silas B. Guggerty, a popular and charming transatlantic visitor who often has the honour of entertaining both Princess Marie-Antoinette of Metro-Schinkenberg and Princess Antoinette-Marie of Metroberg-Schinken in her fascinating London home. All six of them, Lord Richard, Lady Richard (Goo-Goo), Mrs Guggerty, Baroness d'Arenheimer, Princess Marie-Antoinette and Princess Antoinette-Marie, are, of course, exceptionally artistic. I met Mrs Guggerty in Bond Street yesterday and thought her looking quite a picture, with her mass of snow-white hair, in a short bolero of blue coney-skin, with a hussar-collar of Trotsky-lapin. Such a becoming toque, too, dark blue, trimmed at one side with little bunches of coque's feathers.'

An Original Hostess

'Dinky writes to me to-day that she immensely enjoyed the interesting party of artistic people that Lady Richard entertained last week at her country home, Little Titterham, Old Twits, near Cinderbury. Situated on the barest parts of the Sussex Downs, Little Titterham was just a small two-roomed cottage, with the dearest old barn, till Lady Richard – who, like her husband, is, of course, immensely artistic – turned out the family who lived there and converted it into an ideal country residence. It is unnecessary to say that she is extremely popular in the neighbourhood. Each guest is given a bathroom, swimming bath, tennis court and croquet lawn of his own, and a delightful note of simplicity is struck throughout. One of a number of charmingly modern touches that mark this unique home is the placing in each bedroom of a little homespun sack full of lavender, on which are depicted scenes from the Soviet-Art Cabaret; these are executed by Lady Richard herself, and are signed "Goo-Goo" in diminutive letters. These little touches, needless to say, are immensely appreciated by Lady Richard's friends.'

An Interesting House-Party

'The artistic party of interesting people at Little Titterham last week included Baroness d'Arenheimer and her two pretty debutante daughters, Angel and Desirée (doesn't she seem young, darling? to have grown-up daughters!); Sir Booster Babboon, the Picturesque Persian Philanthropist (who is taking such an *interest* in the bazaar that the Baroness is getting up in aid of the "Superannuated-Money-lenders'-Children-Benefit-Fund." He can always be depended on to help forward any worthy charity); Mrs Guggerty; Mr Matthew Dean; Mr Valentine Leviathan, the clever and popular young writer on international topics; Mrs Kinfoot, the well-known hostess, who has just returned from her first lion-hunt in Africa; Lady Selina Moonbury; Adèle Lady Fortcarrick (who is supposed to have gone round in four); Mr Edward Tush; Mr Charles Rotumjhy, the famous Hungarian portrait-painter; Mr Freddie Parkinson, and others equally well known. Lady Richard, who, besides being *exceptionally* artistic, *adores* music, delighted her friends by a rendering of the "Jewel Song" from *Faust* on the water-whistle and has now left for Aix-les-Bains. It is hoped that she will be back in Little Titterham, where she will be much missed, by the middle of next month.'

Valentine has re-entered the room, and is wildly opening and shutting various drawers, and ringing wireless-electric bells, which he knows quite well will not be answered: a form of neurasthenia resulting from a long period of underwork, for he does not really in the least mind how late he is for an engagement. As he moves about, very swiftly, half-dressed, it is difficult to grasp the salient features of his appearance. He is youngish, perhaps about twenty-seven, and taller than the average. Though still somewhat flushed from the bath, his skin is yet rather yellow and very smooth, his eye of that vacant blue which clearly demands a monocle; but in this case the demand is unsatisfied. His toneless fair hair is brushed back, sleek and shining, and he boasts a moustache, short, fair, rather more bristling, drooping, and untidy than one would expect from the rest of his aspect; for, as his dress grows more complete, a certain rather insect-like elegance evolves round him. Clothed, brushed, polished, he has a suave yet overblown quality, like the scent of syringa or the glossy, rounded, and enamelled form of certain beetles. The rather shabby moustache, therefore, detracts from this, making it more bearable, like a flaw in a precious stone, though, at the same time, it imparts an air of premature age.

The rooms, usually noisy, are very quiet at this instant. Obviously, then as now, the taxicabs are in hiding, the drivers playing piquet in a thousand obscure shelters, happy in the knowledge that this should be their busiest hour. Hastily snatching coat, top-hat and cane, Valentine dashes out to retrieve one.

*

Half-a-mile away Lord Richard Cressey is presented to us in an upper bedroom of Kirkcudbright House, the family mansion in London. He has arrived back, rather late, from the Foreign Office, and is tired. The swelling waves of the treetops, now in their full green spray, stand frozen below, as if some wizard had thrown a spell over them just as they were about to flood the wide-open windows of this gaunt, severe mansion. Led by one of those small grey puffs of wind that are a feature of the London parks in summer, they advance once more; this time, surely, they will invade the house, for the leaves are tilted up by the breeze, overturned for a moment with a flash of silver till they become the white-horses of this green sea, or the outriders of such an army as marched against Macbeth. Beyond the park, above the droning, groaning clamour, broken by shuddering hoots, of the distant traffic, beneath the softer dragon-fly note of the hovering aeroplanes that pass every second, Lord Richard's wandering blue eye is rested by the stiff cubist arrangement of slate-roofs, gables, spires, huge flat square warehouses, looking like magnified Roman-tombs, and angular towers, that constitutes the London horizon. In among these, contrasting with the great width, heaviness, and solidity of these buildings, rise the giant but slender wireless-masts, which, growing thus in clumps, look like cuttings of bamboo waiting for the spring to touch them into leaf. The prevailing colour of the outlook at this hour is soft grey, softer blue, and a little gold, while over these pastel-tones is superimposed the patine of light and shade that London has breathed on them, blurring and silvering them gently, as the breath of man lingers for a moment on a mirror or pane of glass. The three square windows that allow these tall buildings to lift their heads above the trees into the room are set in a large square chamber that has a steady air, like that of an old-fashioned butler. There is much solid mahogany furniture and a singularly respectable wall-paper. The air is pervaded with the familiar smell of ancient polished wood, and in this evening light the walls are enveloped in a rather thick golden-glow, like the varnish on one of those screens composed of scraps, prints and Christmas cards, which, made in the early decades of the nineteenth century, still show boldly in the messrooms of old regiments, or lurk abashed in the lumber-rooms of decaying country-houses. No sign is here of Lord Richard's modern taste in decoration; but then this is not his house, for Lady Richard is away at Aix: his house is shut up, and he is staying here for a few weeks with his brother.

Under the shadow of a large mahogany four-poster, placed on a thick white counterpane, white as a winding-sheet, lie the folded corpses that will soon be quickened; black clothes that, as they lie there in the strong light, seem green, rather mouldy with age, but, when once more in contact with human vitality, will become fresh again, almost smart; for clothes are essentially vampiric, taking part of our life, though in return they give us something back. There lie, too, a white shirt, rigid and shiny, and a white collar like the section of a drain-pipe, stiff with death. On the dressing-table are a black tie, folded and looking like a large, frayed moth, a square folded white handkerchief, and a little mound of copper coins. These latter suggest, by their presence, that in due course a professional is coming in to lay out all these corpses in the proper manner, weighting down their empty eyes with these coins. And, indeed, the professional (Barnacle, Lord Richard's valet) is waiting outside even now for a summons.

Above the dressing-table, supported by two pillars, is balanced at an angle the reflection of what is apparently some sea-creature, some light-blue and deep-pink sea-monster, but is in reality merely a rare edition of Lord Richard – Lord Richard as he appears each day to his valet but not to the world, blue as to underclothes, coral-pink from his bath, while little sequins of steam glitter like sea-water on pink face, feet, arms and calves. This deepening of colour, accentuation of light and shadow, rather obscures the face, so that at one moment he looks in the later twenties, at another in the late forties, and is probably somewhere between the two. We notice a rather bristly downward moustache, fairish, rumpled hair, and blue, blue eyes. The mirror reflects hurried movements: in it we see Lord Richard plunging headforemost into his white shirt. There is a rattle of white spray, and he comes up to the surface, his head showing again at the crest of this foaming, flashing wave, like the moustached countenance of a seal revealed from some breaker. As if he had really just returned from the salty depths rewarded with precious trophies of his skill in that other element, the reflection presents to us a pearl, round, fair, and velvet-soft, being secured by red fingers, like crustacean pincers, in the centre of a flat surface of white foam.

Piece by piece the corpses assume vitality: the warm, magnetic flow of life courses through the fibre of shirt, collar, socks, trousers, waistcoat; and even the frayed moth takes the air again with a certain jauntiness. Lord Richard looks, on the whole, rather well dressed, but in contrast to our first hero, as if he did not care very much about such things. He glances anxiously at his watch, dashes with short, very quick steps downstairs, where he is helped into a large overcoat, his own quickness of movement being in such contrast to the leisurely actions of his valet, that he is nearly strangled in the process. He runs into the waiting taxicab, shouting to the valet: 'Don't wait up for me, Barnacle. If anyone radios me, tell them to ring up 9234 Holborn, Mr Dean's. And you might let them know at Mecklenburg Square that Her Ladyship won't be back until the middle of next month. Good night!' And, heralded by a startling series of rattling alarms, is borne out of the large sombre backwater into the choked streams of traffic beyond.

*

Westward, Freddie Parkinson is nearly dressed, but in no great hurry. Valentine is sure to be late. The small, demure house always smells as if it had just been painted. The walls are nearly always grey, the carpets invariably green and self-coloured. There are, placed about in the rooms downstairs, several subtly ugly and completely undecorative little pieces of early Chinese pottery, which have either been snatched out of the sacred earth by tomb-plunderers and handed on through dealers at a price completely out of proportion to their value, or have, perhaps, just been made at that new factory outside Pekin, where they will busy themselves with such things. Freddie is devoted to these 'pots' – pronounced 'pahts' – and is constantly caressing them with rather insensitive, blunt finger-tips, imagining that he can determine their age by the feel of their glaze, or get some æsthetic pleasure out of the handling of them. These things are now everywhere inheriting the place of willow-pattern plates and long-ladies. Very few pictures hang on the walls, but there are a few etchings and woodcuts, simple and at the same time very fussy. It is curious that Freddie should collect both these 'pahts' and these etchings; it is a curious combination, for though he takes both seriously, one completely denies and cancels-out the artistic principles of the other. But above all Freddie collects the scandals of the day; on these he is a recognised authority, a connoisseur who is consulted upon scabrous discoveries, just as a great authority on early Italian pictures would be asked to pronounce his opinion upon some new and precious find.

Upstairs, on the second landing, the door is open, and Freddie is fastening his collar. In appearance he is taller than either Lord Richard or Mr Leviathan, and older, about ten years older. His face is more furrowed, and is becoming somewhat leathery. His hair – for he shows no trace of baldness – is more stubborn, his eye of a more faded, and therefore a more piercing, blue. Eyebrows and moustache are very definite and stubborn. He carries his head rather forward, peering a little, as if scenting some new scandal, and already well on its track. He comes out of his room to shout to the maidservant that he wants a taxicab; and it is noticeable that as she comes nearer, he shouts louder. Freddie looks rather tired; for, in this respect totally unlike Valentine, he works hard in an office all day for money that he does not need. He is well known in the social world – in fact everybody knows him because he knows someone else. Two gaunt sisters, tall as grenadiers, are his companions in the house, sisters who adore yet despise him. He is very fond of them, but is not attached to his numerous other relatives, of whom he is really rather ashamed, apt to avoid, however willing are they to see more of him. His voice getting ever louder as he goes downstairs, he bears off an old opera hat, which he opens with a snap, until, like himself, it is tubular in form. It elongates him, as if a snake had added to its stature – completes his appearance. He is seen sitting in an open taxicab, its wheels grinding slow, like the mills of God, until it has disappeared round the corner.

*

At this moment Mr Matthew Dean, R.D.O. (Royal Dodonian Order, 2nd Class, Grand Cross), is waiting rather agitatedly in his house near Queen Anne's Gate. There is little reason for agitation, but Mattie cannot bear being kept waiting; it is bad for his nerves. He walks from room to room, gazing vaguely, without seeing anything, at the pictures old and modern which are so numerous as almost to blot out the gaily-painted panelling. The blinds are drawn, though a faint, cold light still penetrates them, and the rooms are lit by old-fashioned electric lamps, well shaded, that throw down rather ruddy circles of light (so much softer and prettier, his guests invariably say, than the hard false daylight of wireless lighting) on the tables where they stand. There are several of these tables in each room: on them, framed in tortoiseshell, stand signed photographs of many social and stage celebrities, reputed beauties, and a few popular, but not *too* popular, poets and writers. Lying about carefully arranged, but with an appearance of freedom, as if they had just been put down for a moment, are various books, political or literary, collections of rather rare modern first editions, novels, or the last word in poetry or the drama. Among these, taken at random, we read such titles as *Down Sussex Way*, by Jacques Rosenheimer; *My Part in the Third Great War*, by the Rt. Hon. Winston Churchill; *Limpet, and Other Poems*, by Ego Aneurism Jones; *Scribblings:* a book of Literary Criticism, by H. Mollycod Moiré; Vol. II of the 'Bloomsbury Painters Series,' *From Giotto to Gertler;* and several rare Squireana, consisting of *Baudelaire Flowers*, by Jack Collings Squire – suppressed by the author; a book of Early Essays by 'Solomon Eagle'; *Collected Parodies* (very rare), by Jack Squire; *Songs of the Slaughterhouse* (early and rare), by Jack C. Squire; *The Lily of Malud* (rare and curious), by J. C. Squire; *Australian Poems*, by J. Collings Squire; *The Soccer Match, and Other Poems*, by Sir Collings Squire; *Lesser Lyrics of the First Half of the Last Decade but One of the Seventeenth Century*, compiled by Ego Aneurism Jones, with a prefatory note by Lord Squire of Chiswick; *Simple Lyrics of the Countryside, with Glossary*, by Raoul Gelding, prefaced by a brief explanatory note by Lord Squire of Chiswick, O.M., and 'A Catalogue of a Portion of the Library of Viscount Squire of Chiswick, O.M., compiled by Professor James Criscross and Ernest Lympe, with a new portrait of His Lordship by Solomon Gluckstein, and an original poem by Mr Edward Shanks.' On another table we see piled up, *From a Library Stool*, by James Criscross; *Drivellings*, by K. Mimicky Murrain; *Heather o' Moors*, a volume of Verse by Vincent O'Coddell; *How I won the Third World-War*, by the Rt. Hon. David Lloyd George; *Myself and Trotsky*, uniform with *A History of my Fourth Campaign in the Dardanelles*, by the Rt. Hon. Winston Churchill; the last six volumes of Verse by Mr Edward Shanks; the last dozen by Mr W. J. Turner, and the last dozen and a half volumes of Collected Essays by Sir Robert

Lynd. On a larger table are several bulky and fantastically-bound scrap-books, in which during his leisure moments Mr Dean, with one or two chosen allies, pastes photographs, and newspaper cuttings, or induces his numerous friends among present-day poets to write a favourite set of verses. There are also several vases of flowers.

It must be admitted from the first that Mr Matthew Dean – or poor Mattie as he is to his friends – is essentially himself and, in spite of a rather feeble character, is reflected by many, while never reproducing the ways or tricks of others. Coming out of a solemn background at once scholarly and ecclesiastic, he has reacted away from it, towards, as he thinks, the worlds of fashion, gaiety, and wit. These he has frequented for over thirty years; so, though his appearance does not suggest it, he must be between fifty and sixty years of age. But, since a man is judged by his friends, he must be counted as an honorary young man – young enough, in fact, to know better. His body, though not stunted, is punily, uneasily built; the shoulders are too broad, both for the head and body, more especially for the neck, giving from a distance an impression of strength that is immediately contradicted by the rest of his physique, and by the face. This latter is sallow in colour, nearly circular in shape except for a slight squaring of the forehead, and a dent, like a nick clipped out of a coin, that marks the chin. The black eyes are alive and kindly; the eyebrows thick and dark, grow up at an angle, ending in a Mandarin-like tuft. These eyebrows, tilted up like the eaves of a Japanese temple, are really the natural feature of the face: but art has helped Nature, for beneath one of them is a round monocle that echoes in miniature the larger circle of the face, seeming to be a young one budding out of it. The hair follows the line of the eyebrow, turning up slightly at the temples, and is brownish-grey. The neck, as we noted, is peculiarly long, thin, and out of proportion to the shoulders, so that when Mattie lifts up his head, with the nervous wriggling waggle that is his way, to talk, it is as if a ventriloquist's dummy is speaking – so thin is the wooden stalk of the neck moving in the too-wide socket of the collar-bone. The voice itself, when with great effort it sounds out, is extraordinarily high, lisping, innocent, and irritating as the twittering of a fluffy young bird that lifts up head and gaping mouth from its nest, expecting to be fed. Like such a fledgeling, too, is the manner in which he raises his head, and moves his neck – or perhaps like a newly-hatched chicken looking up out of its broken shell! – while the bright nervous eye, which seems to twitter also behind its glass section, has something of the bird-effect as well. On the other hand, when in a very good mood, his face and shoulders remind one a little of a smiling, purring cat. At this moment, however, he is more bird-like than cat-like; he is obviously waiting for someone, and as obviously dislikes the process. He is now dressed in a black dinner-jacket, black tie and white shirt: his clothes are always well made, almost too appropriate for the occasion, and must require an amount of attention.

Mattie, as we have noticed from the furnishing of his house, is a great patron of the arts, ancient and modern; a patron of advanced art even – as long as it has not advanced too far to make safe its retreat. In the social world he is one of the acknowledged arbiters of taste, especially of things new, and is being constantly implored in the drawing-rooms for help and advice on matters concerning art and literature, what pictures to invest in, what books to borrow. 'I'll ask Mattie; he'll tell me what to get,' is to be heard on all sides. He is on every board and committee that exists for the acquisition of modern works-of-art, or for the reward of virtue in literature, and is one of the permanent judges who each year assign the Pecksniff Prize to some suitable neophyte. The latter consists of a cheque for £200, awarded to the writer of what is, in the opinion of the judges, the year's best piece of imaginative writing, whether in poetry or prose. Mattie therefore is essentially for Safety-First in literature and the arts, for though he must startle his friends occasionally, and can afford to be a little daring every now and then, he does not want to risk the reputation for sound judgment which he has acquired among those friends who know less about such things than himself. His own personal inclination is toward an affected simplicity in art, just as the dyspeptic finds more enjoyment in plain food than in complicated dishes. But his own natural impulse has somewhat broken down. For, in spite of a genuine instinct and love for art and literature, he was originally a prig; an artistic prig, no doubt of it. But now success has made him a snob instead. He appears terrified that his past will be revealed, that his smart friends will know him for a prig! Thus he is battling always against an unspoken accusation, anxious to prove it false. This process has made his taste muddled and flaccid, for he has been forced to talk of musical comedies as if they were as important as the greatest operas, of music-hall comedians as if they were the greatest executants in the world; and in a voice so high, that like a bat's note it is scarcely audible to the human ear, he is for ever singing inane little jigs and jingles to prove how up-to-date he is, and how much he enjoys these entertainments. And, as a matter of fact, he has really grown to like them. He attends every theatrical first night, of whatever kind, which gives him an opportunity to show his tact, for his clothes must ever be appropriate to the occasion, and yet he must differentiate according to the status of the theatre. A Lyceum melodrama demands from him quite a different turn-out from that which is necessary for a musical comedy, or Covent Garden. But if two first-performances at the theatres occur on the same evening, then his grief and perturbation know no bounds! He becomes a baby claimed by two mothers and awaiting the judgment of a wiser, more merciful, Solomon. Altogether, in order to prove that he is no prig, Mattie has had to cultivate that odious, authority-sapping theory of relativity in the arts that is so much in evidence. The chief symptom of this softening of the mental fibre is the series of tremendous attacks on such men as Dante, Shakespeare, Virgil, and Titian, delivered by such 'high-brow' journalists as write every week for 'low-brow' readers. I am as good as you, Tchekhoff as great as Dante, Lord Squire as Shakespeare, McEvoy as Mantegna, Grock as Greco. This trait of Mattie's, this equal devotion to God, Demigod and Beast, is the most modern thing about him, since, though he would never admit it, he actually belongs to the period of the first Great War – of Illustrated Society Papers and 'Jazz Bands.'

His position as a man behind the scenes in politics helps his prestige as a connoisseur of art, and is of use to him generally. He is of the type that, like certain Orientals, enjoys obscure power, loves power without the public appearance of it. Not for a moment does he wish for any more prominent position that than which he now occupies. Politically he has had much experience, has acquired much knowledge. His career had begun, as a matter of fact, many years before the violent disruption of the old Party System by the Press Barons, as they are called. Those of my readers who are old enough, remarked for themselves, doubtless, that steady increase of power which accrued to the Newspaper Proprietors over a period of some thirty years – a steady development only set back occasionally, or even tragically, by some such incident as that which befell Bottomley-The-Martyr. The first sure sign of the new power was the substitution of Newspaper, for National, Insurance. It was not until that momentous meeting in the spring of 1934 that the Press Barons openly claimed the right of the Journal with the Largest Daily (Net)

Circulation to govern the country. They pointed out that the time had come for a more modern, more democratic, form of Government, and that they were the fully-developed heirs of the old system. For the old Party System had over a period of a century rightly attached supreme importance to universal education; it had taught every man and every woman to read – and what they read were these journals. Thus the power of the Press was proved to be the offspring of compulsory education.

And the politicians, or Elder Statesmen, as they are now officially designated, welcomed the change; before the *coup d'état* they had been the targets at which had been constantly fired the most poisonous darts of the Press. The latter would insist simultaneously on such things as Retrenchment and the most expensive Social Reforms, a great increase in armaments together with a reduction of 5s. in the £ on the Income Tax, Peace and a policy which would inevitably lead to War, thereby pleasing, by one proposal or another, every possible reader of their papers. As for the politicians, they had neither the strength nor the desire to struggle against these contradictory demands. At the same time, in order to keep up, or to increase, its circulation, the interest of every newspaper was really in the direction of greater excitements – more frequent and more brutal murders, vast explosions, huge conflagrations, gigantic battles on land and sea. Even Nature itself seemed anxious to please the omnipotent Barons, presenting them with tidal waves of unusual size, thrilling earthquakes, devastating eruptions.

Before the new system was declared, each succeeding Government was in turn exposed by the Press: Government succeeded Government with a bewildering rapidity – a rapidity made more bewildering, indeed, by the fact that, though differently labelled, the personnel of each Government was nearly identical with that of the one which it had replaced. The combinations of politician and politician were infinite and kaleidoscopic. At one moment they would be abusing each other like fish-wives in the market, at the next they would 'Achieve Unity' and embrace: within a month they would together form a new Government. This, in its turn, would fall within a few weeks, to be succeeded by a new arrangement of the dear old faces. Elderly ponderous peers would tread weightily from one party to the other and back again; but at each change the country would be put to the expense of a General Election.

Thus, when toward the end of the Third Great War (the French One) the Barons seized the executive and proclaimed themselves the Trustees of the Nation, the politicians welcomed it, actually, as a release, for they were still to carry on the actual work of Government; but now the Press assumed openly the responsibility, and there would be no need for sudden changes of policy and, better still, no possibility of an election. The same old faces, under the Guy Fawkes-like masks of the Press Barons, still make our laws; and owing to the prolongation of human life made possible by the great advance in biological and surgical knowledge, it seems as if we shall be able to benefit indefinitely by the ever-increasing wisdom and experience of these Elder Statesmen.

The latter, it was arranged, were to be paid large salaries by the Press Barons, though liable to instant dismissal if they failed to please their masters; heavy penalties also were incurred by any attempt at insubordination. Till the new system was in proper working-order, the two proprietors of the two journals with the Largest Circulation (Net) formed a coalition in order to draw up the New Charter. We owe much to these two patriots, who sank their differences for a common purpose, Lord FitzBison and the old Duke of Badgery St Lawrence. How typical it is of that admirable British spirit of compromise which has always influenced, for the good, our Rough Island

Story, that these two men should have chosen to govern on their behalf those very same politicians for whose impeachment they had been clamouring but the night before!

The New Charter was drawn up with great moderation. No change was made – or even contemplated – in the Constitutional Monarchy, for, apart from any question of the relative merits and demerits of the monarchic and republican systems, the King grows, if possible, ever more popular as the years pass. Measures enacted have still, before they become the law, to receive the Royal Assent. But the Press Baron of the moment is, like the King, advised by his ministers, and can now do no wrong. Let it not be supposed for a moment, though, that by this I am suggesting the possibility of a newspaper peer doing wrong before his infallibility was thus legally established.

The old House of Commons was closed and converted into a Museum of Progress – showing the invention of the printing press, and its subsequent developments. The House of Lords, which had, some years before the coup, been reformed, was allowed to continue its deliberations and to a degree, to increase its power. Since 'the backwoodsmen,' as they used to be termed, had been removed, no rancour was felt in the country at the influence of this august assembly, for the latter had taken care to make it obvious that not one among them could be accused of being a gentleman. It had become, in fact, under the final Labour Governments, a more democratic institution than the House of Commons.

Financially the Charter established important reforms. The National Debt now amounted to £1,000,000,000,000,000,000,000,000,000,000,000,000,000,000,000,000,000,000,000,000,000,000,000: it was necessary, therefore, to increase the taxation on small incomes. Tax-payers with incomes of £50 per annum had, of course, to pay £25 a year in taxes. Though this at first seemed hard, the Press Barons felt it to be a necessary measure, and were not afraid to govern justly. Alleviations were made in other directions. The tax on incomes of over £100,000 was halved, the Super-Tax abolished, and taxation on incomes of over £200,000 done away with altogether, in order, as the Charter phrased it, 'to encourage thrift by a sane measure of economic democracy.' On the other hand, it was made compulsory for every citizen with an income of under £5,000 per annum to buy a newspaper every morning and every evening (after this measure had been passed, it came as a surprise to find how many men there were in the country who admitted to an income of over £5,000) and, on leaving his home for the day's work, to stand still in the street, at attention, and doff his hat three times to that foreign power to which, on this particular day, the governing newspaper had decreed the compliment. This – as we are all aware – one ascertains by opening the day's paper, which will have in large letters, at the top of its principal page, such captivating captions as 'Salute Denmark' or 'Hats off to Holland.' The enactment of these daily greetings, too, has done much to improve our relations with the Continent. Sometimes individuals are substituted for countries or the actual compliment is varied. A Two-Minutes' Silence may be proclaimed in honour of some more than usually public-spirited millionaire, Sir Booster Babboon for instance; while a silence of Ten-Minutes is imposed each year in memory of Bottomley-The-Martyr. Indeed, one of the decrees to which the Coalition attached the greatest importance was the setting up of a statue of heroic size to Bottomley on Parliament Green. Of gilded bronze and nearly fifty feet in height, it was erected as a tribute to the memory of that pioneer who had first both divined the power of the Press and exploited its financial possibilities. Alas, since public opinion had been in his lifetime so backward and ill educated, Bottomley had suffered for the cause, had paid the price for his initiative, as had many a martyr before him! But there were many glad faces in London when the Bottomley Shrine was publicly unveiled four years ago, by the venerable Duke of Badgery St Lawrence himself.

The three most important clauses in the new Constitution we have left to the last. Firstly, a ban was placed on the development of loud-speakers for newsgiving, since it was thought that these might interfere with the legitimate power of the Press. The use of the radio was thus confined to purposes of business and communication, and was made, for political ends, dumb as the old telegraph wire. Secondly, it was made illegal for any British subject, or any foreigner domiciled in Britain, to start a new journal without the permission, signed and sealed, of the Governing Baron. Any infringement of this law was punishable with imprisonment for life – a more serious sentence now that the length of life has been so much increased. For though, as we shall see, the lengthening process has not been made compulsory outside the prison wall, yet it is felt that to allow a prisoner to die at his natural age would be to defeat the ends of justice – equivalent, indeed, to the encouragement of suicide.

Thirdly, it was decreed that no mention of public affairs was henceforward to be tolerated in the Press: these mentions, it was felt, would only serve to inflame public feeling, to stir up discontent, since, in order to conquer the Largest Circulation, and thereby the Government of Great Britain, the rival newspapers would have to make politics too thrilling to be truthful or healthy. This, the chief rivals agreed, was in the present circumstances undesirable. Royal speeches, accounts of the Royal Tours of the Empire, the epigrams of the various guests at the Mansion House Banquet – these can still be reported in full – will kindle the flame of loyalty, tend to keep public opinion patriotic. But such matters as Social Reform,

National Finance, or Armaments, were, it was decreed, never again to be mentioned in the Public Press. This wise law has been of inestimable benefit to the nation in the increase of stability it has given, and could have been enacted under no other form of government. Yet, to those of us who are old-fashioned, and remember the reign of Queen Victoria, there is perhaps something a little dreadful in the thought that, since the Government of Britain goes to the journal with the Largest Daily (Net) Circulation and since no matters of public importance may be mentioned in the Press, the ruling and administration of the country actually fall to the owner of that paper which for the moment reports the most divorces, gives the fullest details of them, gets the first news of some really first-rate hold-up, enthralling murder, extraordinary villa-mystery, entrancing poison-case, curious suicide, or holds the most successful beauty competition of the year.

The Government, on behalf of the Barons, were still to speak and act as if they possessed the executive power. The old Civil Service, the Permanent Officials. still served the country as before; and Mattie, in his capacity of private secretary, still serves a minister; and being a kindly, timid little man, it has invariably been his fate to be the slave of the most filibustering, bellicose, and braggadocio minister of whatever Government, or whatever form of government, was in power. These several swashbucklers he has served with the reverence and loyalty born of mingled love and fear, and with a surprising competence. They teased him, bullied him, made a butt of him, yet it was he, in every case, who composed their most fervent, characteristic, and effective speeches (for though the Barons dictated policy, they encouraged the oratory of their ministers so long as it was understood that it must not be reported in the Home Press); his piping falsetto it was that first rehearsed and recited their most baying and leonine utterances. For example, that famous fanfaronade that once roused a weak-kneed Britain was, in reality, poor Mattie's: out of this sweetness came forth strength:

'Ladies and Gentlemen (thump), let me put it to you (crash and cheers): ARE WE to Meet the Menace of Armed Might (shame!), yes, Armed and Hostile Might, with a weak, and what seems to One here to-night (gesture) at any rate UNBRITISH, shrugging of the shoulders (long and painful silence)? ... Or shall we look our foes Undaunted in the face, relying on the Strength of that Great Fleet whose ships crouch low (shudders) in the water, their iron prows curved like the Backs of Giants bent in prayer, ever on the Watch (frantic cheering and even more effective gesture)? Shall we, for fear of risking a few hundred thousand lives – a fear which I think, Ladies and Gentlemen has never yet swayed a British Government Worthy of the Name – discard that National Honour which has been built up through so many centuries? Shall we, I say (I say it and I REPEAT it again), shall we lightly throw that away? England, look to your laurels! (Fine bull-dog grimace by watchful and expectant orator. Transcendental cheering, whistling, cat-calls, and unfortunate cry of "Good Old Bottomley!" from rather muddled old gentleman in corner who remembers better days.)'

Yes, it was Mattie's! and this political connection gives the panelled rooms, in which we are waiting, a character and fame of their own. There would be, continually, little political, social, and artistic parties, for it was Mr Matthew Dean's pleasure to present the writers of nature-poems to politicians, to mix together several minor musicians, a duchess, musical-comedy heroines and young revue writers, to introduce obscure and penniless painters with-a-future to prominent and penniless ladies with-a-past. Little parties, not too big. There must always be a nucleus of young genius – pudding-basin hair, straight fringe and all the familiar apparatus of unprejudiced voice and vague, wide-open eye. Elegantly dressed shadows would engage in intellectual converse with rather untidy geniuses, would experience a thrill of excitement as if they had been talking to a bandit; though the bandit is of an origin as bourgeois and respectable as their own. Occasionally a real Whitechapeller would be called in, and oh! what flutterings would follow. *Such* an extraordinary-*looking* man, and what an interesting life! And the shadows would shudder and tremble with delight. People would come in after the theatre or opera; exotically-dressed young men would be seen talking to tweed-clad, bearded critics; musical-comedy heroines would giggle artistically to earnest-eyed writers; our bull-dog politician would discuss Modern Art with Lady Carabas and Professor Criscross; Lord Fitz-Bison, the reigning Baron, would ponder on the more obscure problems of literature with Bébé Milson the, leading lady in *Whatever Are We Coming To*? – while their host would sit there, smiling and feline, his eyeglass apparently budding from the outer circle of his face, his eyebrows uplifted as by a Chinese wind, wriggling his head and neck, laughing or talking in a twittering bat-like voice.

It was supposed that these gaieties were of use to the mop- or bobbed-haired, the earnest-eyed and tweed-clad; but their effect was more to benefit Mattie, bestowing upon him an importance in the eyes of both sides. The Ghibellines would welcome this whiff, as they thought, of the East End; for, while it made their flesh creep, and reminded them of the French and Russian revolutions, they yet experienced a feeling of pleasurable excitement. And really how clever Mattie was, so-modern-and-all-that, and such interesting people, always! The Blacks, for their part, would be overwhelmed with the lacquer and varnish of these elegant shadows and exquisite reflections, though sometimes surprised by a frankness of speech to which they were unaccustomed in their own almost Victorian homes; slightly intimidated, perhaps, but happy in the feeling that they were seeing life, and for this they would thank Mattie in their hearts. Then there was always a hope – always an unfulfilled hope – that one of the shadows would commission a portrait or buy a landscape, would give a concert for that new string-quartet, or buy the latest volume of verse. But the shadows preferred speech to action. They enjoyed talking about these things.

At this moment, however, the room was empty even of shadows, and Mattie is pacing irritably up and down, stopping every now and then to touch a book, to open and shut it swiftly. The lamp is brighter, or perhaps it is merely that the cold squares of light behind the blinds have faded out.

Suddenly, with no murmur leading up to it, sounds out the tinny rattling of several taxicabs, and, as if arriving down the three crowsfoot-alleys of the old conventional stage, three of these vehicles converged from three different directions on to the doorway below. They arrive there at the same moment, as though a careful stage-entrance had been contrived. Three taxi-doors were slammed simultaneously. Mr Dean remarks to himself expressively, if not grammatically, 'This must be them,' as an immense booming, roaring, and daft, cackling laughter floods the house. The sea, surely, must have burst in, and be whirling and swirling down in the basement. The flood mounts higher, sweeps relentlessly up the stairs, for a second dies down as the door is flung open, and a loud voice with no trace of comment in it, the voice of a machine, announces sonorously:

LORD RICHARD CRESSEY
MR PARKINSON
MR VALENTINE LEVIATHAN

When the three guests are in the room, the wave of sound

leaps up into the air again, punctuated by little jets and spurts of talk from Mattie. In this confusion only a few sentences can be isolated. 'Mattie, I am so sorry, but it is this beastly Daylight Saving Bill. When it was one hour, I could manage it, but now that it's three – ' '... They kept me so late at the F.O. One never gets away now till about eight.' ... '... Had to write an account of the reception of President Trotsky at the Champs Elysées for *The Morning Star*, and only got back at seven.' Mattie seems rather overwhelmed by the sheer volume of sound. His voice seems less now to spurt up, than to come down from above, as if a bat were bumping blindly against the ceiling, as if the invisible ventriloquist had just made up his mind to speak from an angle of the cornice.

The guests were still standing near together, side by side almost; and out of this juxtaposition gradually the fact of an extraordinary resemblance between them emerges. In opposition to, the generality of persons encountered, among whom, as we have remarked, but one or two out of a large gathering are definite individuals while the remainder imitate them, copy others who are not present, or are even content to reflect these mimickings, we have here in front of us three persons who, though when apart from one another they present little personality, yet together, and in combination, seem to possess a collective character. Not so much that they are exactly alike, these three, as that out of their present proximity to each other it can be seen that through them runs a common denominator: three flowers from the same stalk or three separate stages of the same disease.

Here, then, in these three friends, we have what may be termed a 'short-circuiting' of reflections. Each member of this little group presents countless mirrorings of the other two, innumerable reflections of these two unconsciously mimicking each other; these are echoed on, *ad infinitum*, among the three, but going no further, not getting out of the group, are always thrown back upon themselves. Yet so used are we to the encountering of shadows, to the feeling that it is impolite to detect them as such, so accustomed to an endless repetition and reflection, that the similarity between them passed unnoticed until Fate itself drew attention to it: and even then, as we shall see, little was said about it, for fear that man should be undeceived about his soul, for fear of lowering him in his own eyes. At present the few who detected any resemblance were only pleasantly reminded of dear Valentine, dear Freddie, or dear Richard.

Observed thus, seen together, they are somewhat like the various phases of development of some insect – caterpillar into chrysalis, chrysalis into butterfly: but the order of this evolution is reversed, as it would be if time were a mirror in which we could see these gradual changes reflected. Valentine is twenty-seven, Richard thirty-seven, Freddie forty-seven years old. Ten years separates Valentine from Richard, Richard from Freddie. But Valentine, not Freddie, is the most perfect expression of the slow transition from caterpillar to butterfly; his is the winged metamorphosis. With the over-full lines of his still-young body, with his rather full yellow skin, sleek yellow hair, small, fair moustache and general false air of prosperity, he yet has about him a certain overblown, insect-like elegance. But soon he, too, will have passed beyond this into that chrysalis stage in which we find Lord Richard. The latter is thinner, his body a little baggy, but sagging, his skin more lined, his moustache more stubbly, his hair less smooth, the aquiline tracing of his features more pronounced, his eye more vague, his clothes less elaborate; obviously his is the chrysalis, the torpid, stage. While Freddie, with heavier eyebrows and moustache, coarsened skin, and a long thin body that wanders uneasily down the length of his shabby clothes, is plainly the caterpillar of this trio. Yet looking at them was like reading a palindrome – the same words, the same meaning, though perhaps not very much of it, manifested through them from whichever end you start. For all of them had the same dusty fair hair and eyebrows, the same dim, blue, vacant eye with an uneasy look, more often found in the eyes of older men. Each has, when talking, the same method of avoiding the eyes of others, without seeming to wish it, of behaving as if this was but a mannerism, the result of intense mental effort. The eye then assumes a sideways and upward glance, as if searching for something within, as if looking up and away from the drooping yet rather bristly moustache, which, in its turn, seems to be looking sideways and down, as it were, in the other direction. Each has the same loud yet hollow voice, as though perpetually engaged in an effort to communicate some item of news into the very impersonal black-frilled nautilus of an ear trumpet, which, like a real shell, can never hold any sound with sense in it, but only a distant rushing of waters in buried caverns, an ominous roaring, a perpetual rolling-round of pebbles on the ocean-bed; and the latter is an accurate summary of their conversation – a continual grinding, rolling, and polishing of pebbles – fashionable pebbles, though!

Yet each of them, as far as any one of them can be said to exist apart from his comrades, is a little more intelligent than the average – who, luckily for the rest of mankind, never exists at all! All the small stories that circulate in the London drawing-rooms, stories that revolve round and round until a feeling of nausea is induced, pass through them, are sifted, sorted, separated, boomed abroad, roared back again, and distributed, finally, for general use, to be echoed, lisped and twittered-at in a thousand homes. In this respect they are like the sorting-machines in the Post Office, or the engines that beat out the chaff from the grain. They never originate a story, not even the most minute of this pygmy race, never initiate a thought; but, again, they never reject a thing of value to them as gossip, never choose anything unsuitable, and launch them, when tested, in the best possible manner. All three friends have the artistic and literary catchwords of the moment – which they are the first to jeer at when uncertain of their success, the first to grasp when successful, the first to discard when worn out – perpetually blowing off their tongues, lightly as bubbles. All three are absolutely saturated in the scandals of the moment. They are the possessors, too, of an endless curiosity, and will return to peck at the same subject day after day, pecking, mimicking and screaming like so many dull-plumaged parrots. Though they do not indulge in unconscious imitation, they have developed a fashionable talent for intentional mimicry which fits in well with their little stories: these imitations are not very realistic, but must pass as hieratic likenesses. With this mimicry, unlike yet recognisable, they usually invoke the memory of very distinguished persons. To those who are acquainted with the victims, and know whom the impersonations are intended to represent, the performance is a quite diverting one: while to those ignorant both of the victim and the intention it is a subtle tribute of flattery, suggesting, as it does, that the audience are themselves very important, very-much-in-the-know.

The actual volume of sound that they make, the sheer loud boisterous thunder of it, has helped to create for them a reputation for being 'so amusing.' And what courage they possess! Not one of them would hesitate to attack, when meeting a man or woman for the first time, the subject most dear and sacred to his or her heart; the topic most unapproachable, and by others the most feared. There are parrots in New Zealand which, though once vegetarian, and that not so long ago, have, since the introduction of sheep into their country, learnt to swoop down from a great height, tear open with their huge, hard beaks the woolly back of that animal, rip open the flesh, and remove the kidneys (their favourite food) all in a moment. The sheep has not time to resist. At one moment it is in a large green field, happy and stupid; the sky is blue and clear, the grass green and sweet; and the next it is doomed, writhing in mortal agony. This too, was their method. They would strike suddenly out of a clear sky; while even if detected in their preliminary swoop, surprise would paralyse their prey. And, though our three friends did not meet their victim again over a space of ten years, yet, when they did meet him, they would at once recall the position and nature of the wound and would proceed immediately to probe and deepen it. No matter how many thousands had fallen victims to them in the interval, they would remember! To watch the proficiency, adroitness, science, yet frank brutality with which they first attacked, veering down swiftly out of the void, was also, in a sense, like watching an operation performed, without the use of an anæsthetic, by some great surgeon. So violently, remorselessly, swiftly, was it done that the patient, overcome by shock, would at first feel nothing. But if ever one of them bungled an operation of this sort, his latest indiscretion, which he would attribute to a childlike innocence of disposition, would add to the volume of fashionable chattering and twittering. Without any respect for the feelings of others, themselves were somewhat pompous, easily offended, easily vulnerable.

By this time Mattie had managed to get his three guests anchored safely in front of their dinner. The dim golden light smoothed out the differences in age, distributed part of Valentine's over-glossiness among the two elder members of his spiritual family, making the likeness between all three of them more remarkable. It is obvious to a stranger, and probably to the host, that they appreciate to the full every peculiarity, physical, mental, and vocal, of Mattie's personal style, and are eagerly awaiting more material for little stories and little imitations. They respect, however, his position both as a source and object of gossip, as a man behind several scenes. The talk, though loud, was not without effort. 'Mattie,' boomed Freddie, as if trying to make his voice heard through a storm, from a vast distance, 'what has happened to that queer, interesting little man I met here last time? A poet, I think he was, or a painter or something?'

'Do you mean Jacques – Jacques Rosenheimer?' Mattie replied in a voice so high that it had an impact on the air like a diamond cutting glass – 'wonderful little man ... exceptional promise ... such heavenly lyrics, full of real June ... real English countryside.' ... The sentences were thrown up into the air, staccato, abruptly, for only with effort could he make even these dying sounds! While to emphasise his feelings, he would let his monocle drop down on its string, clashing against his stiff shirt-front like a cymbal; and then he would go again through the ritual of fixing it in his eye, like a schoolboy trying to hold a penny there. '... Understands the birds and natural history.'

Lord Richard intervened. 'I believe he's going to be at Old Septua's to-morrow. I've promised to take Valentine and Freddie down to Dodderingham to-morrow in my new 'plane. (Oh yes, I've got a new one: haven't you seen it?) I thought she'd amuse them. She's hardly ever in London now and has the most extraordinary people there.' (Mattie produced an angry spurt of sound. 'Well, you won't ... find Jacques at all extraordinary ... I'm afraid.' ...) 'She goes in for farming. I think it's a great mistake. They neither of them understand it; the sheep have got something wrong with them this year, and walk about all over the place on their knees. One Sunday the Bishop came over and asked if he might hold an open-air service in the park – one prayer and a sermon; there wasn't a large congregation, but when he had prayed he looked round, and there were all the sheep on their knees! As he got up, they got up too. Septua was furious, and blamed poor Tootsie for it.'

'I can quite believe it!' Freddie roared, 'because I remember that in my grandmother's lifetime we used to have family prayers. When she said "Let us pray," all the servants got up from their chairs, arranged in line, and revolving silently, as if performing some well-practised exercise in Swedish Drill, went down on their knees; and an old parrot, standing in a cage in the corner, would invariably revolve through its hoop and then fold one claw over its eyes as if joining in the worship.'

'... Wonderful thing, birds' intelligence,' lisped Mattie; but his friends intended to escape romanticised natural history for the moment and essayed to trail a red herring. 'Isn't it true, Richard,' Valentine asked, 'that there has been a serious outbreak of Hand-to-Mouth disease at Doddering-ham? I heard that Lady Septuagesima, wandering in the lanes, met a sow that was shortly going to suffer an accouche-ment. Being awfully kind and generous, she asked it to stay, and took it in at once. The bailiff warned her that the disease was very prevalent, and extremely infectious, but she wouldn't turn it away. Not, of course, that it mixed much with other people. She gave it a separate bedroom and all that sort of thing, but directly afterwards there was a fearful outbreak.'

'Poor Septua,' Richard murmured, 'I'm afraid she'll lose a lot. But she will do these things.'

'Talking about grandmothers,' Freddie prepared to embroider his theme, 'it appears that poor old Hetty Wardeburgh has developed a passion for deathbeds – a regular complex! They say she positively breaks into the bedrooms of the dying. She got in ... ' But Mattie had got his voice under way and meant to be heard this time.

'... Wonderful thing, birds' intelligence,' he lisped again, 'and Jacques is the only man who understands them. In confidence, as you have promised to give the prize, Richard, I'll tell you, though I oughtn't to really, that we've decided to give the Pecksniff to Jacques. Don't forget, Richard, the 12th of July ... I rely on you to whip people up for it ... so important that the prize should be a success. Naturally Goo-Goo will be there, but we must make other people come. Goo-Goo must be made to bring all her friends. Can't you persuade Lady Septuagesima to come up for it? I don't mind even if she brings some of those people with her – though (and he winced) I must admit they are a little too advanced for me – but I suppose I'm getting an old fogey,' and he tittered in expectation of a friendly denial. Since none came, he continued, 'And Jacques really deserves support, ... such lovely poetry, ... simply steeped in beauty ... steeped in beauty; do you know that last poem, *Denial*? It decided us ... lovely ... I think ... I'll try to remember it.'

The guests exchanged looks of self-compassion; and Mattie, throwing his head back and up, produced those high little jets of sound that bumped against the ceiling like a bat flying into a sudden light, and at other times was the cry of the bat, the fluffy twittering of young birds:

I would not, if I could, be called a poet,
(Oh, tweet-tweet, feathered friends, how do you go it!)
But rather would I cricket in the sun,
Share in the genial crowd's warm-hearted bun
And ginger beer – go into politics and play
A man's stout part; let no man say me nay.
(Oh, dear, how does it go?) Say nay, me nay, say me nay.
(I've got it.) Let no man say me nay
Build empires, or in some rough country place,
Throw silken flies, or tickle silver dace,
Watch happy pigs a-waffle in the weir,
The mornings come, the evenings disappear.
Like grains of sand!
Come, friend, your hand!

PART II

No more perfect morning for a flight could be imagined – blue sky, with little cool bunches of white cloud knotted together above the horizon, waiting as if afraid to advance alone into the emptiness. They seemed, these white clouds, like ballerinas against an over-painted back-cloth of blues and violets, a cloth painted so brilliantly that the colours have split into refracting and scintillating fragments, a haze of diamond dust, while the dancers themselves are for once nervous, loath to respond to the music's invitation, fearing the huge empty stage in front of them, with its circle after circle of eyes, dull or mocking. Occasionally a grand cloud, a giant, flaunts across like an iceberg seen from under the transparent depths of water beneath it, so that its full thickness of ice-greens, ice-blues, and faint rose colourings is visible to us, and it becomes a matter of wonder that the weight of this floating mountain does not overturn it. The air is warm, yet so coldly white is this giant that if it were only nearer, the polar animals, bears whiter than snow, and all the other creatures that have fashioned for themselves skins out of their native element, would show on it, horrified at its breaking away thus from their home in the frozen seas, looking down with wonder and resentment. The trees are very still. In the open space in Hyde Park where stretches the public landing-stage, the plane was waiting for them. The vast cement quay glares out, painted crudely with signs and symbols, placarded with gay if somewhat hideous advertisements. A great droning rises round it, as a thousand planes are launched on one side or come to anchor on the other, coming and going like a horde of dragon-flies, a swarm of bees, round some tropical plant. Lord Richard's plane was at the near end, looking in the morning light as if it were a swallow-tail that had fallen into a tub of liquid silver. The driver, whom they were not taking with them, got out, and Lord Richard sat down at the wheel with Valentine and Freddie behind him. Suddenly the driver, standing on the quay to see them off, grew smaller and smaller, as though performing the Indian vanishing-trick, but climbing down, instead of up, his long rope, and the earth swung away from them. The whole width of London swung beneath them, revolving round St Paul's, the dome of which stood out as the hub of the wheeling city. A myriad grey ribbons, grey ribbon after grey ribbon fluttered and swerved beneath them, and, over these, crawled and hurried minute ant-like creatures, ever diminishing in size, fetching and carrying, dragging or propelling great loads. So much did the ribbons flutter and wave, that it seemed a miracle that those tiny creatures could keep their balance at all. Now the wheel of London trundles itself away into the distance, and they hang apparently motionless, over the open country, which slides beneath them, pushing them on, like a moving staircase. This prospect changes in the space of a few minutes from a landscape into a realistic but metallic-coloured map. Occasionally the atlas would be hidden from them, as they traversed white seas which, though floating in air, looked so solid that a man, willing to face the coldness of their breakers, would surely be able to wander among the hillocks of these waves, snapping off, here and there, a spring of frozen spray, pure and flowerlike: for the waves had been crystallised, seemingly, in the very rhythm, the very tilt of their life, the foam still leaping upward from their rush caught in attitudes as true yet conventional as the uplifted springing claw of a wave that leaps at you from a screen by Korin. And these seas were but what appeared from the city as timid little clouds! Now, again, the air below grew clear, and the ocean, the real ocean, reveals itself below; the whole line of east coast and Thames estuary showed there, as far as you could see, and the geography that had been to them as children so improbable, assumed for a space a reality of its own. Exhilaration seized Freddie and Valentine, and they roared and boomed loudly at each other, forgetting for a moment that no sound is audible up here, until each wondered at the other's mute grimaces.

Deep down under them grow tufts of grass that are really trees, spreading and noble, ant-heaps that are hills. The diminutive pediment, the prim dovetailing of grey slates would mark a Georgian mansion; and little figures would walk under the grass-blades or move over open spaces of green baize. And, as the plane passed over, it cast down on them a blue or mauve winged shadow, a small shadow that skimmed like a dragon-fly just brushing the still greenery with a breath of coolness. And within that flying speck, high up among the drifting white clouds, cheerfully roaring to themselves, Lord Richard Cressey, Mr Freddie Parkinson and Mr Valentine Leviathan are in the clutches of those Demons of the Upper Air, who, unappeased by any sacrifice, can still be heard howling, far away above us, on a dark winter's night.

*

Dodderingham Old Hall, their intended destination, lies beside the Cam: a simple, Queen Anne house, like a pavilion of red velvet, with a long and wide staircase leading up to it, and down from it, on to stretching green lawns. It seems to have been improvised for some pageant that has passed long ago, lies embedded in all this intense verdure, sinking slowly into the flat country which is as rustic now as before the house was built. Only the avenue of wireless masts at intervals of five miles, rising to a thousand times the height of the huge old trees, shows that the age of the Virgin Queen is over – for so Elizabethan is the countryside that Dodderingham Old Hall seems as much of an anachronism as the masts that join it to London.

The present regime in the house appears to have something Gothic still lingering about it, strange and fantastic. For Lady Septuagesima patronises the advanced guard of art and literature. The large panels of the walls that had before shone dully, grey or brown, full of low lights and mouse-like colour, now blush under bedizenments of purple, scarlet, and apricot, are blazoned with stripes, are chequ-ered, or have gathered constellations of gold and silver. The pictures that liven, or sober, these walls are either frighteningly old or terrifyingly new; illustrating the theory of the most modern painters that their wagon is hitched on to such stars as Giotto and Duccio. On the other hand, Raphael, who had enjoyed a temporary popularity with the vanguard, now bows the knee to Guido Reni and to Carlo Dolci, once again the last word in æsthetic thrills. A small picture by Sassetta would hang side by side with the work of the youngest self-taught genius; Guido would pair with Renoir; a huge, early Matisse faces a chiaroscuro altar-piece from Bologna; yet all the pictures, all the furniture, are arranged with a dramatic sense that has enabled Lady Septuagesima to mount herself superbly.

This remarkable lady came, as can be deduced from her name, of a peculiarly religious family. Her father, the late Lord Fortcarrick, one of the richest land and mineral owners in Lancashire, had harnessed his portion of a notorious family eccentricity, and turned it into religious energy. This, though trying to his relatives, was in the end perhaps to their advantage. 'An odious bore,' old Lady Fortcarrick used to characterise it, 'but better than gamblin'.' To an extent she even encouraged this fervour, while, at the same time, keeping it in bounds. In her life-time he was merely aggressively Low Church; but after his wife's death he became more imaginative. He would spend his time now, with enormous notebooks in front of him, reckoning out the precise date of the Second Coming; a calculation based, even more elaborately, upon such foundations as Joanna Southcott's unopened box, and statistics of the growing Catholicism in England, and inextricably intertwined with the fact that the Kaiser Wilhelm II. of Germany was the Beast-in-the-Revelation. As time went on, as he became older (for this was before the prolongation of life had become such a simple affair), his mind became ever more original in its working. He would invariably invest his income (he was a very rich man) as it came in, and then, forgetting what he had done, would declare, would insist, that he had no money to live on unless he raided his capital. The necessary sums for his support he would borrow from his children. Finally, in a fit of prophecy verging on apoplexy, he identified poor Lady Septuagesima, to her face, with the Scarlet Woman of Babylon, and, shortly afterwards, passed peacefully away.

His daughter had started life by being as religious as her father. Devotion was bred in her; and many farmers and miners, who owe their conversion to her, would be surprised if they could see her now – which is improbable, since, whereas the late earl accused his daughter of being the Scarlet Woman, the present one, her brother, has proved her to his own satisfaction a Bolshevik; and the latter, however popular politically in London, is still a word of reproach in ancestral halls.

But in the early days of which we are writing, not even her brother could have brought against her such an accusation. She affected, then, an almost Salvationist simplicity of dress, demeanour, and speech. This continued until she was about thirty-five, and then a change came. The scene of her charitable activities had gradually shifted from the country village to the poorer districts of London. Another transformation, and she began to do her slumming in the studios of Fitzroy Street and Chelsea. It was a miracle. At once her religious zeal was converted into an artistic one, but equally

Protestant, equally unyielding and fanatic in its new direction. At this time she would surely, without scruple, have started a crusade, a holy war, against the Royal Academy. To her they were now what the Church of Rome had been previously. Even the ever-present, farcical spectacle of these poor old men, in their greed for money, rushing out after Modern Art like a fat man after a passing omnibus, and always failing to catch it, could not soften her. Yet at the same moment that this miraculous conversion took place, herself became transfigured. The former possession of ordinary, simple good looks she now bartered for a grotesque yet actual beauty; while from her previous austerity of dress she blossomed into a garish glory of clothes, such as was never seen in this world before. Her language, her conversation, too, now threw off their swaddling clothes and came of age in a day.

Of impressive height – a height that was over life-size for a woman, so that without looking a giantess she might yet seem an animated public monument – Lady Septuagesima had an almost masculine face, deep-set flowerlike eyes with a golden calyx, a long, definite nose, and cut-out chin; strong, large animal-like teeth, which showed when she laughed, and a mass of red-brown hair, cut short but not cropped. Many of these features do not sound attractive, but it is certain that there was about her a quality of crazy, ludicrous, abstract beauty that few, happily, possess. Her voice, personal to herself as her looks, was equally absurd, and in it mingled the peaceful lowing of cattle and the barbed drone of wasp and hornet. As she moved (never afraid of attracting attention – indeed apparently oblivious of it) through the London streets in her gaudy clothes, large hooped skirt and vast hat loaded with feathers as that of any coster's wife, many who stopped to stare supposed that she was staggering-by under the weight of odd-lots that, now past their use, had been bestowed upon her by a charitable theatrical costumier. Every year her appearance became more eccentric, more grim, and yet more decorative, having the desolate yet rather extravagant beauty of a ruin-picture by Pannini; of severe classical remains decked out with bunting; of the Colosseum seen alternately under soft moonlight and by the fire and fizzling glitter of fireworks. In vain the crowd of dirty wide-eyed children, who would accompany her when she walked in London, raised their shrill anthem in the air –

> I see no reason
> Why gunpowder treason
> Should ever be forgot.

For Lady Septuagesima these words contained no hidden implication. She liked children and, alas! had none of her own. She would merely remark, casually, on arriving home, that the children in London were so friendly and would walk with her all the way, singing.

At Dodderingham Old Hall the individual note in her clothes was accentuated still further. She would walk down the deeply-hedged lanes, the flat roads, accompanied by her noble-looking, rather horse-like husband, and by a perfect menagerie of young artists and intellectuals. In winter or summer she would be supported, apparently, by the same court. But though identical in voice and look, these strolling companies were, with the exception of her husband, never the same in their composition for more than one quarter of the year: she quarrelled with them regularly every three months, and then no abuse was too bad for those for whom, only two months previously, no praise had been good enough. 'Never in my life have I been treated like that before,' was invariably the burden of her song to the next assembly. The latter, this permanent though shifting circus, cultivated always the look of its part. One inevitable ingredient in it was a group of undergraduates from Cambridge, which, in its turn, could invariably be divided into two portions: one division consisting of youths painfully well-clothed, too precious in manner, with eyes too liquid; while the other was made up of callow young men, intolerably dirty, whose friendship was valued because of their simplicity. Then there were mop-haired, moist-handed individuals with greenish faces, grotesque and damply chilly as deep-sea monsters; art-critics, like sea-anemones, with circular floating fringes of red hair, or with matted beards that seemed tentacular as the arms of an octopus; a superannuated bishop who believed in seeing life and making the best of things; one or two stray individuals from London, with no particular point; and several young women with golden hair and strawberry-and-cream complexions, who had, therefore, to insist on intellect by the cropping of their hair, by wearing breeches, and by speaking about peculiar subjects in a peculiarly frank way, in voices whose even tones displayed no trace of emotion. Then there were oldish women with short, grey hair, tweed skirts and green-leather football boots; middle-aged ones decked out with pince-nez and crowned with plumes – synthetic ones, though – of victory, like the goddess Bellona. This perambulating group was further augmented by a few stray 'studio-sweepings.' As they walked, one could see that some of them were tall ... much too tall – others short ... far too short: but all, as they marched through the rustic landscape beside their hostess, assumed an air of bourgeois respectability, of utter commonplaceness. And though in London the children followed her here, they were respectful and subdued. As she swept along, her clothes lent colour, an unusual quantity of colour indeed, to the insinuation of her enemies that in order to find such garments she must attend secret rummage-and-jumble-sales at the Local Asylum. But there was something splendid about her appearance; no snowball greeted her even on the coldest winter day, nor, as she sailed past, was any cry of 'Aunt Sally!' wafted to her ear by the spring breezes.

And the course of her previous progress through the countryside was afterwards easily to be traced by strangers; for, as she went, the most extraordinary, the most extravagant, objects fell from her and were lost. These, if left for future generations to discover, will greatly puzzle posterity. What strange race, it will wonder, what extinct civilisation had its centre, as testified by this accumulation of grotesque objects, in this flat, green, peaceful land? Even now the passing pedestrian is filled with awe and surprise. Tall trees rise up, covered with leaves from head to foot, every tiny twig of every branch flooded with leaves, the very trunks and arms green with moss, gold with lichen, as if they had just risen, dripping, cool, and watery-green, from the ocean bed. Under them are whitewashed cottages, very white and crumbling, with windows, like wide-open eyes and thatched roofs that jut out over them, hair, brow, and eyebrow combined in one slanting, moss-covered greenness. The whole area is calm, sleepy. Cottage gardens, raised above the road, are bulging with stocks and sweet-blowing flowers of many colours, are full as cornucopias. Even the windows of these cottages are full of flowers, whose faces, red and hot, are flattened against the windows, as ever tightly shut; the blossom in each pane seems the iris of an eye, alive and vibrant. Against this background, pasted on the boles of trees so ancient that they are antlered like king stags, or pendent in the boldly-curving bow-windows of a village post office, among open boxes and glass jars of sweets like small over-ripe fruits, among barley-sugar gold as corn and twisted like the pillars of the Temple, among bundles of brown and black bootlaces hanging up like hairy scalps, among pyramids of snow-white sugar or mounds of honeyed Demerara, rods of coloured sealing-wax, rusty steel pens, and all the other familiar properties of village life, he reads some such notice as this that follows :–

LOST

LOST between here and Dodderingham Old Hall on the afternoon of May 2nd, 1948:

Seven herons' plumes set in brilliants.

A green ostrich-feather fan with tortoiseshell mount.

An Elizabethan whale-bone hoop.

One crimson shoe-heel with cairngorm inset.

A tartan shawl.

A Japanese embroidered bag, with panels of flying storks worked in salmon-pink and rose silks, containing:

A stick of orange-coloured lip-salve, with black onyx-mounting and

A purse with platinum fastening, in which were:

A card of permanent invitation to the Trafalgar Gallery of Modern Art, London.

£3 12s. 6d. in silver, and

A paper bag full of bull's-eye peppermints.

ALSO

LOST between Skipton and Dodderingham Old Hall:

A blue-silk cushion of native workmanship.

A Congo Fetish in ivory.

A first edition of Milton's *Paradise Lost* (Simmons, in 10 books, 1667).

A volume of Jules Laforgue's poems.

The second volume of the Bloomsbury Painters Series – *From Giotto to Gertler*.

A photographic miniature of Cézanne, presented by the painters of the Black-Friday Group, set in half-pearls.

A green amber amulet.

A New Zealand Totem Pole, converted into a walking-stick, and

A wisdom tooth, mounted in turquoises, and inscribed 'To Septua from Tootsie, 1943.'

The Finder, on returning these items to their owner,

Lady SEPTUAGESIMA GOODLEY, Dodderingham Old Hall, will be SUITABLY rewarded.

Tootsie, it must be confessed, was Thomas Goodley, her husband. Thus, in her progress round the countryside, would Lady Septuagesima distribute regal, if involuntary, largess.

On this fine Saturday morning, however, she indulged in no ambulatory adventures, preferring to stay in the garden surrounded by her court of the instant. Seen from a little distance, it was quite a spectacle. The entire assembly was broken up into knots of two or three persons; but all these groups were yet near together, as if each one feared to be out of earshot of any other; each listening to the conversation of the one furthest removed from it, while, at the same time, carrying on a conversation amongst itself. Some members of these various court-factions were sitting on garden-seats painted in sugar-stick stripes of red and white, some were lying curled up, or were crouching uncomfortably, hands clasped round knees in the manner of those rigid mummies of pre-dynastic Egypt, while others were sitting easily on the ground, as if never accustomed to any more comfortable posture. Under them were square rugs decorated with large square patterns, and over each knot spread a large striped umbrella. The light dripping through these, and cast up again by the rugs and flat stretches of green grass, spattered them with vivid patches of scarlet, purple, blue, and sea-green, till they seemed hotly-coloured insects nestling under the shade of a clump of iridescent, rather deleterious toadstools. A cloud floating overhead reduces the colouring, lowering it a tone or two for an instant as if a tinted glass had been interposed between the groups and the onlooker. The cloud would pass and the tones would jump up again to their normal violence. From under the fungi rose a continual droning, shrilling, hoarse cackling, and shooting-out of the tongue, as the chameleon-coloured groups conversed. Little spirals of smoke rose, coloured too, by their surroundings.

Nearly the whole day was spent here, and in this manner, for Lady Septuagesima was expecting three guests down from London. They should have been here by twelve o'clock or in time for luncheon at the latest; but there came no sign of their arrival. In the garden it was very restful; the lowing, whinnying laughter of the hostess fitted in with the prospect disclosed between the high green trees, pillars that framed-in the view, with its foreground of sun-baked, red-brick walls, seeming already to breathe out the honey-sweet scent of ripe fruit, though at present the flattened forms of espaliers, that clung to them like green cobwebs, bore only small constellations of delicate blossom, apple and peach, pear and plum.

The conversation was woven equally of high art and low scandal. An enormous man, with a blue shirt, an open coat, no waistcoat, and a belt, a costume singularly courageous for so large a person, was, though he had an air of easy well-being combined with little intellectual effort, taking a severe line about æsthetics. The cropped-haired young women were voluble too; their voices, calm and even, indicated clearly a conscious superiority which enraged the large gentleman; for as the Quakers are confident of the spiritual revelation within them, so were all these combatants sure of their essential rightness. The undergraduates were present as usual; the untidy spoke seldom but loudly, and when they spoke would not be silenced; the ones elaborately groomed and dreamy eyed gazed on mutely, lost in some adolescent stupor. Jacques Rosenheimer interrupted occasionally, with abrupt, authoritative, and rather snapping utterance; short, dark, and thick-set, he was curly-haired and curly-nostrilled. Then, distributed among the groups, there were some cosmopolitans: a Danish dancer, a Spanish gypsy, a Russian artist, swelling out of his clothes, full of compliments, ever so gallant; and all the usual court, except the bishop, who was resting within. Tootsie, monumental, like one of the togaed statues outside the old House of Commons, remained immersed in his own nobility of mien and character.

All day the conversation wove its arabesque design, a design barely traceable, seldom leading to any very definite pattern; but the threads, drawn up above the several umbrellas by one hand, would have a certain vague significance.

The fat man's voice, loud and distinct, sounded out his bass theme. 'Give me Giotto, give me Giotto,' he reiterated solemnly. 'I don't see how you can compare Guggenheimer with him.' ...

'It isn't that' (and a feminine hand was waved descriptively), 'it's the solidity, the *pure* painting, if you know what I mean, the actual *pure* painting ... like Defoe or Stern,' and her voice drooped back into the general shrilling.

The threads are drawn closer, so that the fabric can be regarded.

' ... Well, of course, if you're going to talk in that way, the argument simply can't be continued ... must compare one painter with another ... But why? There is a likeness, don't you think, the same definite hardness, you know ...' (Fresh theme announces itself.) 'Well, all I can tell you is, *he* told me so himself. I know she didn't. She didn't want it talked about, naturally ... but he happened to tell me himself ... After all, it had been going on for years, hadn't it, Septua? You know as well as I do ... Oh! Breughel's not to be compared with Giotto ... not in it simply. Besides, I don't like Ingres's drawings, I only like the *drawing* in his *paintings*. ... Well, I'm glad he left her: came down here for two nights three years ago, stayed ten days; poor Tootsie was nearly driven off his head and played the electric organ for seven hours without stopping. So exhausted that the doctor ... immensely improved ... fine thing that, at the Black-

Friday Club ... Impressive design ... I shall be out if she comes again – such a bore ... She always was one, and quite crazy into the bargain, now. Why should one be lumbered up with people like that? ... all I can tell you is this. Giotto and Tolstoy, they've made the difference to my life ... don't see that Blake's a bit like Cézanne ... and when she's got into Italy, they had to come back again ... very queer and interesting ... and in Petrograd we (how you say it in English?) sledged down the Neva ... what I wonder is will Mingler become a SUBJECTIVE or an OBJECTIVE writer? That is what I ask myself ... judging by the last one, subjective and objectionable, I should say ... that's merely silly. Of course, I like him, but he is pompous, isn't he? Goo-Goo is charming ... pretty, and personally I like her accent. Of course no talent, either of them ... Aix-les-Bains ... no, I haven't seen the ones in Vienna, but in any case Breughel had no sense of form ... Mattie ... ridiculous but kindly. (Giotto and Tolstoy, Giotto and Tolstoy, Giotto and Tolstoy ...) The minister had to disarm him. It simply wasn't safe to let him shoot. But he was allowed to carry a white sunshade; and the very next day he was charged by the only White rogue-elephant in Africa ... never been the same ... and the minister only laughed and said (Giotto and Tolstoy) that Mattie had got a white elephant in his sun helmet ... well, you may not agree with me; but there it is Giotto and ... I can't bear that barn. It would drive me mad if I had to live in it (Giotto, and give me the Primitives). Doesn't look lived in somehow ... for his children, but now they've had to abolish death-duties altogether ... not quite so pleased ... solidity, that's what I mean – pure painting ... like Mozart.' ...

But the fabric was torn suddenly by a maid, who hurried out of the house to tell her ladyship that she was wanted on the radiophone.

'The Superintendent, Cambridge, speaking ... speaking ... yes, yes. Is that you? Three miles away ... like a lump of lead?

Terrible ... terrible! Yes, radio at once. Are you ready? Lady Richard Cressey, Hotel Splendide, Aix-les-Bains. Return at once Richard unwell will meet you Cambridge Septua. And one more, please; yes, Superintendent. Sir Vincent McNabb, 142 Wimpole Street, Inner London. Please engage Express Flyer Cambridge at once grafting operation Lord Richard Cressey most important on no account fail me. Stay night here Lady Septuagesima Goodley, Dodderingham Old Hall.'

*

One of the most pleasing features of the progress of civilisation during the last quarter of a century has been the immense advance in the art of surgery, as well as in healing, mental and physical. If the dominating features of the nineteenth century were concerned with mechanics – with machines and mechanical inventions – this one surely will be remembered always as the Biological Century. Biology has disclosed to us miracle after miracle, and has not yet bestowed upon humanity the last of its gifts. To those who were children during the course of the First or Small 'Great War' (that one which, beginning in 1914, lasted until 1918) – still more to those born since that event – the extent to which the old pre-war world of 'statesmen,' 'newspaper proprietors' (as they were then called) millionaires and philanthropists, was dominated by death, and by the idea of death, can hardly be credible. However accustomed the new generation may be to the prospect of that triple span which holds life for them, to us older men it must remain a continual cause for wonder, making us rub our eyes to see if we are awake. Nor are the full implications of the life-lengthening operation fully grasped even now. Because, since the first operations were performed barely twenty-five years ago, there are still with us but few men who have achieved over eleven decades, whereas in the future there will be many, mentally and physically in the prime of life, at the age of one hundred and eighty. To remind us that we are not dreaming (if one may still, without impropriety, mention that word ...) there are, luckily, certain concrete facts constantly before us. When I first began to read the newspapers as a child of seven – for in those distant days the reading of newspapers, far from being compulsory for children, as it is now, was discouraged or actually forbidden – it was noticeable that hardly a day passed without the death of A Last Great Victorian having to be recorded. It was very depressing reading, that list of obituaries which became like the accounts of the-positively-final-farewell performance of some great stage favourite. Suddenly the torrent was checked, and, as we know, many of the last really great ones have been declared 'public-monuments,' and are with us yet.

Another proof that the miracle has actually been achieved is to be found in the abolition of death duties. Curiously enough, it was the iniquitous and vindictive incidence of this taxation – aimed solely at one small class rich enough to pay it – as much as any single fact, that in the end, perhaps, was responsible for the lengthening of life. An inevitable evolution it was, comparable to that neck which the giraffe has developed in its continual search for food at a considerable altitude. Each rich man was determined for the sake of his family, nay, of his country, to live as long as lay within his power. Each wealthy pioneer of longevity – for, as in so many other charitable causes, it was the millionaires who took the lead – made a public declaration that it was not the fear of death (on the contrary, such were his responsibilities that he would welcome a release from them) that made him wish to postpone the end, but the fact that if he surrendered to care, illness, and old age, a disgraceful and punitive impost would fall upon his children. Nor, he would add, was this bad for the family alone, since the Family is but the Unit of the State!

What, therefore, is injurious to the family, damages the State; what impoverishes the family, though it may at first appear to enrich, yet surely in the end impoverishes the Motherland. I remember what an effect a certain simile made on me in this connection: it has often been noticed that powerful and original minds work in much the same manner; and several of these grand old men said to me, oddly enough, the same thing in almost the same words. As they pronounced their faith, with a fervour that was convincing, there was about them something, perhaps a little ponderous, yet noble and statesmanlike. 'You cannot,' they would say, 'you cannot both have your cake and eat it! And one felt, somehow, from the fact that they had thought out and pinned down the same phrase, that deeply, deeply, must these pioneers feel the truth of it. Great was their courage and resolution. No matter how their sons gave way to their own feelings, crying and imploring their fathers not to sacrifice themselves, not to pass this stern, self-denying ordinance, urging them to release themselves from this bondage of family feeling which required such inverted immolation of father to son, the old gentlemen remained firm in their resolve. Patriotic, as well as family, scruples had entered into their decision; they could not, therefore, look back. Nor even did the threats of the Church intimidate for an instant these patriots. The Church, as ever behind the times, began by denouncing the surgical prolongation of life as a sin against God's ordering of the world, and one that would entail damnation eternal, the complete conquest by Satan of the soul of each man operated upon. A breath of humour was brought into this controversy by the declaration of old Lord Badgery St Otter (as he then was), now the Duke of Badgery St Lawrence, who, being eighty years of age, and about to submit to the operation, said: 'If the devil waants me, 'e can coome an' fetch me, an' a devilish touff job 'e'll 'ave!'

Such was the spirit of these men, willing to risk a presumable certainty of eternal happiness for the sake of another span of worldly care and sorrow in which to help their fellows. Undaunted, these fine old Die-Hards damned the consequences, flinging themselves down on the operating table in the same spirit in which Abraham had sought to sacrifice his dearly-beloved son. And the sacrifice has not been made in vain, for the substitution by the Press Barons of the 'Re-marriage' – or, as they are popularly called, 'divorce-duties' – for Death-Duties, has been to many a great relief. The Death-Duties had, as a matter of fact, long ceased to bring in much revenue; and the new ones are both less heavy and less easily avoided – for a man can, after all, avoid death more easily than marriage. But if the tax should become too heavy, it is not to be doubted that – ever at the call of patriotism and the family – the same grand old pioneers will no more hesitate to give up making a fresh start in their new life, than, on behalf of the same ideals, they feared to give up making a fresh start in death.

The Press Barons were among the first to undergo what was at the time a dangerous experiment; and while we owe our good government to them, and to the increasing wisdom and generosity with which the passing years have endowed them, it is right, surely, to admire that very British spirit of freedom which has actuated them throughout. Never, for an instant, have they sought to force these discoveries on others, to thrust them, for example, upon the poor! From the first they understood that the world was over-populated, and for the sake of those same ideals, for faith, family, and fatherland, the workers should be permitted to die at that age at which they had formed the habit of so doing – or, if they wish it, at one yet earlier. For, in effect, they are too old at forty. Thus it can never be said that the men with responsibilities sought to shift their burden on to the shoulders of those free of them; and it remains one of the consolations, the compensations, of poverty that a double – or even a full – span of life is not obligatory.

These political and social benefits are all due, in the first place, to the marvellous science of human grafting, the effect of which has been increasingly toward national stability. The workers must realise by now, one would imagine, that the holding of wealth, with its privileges and responsibilities, in the hands of a few permanent, indeed almost eternal, individuals, is a guarantee that while the former will not be abused, the latter will be respected. Apart from this self-obvious conclusion, it is one of the blessings of our present form of government that every day, in every way, in every paper, this thought is enunciated, this lesson taught. Again, it had long been noticed in every country where hereditary monarchy survived, that there was never a revolution against any king who had reigned for over fifty years – however good a ruler he may have been. And since 'O King, live for ever!' is now hardly an exaggerated expression of good-will, since reigns of two centuries will automatically become quite normal, the fear of revolution becomes continually more remote.

The first operation that proved the value, and advertised the miracle, of grafting was that performed upon Prince Absalom, son of the Emperor Dodon of Aquitania. It is not yet twenty years, though it may seem more, since that well-beloved prince, the darling rival of every cinema-star, and scion of an ancient and august house, which had in an amazingly short period consolidated one of the greatest empires – and by making no use of it had managed for an amazingly long time to keep it – met with a terrible, an appalling, accident. Though possessed of immense charm, he was of a puny, frail physique, that contrasted forcibly with his marked mental powers and attainments. While seeking recreation one evening, in those few moments of leisure spared him from Empire's Call, by performing in what was then called a 'Jazz' band (a fashion that had spread to Aquitania from America via England), he fell into one of the noise-contrivances, his right leg being terribly lacerated. At the news, a thrill of horror passed, not only through his own people, but through the whole of the civilised world. At first the contraption refused to let go of his leg, but eventually its jaws were broken, and followed the tragic announcement that the surgeon had found it necessary to amputate the injured limb. Day after day enormous crowds, some of them sobbing or weeping hysterically, would gather outside the Emperor's palace in Atlantis to read the latest bulletins.

Then, one day, with a burst of joy, with such startling demonstrations of loyalty, such outbursts of shouting, dancing and singing as usually only mark the periodic declarations of a war to end war, it became known that one of the duskier players (or coons, as they were called) in the orchestra had come forward to give his leg in the Cause of Empire! And that operation, first of its kind, was successful.

In those inspiring days I happened to be in Aquitania, and through the generosity of Lord FitzBison, who had just at that moment appointed himself English Ambassador at the Emperor Dodon's court, was enabled to be present at the Solemn Service of National Thanksgiving at St. Andrews', which celebrated Prince Absalom's recovery. The discourse of the Archbishop of Atlantis was particularly impressive, full of original thinking, and I translated some portions of it.

'We are gathered together to-day, brethren,' he said, 'to celebrate the recovery of one beloved beyond all princes – by the people of this mighty League of Free Peoples, Nations and Commonwealths which we call Empire. And in him, for whose recovery we thank our God to-day – for whose recovery humble couples in their forest homes, in log-cabins and cottages, men gathered in the Service of Industry, and the darker peoples who kneel in their tents of grass and wattle, thank God too – we have more than ever, in his own person, what he has so long been called "The Ambassador of Empire." In his own body blends he now the fair people of Atlantis and the northern states, with the dusty – dusky, I should say – dwellers in the jungle. One foot is set in Africa, the other in the Northern Isles. In his own body he binds together every class, every colour, nay, every creed; and the Thin Red Line of Empire cements the union. And, brethren,' and his voice sank dramatically, 'it is only right that' (crescendo), 'in this hour of triumph, our thoughts should go out to another son of Empire, to one of lowly condition and perhaps of but modest pretensions, yet one who, in his humble way, has done much to make possible this Union of Peoples. Hath a man greater love than this ... that he lays down his foot for a friend? ... can we not put it like that, brethren?' (Hissing slightly.) 'In that dusky and obscure player, too, was found the heart of Saint and hero; and there may be many of us amongst this great congregation who, though we have not appreciated the music of jazz bands in the past, will never be able to hear the sweet tones of the Swanee Whistle or the deep, melodious notes of the saxophone without heartfelt sympathy and emotion, roused by the memory of a great and gracious deed.'

But, though the happy recovery of the prince was everywhere acclaimed, yet from that moment, in spite of the Archbishop's prophecy, syncopated music began to lose its grip on the people of the world. Jazz, it was, that died.

This same accident was responsible for a curious fashion among royal princes, and one which is still prevalent, though it may seem strange to the Victorians who survive – that fashion of having the limbs variegated in accordance with the people of the dominions over which they rule. Thus they have now become, in their own bodies, walking examples of Representative Government.

In spite of the fact that the most important of these grafting-operations is still known as the 'monkey gland,' it ought now to be needless to point out that the use of these simian cells has long been abandoned. For the introduction of any element foreign to it into the human body, inevitably sets up an irritation, which is sure to develop into some serious, and possibly fatal, trouble. Whereas the same operation, with human material substituted, is without any possibility of danger. In view of this, special laws were passed, many years ago, to ensure an adequate supply of human material and a proper use of it.

As we know, every young man killed by chance, in street accident or sudden explosion in a factory, is sent at once to the Royal Analysing Institute, whence, if his remains are found to be satisfactory, they are passed on, for the necessary treatment, to the nearest Young Man's Dissecting and Cold Storage Association (Y.M.D.A.C.S.A.). Here, if his relatives so desire, a funeral service can be held by Royal Licence; and many relatives have found a funeral without any corpse – and with no actual expense, save that of the service – most comforting; preferable, indeed, to the ordinary arrangement. In the building of the association, each limb, each cell, waits till the time comes for it to serve its purpose with Elder Statesman, millionaire philanthropist, or famous general. Wars, even, have ceased to hold for the civilian population their former terror. For the essential horror of war was its utter waste and uselessness; but now, after each battle, there is a short armistice, and the slain are swiftly collected and laid by, that we may benefit – and our enemies as well – by the ever-increasing wisdom and ripe experience of those who have guided us through, and themselves survived, so many crusades to end war. Surgeons, as well as statesmen, may now declare: 'We will not lightly sheathe the sword. ...'

In spite of these well-thought-out preparations, it has been found that freshly-dissected limbs are more effective, safer to use, more swift in their results, than preserved ones. So, when Sir Vincent McNabb was warned of the accident that had befallen Lord Richard Cressy, he determined to patch the patient together – if it should prove possible – without the use of any but his own limbs, glands and other material. This might mean that the actual reconstruction would be a more lengthy affair, but in the end it would be of the greatest benefit to the patient, aiding his speedy recovery. In order, however, to be ready for any eventuality, the great surgeon brought down with him from London a complete regulation set of anatomical sections.

Within a half-hour of his urgent summons, Sir Vincent had arrived at Cambridge. There he was met by the Goodleys' agent; for Lady Septuagesima and her husband had been forced to stay at Dodderingham to make arrangements for the nursing of Lord Richard and the reception of his wife. The menagerie had been hurriedly dispersed, the striped umbrellas had been struck, the raggle-taggle gypsies were on the move once more. The wolves and jackals were already howling in the outer wilderness of London, the hyænas were laughing more hysterically than ever in their own homes, and the few lions that there had been were back in their dens, roaring sardonically. Everything had been tidied up, under the supervision of two trained nurses; and, as soon as the preparations were complete, Lady Septuagesima would join Sir Vincent. Meanwhile, the agent conducted him to where, among torn brambles, smashed hawthorn bushes, and earth thrown up as by a miniature volcano, lay the wrecked flyer, guarded by police. Several nurses were on the scene, in readiness. It was now getting dark; but with that rapidity and sureness of judgment, which, in surgery as in other professions, is the very stamp of genius, Sir Vincent was soon able to decide that it was possible, as he had hoped it would be, to operate with the material on the spot. The mutilations and injuries were terrible: but a reconstruction was undoubtedly feasible, however formidable the difficulties. A theatre, fitted with the new wireless lighting, was hastily improvised. Everything, now, depended on swift, on determined, action.

During four hours the remains were under an anæsthetic, while the great surgeon grappled with the problem of their reconstitution. But, in the end, the problem was solved, and Lord Richard Cressey was given a chance of a remodelled but adequate survival.

So immersed had Sir Vincent been in the pathetic and perplexing work before him, that it was not until the long process of his art was completed that he observed, with considerable surprise, the presence among the wreckage of what were apparently, in his technical language, spare-parts. This astonished him; for not even the most thoughtful – or morbid – of airmen would prepare for eventualities in this way. Superstition, alone, would forbid it; nor, in any case, is flying sufficiently dangerous to warrant such an outlay. And, strangest thing of all, the texture of the skin, the tint of hair, the structure of bones, the composition of the flesh – all at once confirmed the first supposition of the trained eye that they, too, must belong to that body that was still lying, unconscious but reconstructed, upon the operating-table. The great surgeon was puzzled ... distinctly puzzled. In the whole course of a long professional career he had never ... no never ... met with a case like it! Was he, then, to conclude, in the face of those very laws of nature by which he was permitted to practise his art, that Lord Richard, like some Hindu divinity, had been the possessor of six arms, had, like Diana of the Ephesians, boasted more than the normal pectoral development ... or, like Janus, with his two faces, like Cerberus, with his three heads, had rejoiced in the distinction bestowed upon him by an unusual plurality? Puzzled was Sir Vincent, distinctly puzzled. ...

The timely arrival of Lady Septuagesima helped to clear up what was apparently inexplicable. Lowing and neighing at him, charmingly, she explained. It was so stupid of her, so careless, she whinnied – but in the sudden shock of evil tidings, in her sorrow for her cousin, her bewilderment as to how to break the bad news to Goo-Goo, she had completely overlooked the existence, and ignored the fate, of the unfortunate Messrs Leviathan and Parkinson. The very fact of there being two such persons had left her. In the same manner in which she was accustomed to shed those fantastic articles we have described about the countryside, so, in that moment, had the lives of that ill-fated pair fallen from her, unnoticed – 'lost between here and Doddering-ham Old Hall.' ... Oh, how tiresome and unfortunate! And really too bad of Tootsie, who had never reminded her! He was getting so very careless and remiss. He knew quite well how forgetful she was! And now it was too late, was it, Sir Vincent, for anything to be done? She lowed entreatingly at him. Alas! it was now no longer possible for him to treat the other two passengers. The police had better warn the relatives by radio. Sir Vincent came forward heavily, and informed the police that, in any case, the fragments were so much injured as to defeat any attempt at reconstruction.

Lady Septuagesima, in order to pacify the two families, who might think she had been careless or inhospitable toward her guests, undertook to use her influence with the old Duke of Badgery St. Lawrence, and the Home Office, to secure for the two victims a special Burial-Permit under Clause 2 of the 'Only Children to Widows Relief from Compulsory Anatomical Service Act of 1936.' She obtained the further favour for them of interment. They were laid to rest in one grave in the cemetery of the Parish Church at Cambridge – in which latter place, too, the funeral service was held – though usually in such cases it had to be celebrated on the premises of the local Y.M.D.A.C.S.A.

*

The return to consciousness of Lord Richard took a more than average time. For ten days he lay in the darkened room at Dodderingham, not speaking, hardly breathing. Goo-Goo watched by his side. His pale face, with its closed eyes, seemed to her, in the twilight of that sick-room, to be remote and strange. Some indefinable alteration had, surely, taken place in him? ... Did he look older or younger – ten years older, or ten years younger? Yet though he remained lying there senseless all these long days, Sir Vincent appeared pleased with the patient's progress. There were no signs of a relapse; the grafting had been completely successful, a triumph such as could only have been achieved by the skilful use of the patient's own limbs and material, the surgeon said. The scars were healing, were disappearing. But Goo-Goo was puzzled by the presence of two birth-marks, one on the neck, and one on the right wrist, which, though they were familiar to her, had been absent, she was certain, in her husband formerly. At any rate, compared with his recovery, the presence of these two blemishes was unimportant.

In the house reigned a great stillness: no rolling-round of tongues sounded from the lawn, and a ban had been placed on the electric organ. Day after day Goo-Goo sat there, dressed as a nurse; for even in her blackest hour she could never resist the lure of an appropriate costume. However admirably a widow's weeds would have suited her – and it must be confessed that in idle and impersonal hours the image of herself floating ethereally in a cloud of black chiffon, with those large eyes and a small black cap, had visited her – yet she was willing to forgo them for her husband's sake. But who knows (her mind took wings, without her wishing it) that she might not marry again? White chiffon suited her better than black; and another image would float through her imagination; large black eyes looking through a white veil, a cloud of white – rather as a mosquito tries to get through a mosquito-net. But the latter comparison did not suggest itself, and in any case she was willing to forgo all these things for her husband's sake. Yet as she sat there, waiting, waiting, everything seemed unreal, and she could not help wondering ... was that really Richard, lying there, white and drawn, upon the bed?

Then one day, about four o'clock in the afternoon, he began to speak a little; he looked round, recognising pieces of furniture and pictures – but ones that were not in the room! Indeed, as far as Goo-Goo could remember, the things her husband saw and described had never been in any room he had occupied; in his talk, rather broken and rambling talk, he recalled incidents from the past – but was it the past of Lord Richard Cressey? As he grew stronger, he would tell the nurses of things that had happened to him at school ... but when they told Goo-Goo of them, she was surprised to hear the name of the school, which was not the one at which he had been educated! Then, one day, the truth (or at any rate a very agitating inkling of it) began to dawn on her mind: for he asked her to fetch his mother and sister (the Duchess had been for many years in her coffin, and Lady Ethel was in South Africa), and added, as if each man was born into the world with several mothers and a variety of species of sisters, 'You know, either Mrs Leviathan or Miss Isabel Parkinson.' Then, again, his mood would alter, and he would talk to Goo-Goo about herself, himself, and their home, very rationally, very sensibly. When she mentioned these inconsistencies to Sir Vincent, the great doctor pronounced that they were nothing, and would pass away with the patient's gaining strength. – 'Growing pains, dear lady, growing pains! That's all. Don't worry yourself. Leave it all in my hands!'

But the periods of insensibility continued, and when he roused himself from them, it took a little time, apparently, for him to focus his mind. He looked up at his wife one morning and said, 'Goo-Goo, when is your husband coming to see us? ... It's very kind of you looking after us, but I can't say that I think *he* behaved very well!' and then once more lapsed into oblivion, as his voice trailed off. What could it mean? In any case there could be little doubt that, as Barnacle put it, 'His Lordship didn't seem quite-himself-like.'

Convalescence was, to those by his side, an eternity. The fortnight was magnified into a hundred years. As the invalid's strength increased, his mind grew more logical; but, at the same time, his aberrations, though they occurred less often, were more concrete and tended to last over a longer period. For days he would be perfectly sure of himself, would talk to Goo-Goo about Little Titterham and how he longed to get back there. He seemed, even, to want to get back to his work at the Foreign Office. Then his wife would leave him, hoping he would sleep a little; but, when she returned, would find him quite different, wild-eyed, as if possessed his bed littered with papers. His counterpane was so completely covered with these white drifts, that at the slightest movement there was a rattling and crinkling and falling as of autumn leaves. He had, evidently, got up (which he was forbidden to do), and had found these sheets, and a pencil as well! These various papers, none of them completed, were all addressed to the editor of *The Morning Echo*, and contained such matter as this that follows:—

'Lord Richard – Cuckoo writes to-day from Dodderingham Old Hall – is making a splendid recovery after his recent serious accident. Lady Richard – or Goo-Goo as she is to her friends – has borne the tragic events of the past three weeks with stoical fortitude, and looks sweetly pretty and piquante in the nurse's uniform which she has adopted for the occasion. With it she wears no jewellery except a large ruby and diamond swastika, once the property of the ill-fated Czarina of Russia, which was given her by her mother, Mrs Guggerty – which reminds me, darlingest, how beautiful we all looked in nurses' uniforms in the last Great War! I sometimes wonder ...'

But the documents differed. One, at least, had an almost sinister tone:

'From Dodderingham Old Hall, where she is the guest of Lady Septuagesima Goodley, or "Mad Septua" as she is known universally to her friends – Grannie writes to me by to-day's post. Apparently Lady Richard – or Goo-Goo as she was to those who were her friends before she took to the water-whistle – has been pretending to nurse her unfortunate husband. It is to be supposed that she likes dressing-up, or perhaps she thinks that a nurse's uniform suits her. One can never tell these things oneself, can one, dearest? Her husband, naturally, is not progressing very fast; and his action in absorbing the two friends who were with him at the time of that fatal flight has, of course, created considerable and rather hostile comment. Lady Richard's common old mother ...'

And here, again, the manuscript, which did not even appear to be in her husband's writing, broke off. But poor Goo-Goo, on reading this brutal reference to herself, and still more, to her mother, fainted away.

Another document was yet harder to explain; it ran:

'The funeral took place last Friday fortnight, at the Old Parish Church, Cambridge, of the mortal remains –

or rather of such as had not been appropriated by Lord Richard Cressey – of Mr Valentine Leviathan and Mr Frederick Parkinson. These two brilliant men – now, alas! no more – were deservedly popular wherever they went, but among ...'

The queer thing was that, though Richard must have written this, he had never been informed either of the fate of his two friends, or the date and place of their burial!

Then there were also lying about several importantly-written disquisitions, of unmistakable style, on the subject of the Détente Cordiale between France and England, and several letters to dim dwellers in the country, people of whom Goo-Goo had never heard. The letters appeared to be in two different hands, while the persons to whom these strange communications were directed were addressed in them as relatives: 'Dear Cousin Toto,' 'Dear Uncle Harry,' or 'Dearest Aunt Violet.' The signature on most of them was 'Your affectionate nephew' (or cousin) 'Freddie,' though some were signed 'Valentine.'

As his vitality grew day by day, the patient's voice became more resonant. And in the middle hours of the night, when so fragile is the dark crystal bowl of silence that any vibration, scratching it ever so faintly, smashes it utterly, making an overwhelming din and clatter, the nurses would sometimes be woken by a roaring of empty, vacuous laughter. They would find Lord Richard sitting up in bed, telling himself fashionable little jokes or stories, or performing one of those hieratic mimickings which we have mentioned. There were questions and answering voices; it was as if a conversation were being carried on between two or three people. But the next morning he would remember nothing about it, and the doctor thought it better not to disturb the patient's equilibrium by asking him about it, or recalling it to his mind in any way.

Ignorant of his night's doings, he would be charming to Goo-Goo when she went in to see him, talking to her affectionately, discussing with her the many subjects that had interested them before his accident. Yet within a few seconds of her leaving him he would begin to act strangely again. He would examine his own looks and character with the nurses, acknowledging things about himself quite needlessly, things which it had not previously been his habit to confess – in fact, he would say such things about himself as was, in his world, usually a privilege confined to intimate friends. He would criticise and laugh at his personal appearance, he would deride his manner very frankly, and neutrally. And, more embarrassing still, he would make remarks about his wife that were as unnecessary as they were untrue.

Poor Goo-Goo, her mind almost unhinged by suffering, had retired to seek a temporary consolation by indulging her artistic and musical gifts (the latter ever so quietly), while upstairs, unbeknown to her, Lord Richard was denying her water-colours and anathematising the water-whistle.

On another night the nurses, hearing a sound coming from His Lordship's room, peeped through the door, having opened it soundlessly, and caught him examining the bedroom china, fingering the glaze, and murmuring soft 'Sung's, 'Ming's, 'Han's or 'Pu's to himself – almost, had they known it, in the manner of the late Mr Frederick Parkinson.

The serious thing about these outbreaks was the fact that they were gradually beginning to impinge upon Lord Richard's consciousness. From being unconscious impulses, they were becoming conscious; and the effort to repress them was a constant strain upon the patient. He underwent, now, trials such as he had never known; he experienced the uncanny sensation that while being one ego, he was yet three people, the three separate branches of the same tree; worse than this, he was often affected with harassing doubts as to his own physical identity, or with even more puzzling convictions of it. In fact our three poor heroes, now surviving in one body, were soon unable to make up their minds which they were — or rather which he was. Richard, though he never openly confessed these uncertainties, became painfully, tragically depressed, or unnaturally hilarious. One day Goo-Goo caught him before a mirror, gazing into its watery depths. 'Funny thing,' he said, pointing to that birth-mark that she had noticed when he had been lying unconscious, 'curious, but I've got a birth-mark here! I'm sure it wasn't there before the accident; but I remember that Valentine had one like it!'

This was the nearest approach to the subject that he ever made. Nor did his realisation of these outbreaks, and of the need to repress them, prevent their recurrence, though he tried to control himself.

A very unfortunate incident took place on the occasion of Lady Septuagesima's first visit to him since his accident. She had been goodness itself; the whole house had been turned upside down on his behalf, and he was always telling Goo-Goo how grateful he was to his hostess, how he felt that such kindness could never be repaid. She swept into the room, neighing sweetly, a very tall and gracious presence, her red-gold mane floating, her large yellow skirt, like a crinoline, swaying a little, as she walked. Lord Richard at first thanked his cousin in the most heartfelt manner for saving his life, and talked to her rationally and intimately — for he was one of the few relatives with whom she had never quarrelled, had always been on terms of affection. Then, suddenly, she noticed an alteration in the expression of his eye, which seemed to become vaguer, bluer, yet more faded: the voice lost its warm tone and became, though the same voice, that of a stranger; he burst into rude, shuddering hoots of laughter, and said, talking obviously to himself, yet as if to a second person: 'Richard always liked her, I know. He used to say to me, "Poor old Septua's not a bad old thing really; she'd amuse you and she's very picturesque to look at!" But she looks to me just like a mad chestnut mare that's got entangled in one of Queen Elizabeth's old dresses!'

In a moment he was again transformed into himself, and Lady Septuagesima – though Tootsie remarked that she seemed rather 'upset' for the remainder of the day – maintained a discreet silence.

Soon Richard asked if he might be allowed to see other visitors. The doctor thought it would be a valuable discipline for him – as well as for his friends! Goo-Goo decided that Mattie was the best subject for a first experiment – bright but sympathetic, dependable and even-tempered. It was, therefore, arranged that he should come down. But he was only granted a half-hour's interview with the invalid, since it was still most important that the latter should not be fatigued. Richard remembered quite well dining with Mattie the night before his accident. He was full of questions about – and seemed to look forward to – the Pecksniff Prize, which would be the occasion of his first public appearance. They discussed books for a while: Mattie brought him down several new ones – a novel by Edward Shanks – the first that writer had published for six months – and a reprint of the earlier poems by the Earl of Chiswick. Richard was delighted with them. Then they reverted again to the dinner-party at Mattie's, and, this time with no change of expression, the invalid observed: 'I thought Richard so very pompous that evening. Of course I'm devoted to them both – though I know they're pretentious – but I think Goo-Goo's the better of the two as long as she doesn't let herself go on that sanguinary water-whistle. But what a pity it is that they neither of them know anything!' Poor Mattie wriggled, winced, wavered, and twittered, and by the time he had managed to produce his voice, Richard had gone back to the more usual incarnation of himself, appearing, luckily for Mattie's peace of mind, to be quite unaware of his words a few seconds before. As Mattie left the room Richard was leaning back; his vague eyes were looking upward and away from his moustache, which was drooping down and under. It was curious how alike those three had been, but till now Mattie had never noticed it!

Goo-Goo talked to her guest, and to a certain extent confided in him. As far as she knew, Richard had not displayed any symptoms of aberration for a fortnight; while Mattie, for his part, was still far too taken aback to recount his recent experience. He urged her, nevertheless, to let Richard fulfil his engagement at the Skimpole Hall in a month's time. It would dispose of rumours. He need not be on the platform long enough to tire himself. The others could make the speeches, while he could just give the prize away. And what a wonderful reception he'd get! Incidentally, from the prize-winner's point of view, it would be an excellent thing; Richard's first appearance since his accident would lend an added interest to the proceedings and ensure a full hall, since, besides all his friends who would wish to be there to welcome him, many people who would not otherwise go to such a function would come to this one out of curiosity – for a man who has met with an accident will always receive both more attention and more sympathy than a poet! One has only to notice the relative density of the crowd that collects round an over-turned hand-barrow, and the one that surrounds a poet disclaiming his verse in public, to observe that! Besides, Richard was much looking forward to giving away the prize, while both Sir Vincent McNabb and his own doctor admitted that there could be no harm in it.

As Mattie went back to Cambridge he reflected how strange it was that he had never remarked the likeness before ... Valentine ... Richard ... Freddie ... He supposed that there had always, yes, he was sure, that there had always, been, a look ...

PART III

THE hall seemed to be filling quite satisfactorily. Not that there was as yet anyone in it, but peeping out from a little punch-and-judy window at the far side of the darkened stage, Mattie could distinguish, beyond the open doors, the shifting white lights (for outside it was a fine summer day) that fell between the flower-like shadows of the assembling audience. These shadows on the floor were agitated as if by some wind, while an insect-like chirping, chattering, and chirruping was borne into the sombre hall, as though this were a Southern night, where the cicadas were so insistent in their crinkling, castanetted music that the lolling stalk of every sun-weary flower, the cool glazed leaves of every cone-shaped magnolia-tree, rattled and sang together. Out of this general seething and murmur it would be difficult to disentangle a particular tune; yet occasionally an individual insect voice shrills loud enough to be heard above its comrades. Thus, too, out of the voices beyond the door, from this distance alike as grains of sand rolled round by an eddy of wind, a particular tone, however infrequently, was sometimes recognisable. For instance Mattie was able to identify that plaintive yet playful neighing as Septua's property.

A few single figures were now making their appearance in the hall – men, nearly all of them, and each obviously a lonely, mocking genius, betraying the stigmata of the consciously inspired and persecuted – overcoats on this hot day, mop, bobbed or pudding-basin hair, pince-nez that made the eyes prominent as those of prawns, or owl-like tortoiseshell circles, open collars and vague distinguished looks, a few beards, and solitary misunderstood voices. In fact they were all remarkably alike – more especially in the persistence with which each protested his dissimilarity from his neighbour. After glowering furiously, but wonderingly, at each other, they sat down in a very determined manner, as if once more publishing their resolution to Make No Compromise with the Public Taste. Then opening their eyes rounder and wider, they gazed through, right through, poor Mattie, as if, by reason of some inner revelation, they were able to use him as a telescopic lens through which to examine some bewilderingly interesting object beyond.

Poor Mattie was already beginning to feel very ill at ease, when the timely arrival of his Chairman, Professor James Criscross, completed his discomfiture. The Professor's face was feline – more feline than Mattie's – but his heavy, greying, downtrodden-looking moustache showed, as well, a certain canine sympathy. A very old dog, he seemed, with a cat's soul, and a cat's stealthy gait and claws. His smile of exquisite malevolence, as he came forward, was an index of his intention, which was, now as always, to throw down, by a form of mental and verbal ju-jitsu of which he alone held the secret, anybody with whom he shook hands. In this drawing-room-sport he displayed an ingenuity and agility completely out of keeping with his years. Mattie went down at his first clutch.

As the beloved author of *From a Library Stool* and a million critical articles advanced across the stage, he looked round constantly, as if both expecting a welcome and fearing an ambush. Next, he allowed the smile to fade out of his face, as though the hall were a large railway station at which he had just arrived, where he was to have been met by some dear friends, but, on looking round, had this moment discovered the long draughty platform to be bare and desolate, with only a plaintive clanging of milk-tins for his comfort. Finally, he arrived in front of Mattie, looked at him fixedly for some seconds, without the faintest glint of recognition in his cat-green eye, then gave an almost too realistic jump, and treated him to an affectionate pat on the shoulder.

These paraphernalia were but the stage-properties which the Professor had, through a long course of years, constructed for himself, without which he never ventured out of his own house – stage-properties at once the disguise and weapon, the cloak and sword, of a curious and intricate terrorism. The method of it was very personal. Certainly he was old, aged indeed, but not so old as he pretended. His vagueness, and the senility which excused it, were in reality part of that armour he had evolved for himself, while from under its protective shelter he aimed his cruellest and most deadly shafts. Thus he made it his rule at first not to recognise his friends, and then, when recognised, to call them by some unfamiliar and unwelcome variant or, if possible, variants of their name. This subdued their spirits at the start; and he would follow up his preliminary advantage by inquiring, in a voice that was painfully sympathetic, after some ailment which was altogether confined to his imagination, some illness from which they had never suffered or even claimed to suffer, talking about it as if it were a permanent disability with which they were well known to be afflicted. This should, if the victim were an instrument sufficiently sensitive, worthy of the Professor's virtuosity, crush resistance and make the rest easy. For example, Mattie was called Mattie. Anyone who knew him well enough to call him by name at all, called him Mattie – and nothing else. Further, he was very timid; while the only peculiarity about him, of which naturally any mention would make him additionally nervous, was that high, jumpy little voice. Professor Criscross began, therefore, by saying to him:

'I'm so sorry, Mark, that I did not at first recognize you; but being so short-sighted and old (too old, too old, my dear Matt*hew*) I mistook you, until I saw your face more clearly, for one of your own geniuses – not one of whom, I may say, is familiar to *me*!' And then, beaming over his gold spectacles, added, before Mattie had time to answer: 'And, poor Mat, how is that tiresome sore throat of yours that gives you so much trouble?'

It was hopeless for Mattie to attempt battle. The only gap in the Professor's armour was an intense snobbery; but, at the moment, there was no title available, with which to hit him over the head and temporarily stun him.

The gloomy geniuses, in their seats apart from one another, had watched the encounter with intense relish, and it was all very annoying. The Professor was just about to start a new skirmish, when the other chief speaker of the afternoon, Mr Ernest Lympe, the well-known critic and man-of-letters, arrived on the stage. The long thin body, shaped like a capital S reflected in a mirror, was surmounted by a small head and a face that was brave, and consciously noble in the extreme. A grey kiss-curl floated down over the upright forehead; and he had a smile, grave yet excruciatingly sweet, that at the same time understood and pardoned everything. In fact he looked like a missionary who had taken the wrong turning and become a writer – which is exactly what had happened. His father was a little-known but decorative clergyman of the Church of England, and enemies cite the son's continually appearing volumes of bright leading-articles, which on their appearance in book-form are immediately converted, by the other critic of the very paper in which they had been served up daily, into 'Mr Lympe's brilliant book of essays' – a miracle as great as that other transmutation of water into wine – as the final, undeniable argument in favour of priestly celibacy. Poor Mr Lympe was terrified of only one man in the world – and that man was Professor Criscross! He dared not try to oust him for, in this era of grafting, the Professor would have a century in which to revenge himself – which, noticing what he could do in this way during a few seconds, was a formidable thought. Besides, Mr Lympe's facade of knowledge was an eighteenth-century library door on which are presented in counterfeit the bindings of many rare books. And the Professor, who had at any rate read very many more books than he could understand, had detected, but not yet published, this fraud. Hence poor Mr Lympe's abject terror.

Leaving the latter gentleman with no straw to catch at, Mattie walked away to meet Lord Richard Cressey, who looked quite well now, in spite of that air of distinction so often bestowed by the winnowing fire of a long illness. On seeing him, the Professor stopped his little games, and became, this time genuinely, solicitous about his health. Mattie thought – and the other two agreed with him – that it would be better for Lord Richard to wait in the small room at the back of the stage until it was time for him to make the presentation. It wouldn't fatigue him to the same extent; while, too, it would be a very dramatic appearance, just giving that necessary touch to the whole proceedings. As they came on to the stage, Lady Richard's voice could be heard outside the door, coming nearer; and then the insect-like chirruping and drone invaded the room all at once, pouring in at the door, giving the room a life of its own, till the lifeless void that it had been began to throb and stir. The light, giving a radiance to the hall without being visible, was turned on, and the drone increased its volume, as if the sun had risen and drawn out the winged creatures from their hiding-places. After infinite hoverings, whisperings, and rustlings, the audience settled; only a few remained standing. Heads would nod together and sigh in rippling waves, as if the wind were breathing down a cornfield, tossing the golden heads together. There would be a silence, and then a sudden movement in one patch of the audience, as though some animal, that had been sleeping among the golden stalks, had stirred and woken. There was, for such a gathering, an unusual air of excitement. These things are hard to explain, and the reason may have been merely that the fine day of early summer outside was sufficient to stir the blood, however wooden, of any audience. Mattie could recognise a great many of his friends, but from where he was seated it was difficult to see 'who everybody was.' Whether it was the light, or this year's fashions, he couldn't make out; but somehow or other from this distance everybody looked the same, shadowy and indistinct. It was very good of so many of his friends to support him, for Mattie could not help regarding it – except when he caught the gold-rimmed eye of Professor Criscross – as rather 'his show.' Over in one corner he observed the familiar grimace, bull-dog and triumphant, of one of his favourite bellicose filibusterers and 'Shall We, I say, yield to the Menace of Armed Might?' rang in his head like the latest successful musical-comedy number. Beyond, in an almost royal seclusion, sat those two rival Trustees of the Nation – Lord FitzBison and the Duke of Badgery St Lawrence. Wonderful old man, that! So small, and yet so dignified with his aquiline, rather curling profile, and little bunches of yellowy-white ringlets beneath each ear. Poor Goo-Goo, he thought, looked rather worried. She must have spent a very trying two months: still, *he* looked much better to-day. With her was Baroness d'Arenheimer, with Angel and Desirée, looking very Spanish, he thought – gypsy-like, almost! Sir Booster's voice was also to be heard in the land: how odd it was, that habit of his of speaking so loudly; but then, like many other remarkable men, he was completely un-self-conscious! As he spoke you could almost hear the rolling 'r's' gathering moss as they rolled; the guttural, agglutinous sound of his voice, like the speech of the ghost for ever imprisoned within an American soda-fountain, could be heard all over the hall; and his genial smile was spotted on everyone in turn, like a limelight, with an orange-slide over it, at a theatre. Able and philanthropic, as he was, Nature, Mattie reflected, had yet hardly treated him as he deserved; and surely it was a mistake on the part of the Press Barons always to put up Sir Booster to lead the attack on Socialism, the defence of Capitalism, when, to anyone ignorant of the sterling qualities of this Persian Philanthropist, his personal appearance must seem ultimately the complete refutation of the very arguments he was advancing. Lady Babboon was with him, looking very young, rather wan and blanched – a little bleached, even, Mattie thought. The strabismal glance of her eyes, when she smiled, was so attractive – a slight cast often helps a face. Behind her he noticed Eddy Tush with Selly Moonbury, and Ned, looking rather like a seal out of water, with a large party of overfed, under-bred friends, youthful revue-writers and elderly stage beauties; the latter looking, under this artificial light, very young and exactly like both each other and everyone else. Many of the shadows were so animated that Mattie could not see who they were. And all those mirrors at the back of the hall helped to muddle one, making a stage-army, reflecting the same people, giving the reflections a certain life. Rustlings and whisperings still ran through the audience as the shadows of leaves move on the ground when a slight wind plays above. Meanwhile Mattie, up on the platform, was communicating with his friends in his own way, shaping sentences at them with his mouth, letting his eye-glass fall or loop-the-loop on its black string, or making daft little beckonings and esoteric signals. Twined in among his gaily-coloured friends, like a dead branch in a rosebush, he noticed two strings of black. One in the fourth row, one at the back of the hall. Gazing intently through his monocle, he recognised the nearest string. It was the Leviathan family! He jumped down at once to speak to Mrs Pulborough, Valentine's aunt. Yes, she said, they had come to welcome poor Lord Richard, who had been in that terrible accident with her nephew. Oh, yes, a dreadful affair! Besides, though she had little time for it, she had always been very much interested in poetry – it was that lovely line ... for the instant she couldn't remember who'd written it, 'A thing of thingamajig is a what-d'you-call-it for ever' – lovely. Oh, yes, Keats, wasn't it? And then, what she really liked was originality; and she was told that Mr Rosenheimer was so original, wasn't he? Perhaps dear Mr Dean would bring him up to her afterwards, and introduce him ... but Mattie had at this moment to get back on to the platform, as the Professor was beginning to get restive. Gripping his monocle with Chinese eyebrow, Mattie peered over the heads of his friends at the other black line. That tall ebony regiment of women seemed familiar ... of whom did they remind him? Richard? ... there was a look, too, of Valentine. ... No, no, of course, it was Freddie Parkinson! They must be poor Freddie's relatives, but how many there were of them, and how few of them had he ever mentioned! Obviously, then, they had come up to London for the same reason as Mrs Pulborough and the others. It was really very nice of them.

The ceremony began. It was Mattie's duty to make a small preliminary speech of introduction. Coming forward, Mattie spurted his jets of sound up into the air in such a manner that only a few truncated sentences were audible. '... and gentlemen ... not going to speak ... only to tell you ... that Professor Criscross (hear, hear) ... in the chair, I need say no more to introduce ... so deservedly beloved ... in literary circles ... Lympe ... later.' ... Then, following a few remarks, quite impossible to hear, about literature in general, Mr Dean sat down.

The Professor, with a really intimidating glance of dislike and disgust toward the audience – a glance much enhanced by an evidently false look of nervousness – then formally took the chair. The audience, quite unafraid, fluttered and preened itself to silence, like a bird alighting on a branch. This stillness, gradually making itself felt, welling up from them, was only broken by the voice of a gloomy genius at the front of the gallery, who was blowing his sentiments up into the air, like a whale spouting water. After rising some distance in the air, they fell back on the audience and the platform. 'Simply doesn't count, you know,' he was saying in a painfully level voice. 'Afraid Leonardo doesn't interest me at all: just l'Art Pompier: has nothing to tell me ...' The Professor looked up over his gold rims, as if ready to spring at this intrepid sparrow – and the consequential voice died suddenly in a violent spasm.

This afternoon the cat had the upper hand of the dog. The Professor looked the sublimation of smiling felinity – as much at home in the Chair as the Cheshire Cat in his tree, purring already, as if stroked by the public applause. Mattie had twisted into the seat on his left, and was trying to look as if he wasn't on a platform at all. Mr Lympe had, like a serpent, coiled himself into the seat on the right. The prize-winner, looking prosperous and curly, sat at the corner of the gangway below, ready to scramble up the side and receive his cheque. If he climbed up, instead of walking round, it would look more boyish and unconventional. Besides, they must all know that he was an athlete. Still, Jacques Rosenheimer could not help feeling that he was not quite the hero he had expected to be on this occasion. The Professor looked down at him for a moment, as if intimating that he would settle him after he had finished with the rest of them. As the speeches proceeded poor Jacques felt, indeed, less and less as if he were there at all. For whereas the prize-giver, the judges, the speakers, the person who presented the prize, were all made much of, the name of the prize-winner scarcely occurred. Mattie had lisped the learning of Professor Criscross, and piped the virtues of Mr Lympe. The Professor, after his own fashion, paid a few cat-and-mouse compliments to Mattie, dealt a few more to Mr Lympe, spoke of the prize, the history of it, dwelt a little on his own life, and wound up with a warm tribute to Lord Richard Cressey. The amiable and brave Mr Lympe, next, sang loudly the attainments, virtues, and popularity of Professor Criscross, presented a verbal bouquet to poor Mattie, a verbal palm-leaf to Lord Richard. He then very nobly denied his own merits. But not one of the speakers appeared to be aware of the existence, even, of the prize-winner, Mr Jacques Rosenheimer.

'Ladies and Gentlemen,' the Chairman began with a literary clearing of the throat, 'I had come here with a few suitable platitudes prepared; but, sure enough, Mr Dean has already delivered most of them to you, and the rest of them I shall leave for Mr Lympe. I must, therefore, confine myself to a few historical remarks. It is but thirty years since the first award of the Pecksniff Prize took place at this hall. And I think that, if we examine the Roll of Winners, we shall feel that it is one that reflects credit on the judges, and on the late Sir Champion Pecksniff, who instituted this annual award. We do not, perhaps, find on it any names famous in poetry; yet we do undoubtedly find the names of many distinguished critics and men-of-letters. Mr Lympe (with a bow) was one of the earliest prize-winners, with that charming if slender little volume of poetry which first established him in the hearts of all book-lovers, and endeared him to all those whose soul is with the birds, out in the fields – I refer to "Crowsfeet".' (Applause.) The Professor's expression had relaxed, for his intention was to charm and captivate. But now his face assumed a more stern expression as he said: 'The Pecksniff has never, I think, stood for mere eccentricity or contortion. It has never – and I think you will agree with me, Ladies and Gentlemen, that it has *rightly* never – been associated with the names of those young men and, I regret to say, young women as well, who believe that to stand on their heads is the only duty of the modern poet. On the contrary from its inception it has been connected with those poets of good heart and upright living, who sing, dulcetly as ever, of English countryside and of those wild creatures that move through it – those poets, modern in the best sense, who are inspired by the sweet English sentiment so well summed up by a predecessor in that exquisite line, 'Llewdly sing Cuccu.' (Rustlings, cheers and cries of 'Oh, how sweet!' 'Oh, how pretty!' and 'Isn't it like him?' from those admirers in the audience who are under the impression that the Professor himself has written the line.)

'It is, perhaps, not yet the moment for me to disclose the name of the winner of the prize, for we are concerned (with a look of mingled hatred and contempt at poor Jacques Rosenheimer) not with the man, but with those principles which, *however unworthily*, he represents. Nor need we discuss my two fellow-judges – or should I say *conspirators*? (mischievous glance through gold rims, and delighted cooings from audience) – Mr Dean and Mr Lympe! – they are too well known to you for any word of mine to help them – but we shall, I am sure, all of us, be particularly delighted to welcome in a few minutes' time on this platform, the Prize-Giver – Lord Richard Cressey!' (Here the Professor's too genuine, sincere, and perhaps not un-English affections – one for a title, the other for an amateur – the force of which is quadrupled by the combination of the two – nearly overcame him. He sips the names, turning them on his tongue as if he were going to pronounce upon the merits of some rare vintage wine – 'generous, fruity, full-bodied.' Tears appear about to spout from his eyes, as from the eyes of those lachrymose loyalists who, when a military band passes, rush from bar-parlour into the street. 'Not only shall we greet him warmly this afternoon because it is his first public appearance since the terrible and painful ordeal through which he has passed; we shall welcome him, also, as one who has already made for himself a name in those worlds of diplomacy and literature to which it has pleased God to call him.' (The Professor's voice took on the lyric note.) 'We owe to Lord Richard – I say it with no fear of contradiction – the solution of that recent crisis between the Yugo-Slovaks and the Jingo-Slavs, which, because Englishmen still believe that right is stronger than might, he had himself done so much to create and ferment. But the strong know when to give way; and by a graceful diplomatic gesture, which consisted in losing all the papers concerned with the matter, he was able to solve the very difficulties which he had himself designed. But we have in him also an author and poet of considerable distinction. Those of us, and I hope we are many, who have enjoyed reading *The Buzzard's Bastard*, have found in it an unaffected simplicity, moral purpose and genuine strength, for which we have to search in vain through the pages of even the strongest lady-novelist – while to many of us, and to me amongst others, *From a Yashmak Garden* brought a new revelation of beauty.' ... After this the speech trailed off into a series of compliments, interspersed with a great many pin-pricks, for Mattie and Mr Lympe. As each bouquet was handed to them, a pin, hidden among the stalks of the flowers, drew blood.

The Chairman sat down, amid considerable applause, and soprano but muffled cries of '*Isn't* Mr Criscross wonderful?', then stood up again, and, as if looking for something he had lost, called on Mr Ernest Lympe to address the gathering.

The latter gentleman uncoiled himself from his chair, and, tossing the careless kiss-curl back from his forehead, proceeded to say a few words about Professor Criscross, who watched him as if willing to play cat-and-mouse again for a minute or two. But, at the lightest sound of insubordination! ... Mr Lympe, however, was far too frightened to make any attempt at retaliation.

'It is a great pleasure to mey,' he said, 'to be on the same platform this afternoon with one who may well be termed the Grand Old Man of Literature. Eminent as is our friend in the Chair, busy as he is, he yet still finds time to come down here among us and encourage the young. Ai will not speak to you about the praize-winner; but Ai should like to be allowed to speak a few words about Professor Criscross. A famous poet, distinguished as a Munofletters even above his contemporaries, one whose learning and whose delicate malice has long endeared him to us (Professor looks pleased, loud applause and stifled cries of 'Isn't he delicious?') in the pages' ... And the speech rambled on for another five minutes.

The Chairman stood up again and gazed, almost benignantly for him, at the audience, now thoroughly settled in their stalls, and with a tone of rapture in his voice, called on *Lord* ... Richard Cressey ... to come forward and present the prize.

Little eddies of curiosity and interest passed through the audience, rustlings of heads like branches swept by the wind, as the tall, spare form of Lord Richard stepped forward across the stage. Applause started with an unexpectedly loud smacking rattle of hands clapped together – surprisingly loud; yet, while continually increasing in volume, the character of the welcome appeared gradually to change. It seemed as if little sighs, sobs, cries and exclamations were mixed up with, and covered by, the volume of sound. The Chairman looked startled and, standing up, gazed toward the back of the hall. Perhaps someone was unwell. The noise was swelling, rising crescendo, like the solemn roar of an organ when first its spray breaks against the stone walls. The noise was swelling, increasing in volume;

a clamour, as when some sudden hit at a cricket match, sudden goal at a cup-tie, or sudden dagger at a bull-fight, rips open the chests of those watching and lays bare their pulsing hearts. The Chairman looked taken aback, this time really old and vague. The applause, ever louder, had yet altered its kind. The change was gradual in a sense, yet very swift. The cries were rising, coming to the top. People stood up on their chairs to see they knew not what, and the very action of standing, peering, increased the expectation and excitement. The cries were rising in it, but feet as well as cries sounded in the tumult and there was movement. The clamorous confusion increased: like a cuttle-fish it seemed both to discharge a cloud of blackness under which it could hide, and then, octopus-like, to stretch long tentacles toward the stage. A tall black line, noticeable among the colourful, fluttering audience, surged from the back of the hall, and rushed up the gangway, waving hands and black parasols, shouting 'Freddie! ... Freddie! ... it is Freddie!' ... Louder and indescribable grew the commotion, fiercer the excitement. The audience were all standing, moving, waving, watching. The Professor's dog-like reproofs could scarce be heard through the uproar, though occasionally an angry barking sound would be audible through the other noises from the platform. Goo-Goo's convulsive calf-sobbing sounded in the air like the gurgling of a fountain. But little attention was paid to these minor manifestations, for another, nearer, black line advanced, waving and shouting, 'Valentine! ... Valentine! ... It is Valentine!' ... and close round the platform which was attacked, stormed, lost in a dark, dancing, whirling cloud of revolving black arms and parasols. Out of it came the far-carrying suctional clucking of kisses, as a hundred unknown relatives embraced Lord Richard and claimed him as their own. Excitement had spread to the gallery, where could be heard, winging up above, the tired, fluttering, bumping cries – like a bird bumping against the ceiling – of poor Mattie lost and bewildered; cries like those of a bird that is trying to escape from a room into which it has flown blindly. Lord Richard's head could still be seen, as he stood encircled by his smaller relatives, the point of the swarming, the centre round which the whirlwind spun its course, distracted, almost hypnotised by the sudden roarings; distracted, pulled, tugged; his clothes hanging in shreds and blown up, as if by winds, with all this fury of sound and movement. A machine working on three gears, slipping back from one to another continually ... Richard ... Freddie ... Valentine ... Freddie ... Richard ... Valentine ... Valentine ... Freddie ... Richard ... Three tunes that were continually being broken and resumed ... forty-seven ... thirty-seven ... twenty-seven ... thirty-seven ... forty-seven ... twenty-seven ... ten years older ... ten years younger ... Yes, he was Valentine ... he was Freddie ... he was Richard. Yes, yes, he was, he confessed. He was. Rival parties of relatives were appealing to the audience to bear witness to this birth-mark and to that, through the gaps torn in his clothing ... Yes. He was. ... The audience began to take sides; and, at the same time, the hysteria was mounting. The confession of his triple yet single identity, completed the work. Everyone in the hall was laughing, crying, and sobbing. No one remembered why he was there, why she was there, or what had happened – for the great truth had dawned on them! The hysteria passed in waves through the assembled shadows. A few minutes before they had been quiet and peaceful, cultivating this smile, that gesture, this voice, that look of the eyes, forming fresh reflections of the same thing, revealing endless vistas and avenues of repetition. But the truth had now dawned on them, and was animating them with a false vitality; like a current of electricity it made these corpses twitch and caper, shudder and jig. With this scene of riotous confusion can only be compared one of those outbreaks of epidemic dancing-mania that seized on Greece and Southern Italy in the Middle Ages, when those infected danced on, whirling and shrieking, in the market-place, till they died. Everyone was shouting, waving, gesticulating, dancing, even. Some saw the tall ghost of Freddie, others the spectre of Valentine, standing, like the angels of Mons, beside their spiritual brother on the stage. The mob surged round the platform, hats lay like trampled flowers, crushed under the triumphant progress of a Bacchanalian rout. Veils were torn, clothes were ripped and dragged, faces were like large poppies, red and angry, or excited and pleased. A few held out, a few isolated towers, like the towers of the nobles in the Middle Ages. Lady Septuagesima could be heard telling the wife of a bishop that she was not her, and never had been. What is more, she did not intend to be! For the confession of identity was spreading, as the figure on the platform confessed he was Freddie, he was Freddie ... he was Richard ... he was Valentine. Yes, he was. He was Valentine. He was Freddie. He was Richard. As if the atom had been exploded, and all the atoms had broken with it, confessions were hurled up into the air, shouted and boasted. The whole miniature world of the hall confessed too. He confessed, and the world with him. At last they realised that they belonged, one to another. The tumult was now indescribable. Handkerchiefs and hands were waving through the air of the hall with one movement, as at an arena during a bull-fight. This one was the same as that; I am as the same as you: only shadows are real in this world of shadows.

*

The starched exterior of Bond Street quieted them. What had happened? It had been enjoyable, very enjoyable, but what had taken place?

'All the same,' said the venerable Duke of Badgery St Lawrence, as he tried to bang out with his fist a dent acquired somehow in his top-hat, 'all the same' – this to Lord FitzBison, his powerful and formidable political rival – 'I don't believe there's much difference between us!'

THE END

FATHER AND SON

Edmund Gosse

700

'A STUDY of two temperaments' is the sub-title which Sir Edmund Gosse gave to this narrative of his early life. One of the two, of course, was his own, the other was his father's, and the quality which gives this classic of autobiography a distinctive tang is its vivid analysis of the relationship between two persons of intense individuality. Gosse Senior was a Victorian zoologist of repute, but he was also a fervent disciple of one of those eccentric religious sects in which his age abounded and his endeavours to reconcile geology and Genesis were a manifestation of this double loyalty.

Young Edmund, then, was brought up in a home where dogmatic theology was a powerful and persistent influence on conversation and behaviour. But he was also encouraged to share his father's scientific preoccupations as well and at a tender age he enjoyed abundantly such adventures as sea-coast expeditions in search of anemones and coral. And no less absorbing to his bright and observant mind were the odd circles of fanatics in which his father usually moved. Through it all, however, the boy learned to discover his own mind and to escape eventually from an environment dominated by doctrines which he grew up to reject. *Father and Son* has some affinities with another celebrated record of a similar relationship – Samuel Butler's *Way of all Flesh*. No more revealing picture of an age exists than this close-up of a Victorian household at the time of the Darwin controversy. First published forty years ago, it now appears for the first time in Penguins.

THE WHITE HORSES OF VIENNA

Kay Boyle

699

THIS volume of short stories is a demonstration of a most difficult kind of fiction, for these are not in any sense the usual run of 'magazine stories'. That is to say, they are not slick pre-fabricated affairs depending on some surprise climax, neither are they little conjuring tricks with well-worn situations. They are all character-sketches of men and women caught in a predicament, microscopic studies of human behaviour in some sharply-defined situation or dilemma. There is, for example, the proud and impoverished old couple keeping up appearances on the Riviera, who remember their manners even when they have lost their wits. Or the dowdy English governess in Salzburg deceiving no-one but herself with the myth of a man who loves her, yet achieving a pathetic dignity in her make-believe.

Many short stories disappoint because they are threadbare in content. They are gone at a gulp. But Kay Boyle observes so deeply the characters she portrays, and has such remarkable powers of evocation, that their brief histories grow to larger dimensions as we reflect upon their poignant or ironic experiences. In this profound and sensitive quality of analysis Kay Boyle will remind readers of Katherine Mansfield and Elizabeth Bowen.

The following are the first thirty titles published by Penguin Books by special arrangement with Chatto and Windus, Faber and Faber, Hamish Hamilton Heinemann and Michael Joseph

PELICAN

MUSIC HO! *by Constant Lambert*

POETRY AND DRAMA

SELECTED POEMS *by T. S. Eliot*
HASSAN *by James Elroy Flecker*

CRIME

THE BIG SLEEP *by Raymond Chandler*
ROGUE MALE *by G. Household*
FAREWELL MY LOVELY *by Raymond Chandler*

HUMOUR

MY LIFE AND HARD TIMES *by James Thurber*
HOTEL SPLENDIDE *by Ludwig Bemelmans*
LOOKING FOR A BLUEBIRD *by Joseph Wechsberg*
NO BED FOR BACON *by Caryl Brahms and S. J. Simon*

BIOGRAPHY

EMINENT VICTORIANS *by Lytton Strachey*
COMMANDO *by Deneys Reitz*
THE SMITH OF SMITHS *by Hesketh Pearson*
THE JOURNAL OF A DISAPPOINTED MAN *by W. N. P. Barbellion*
FATHER AND SON *by Edmund Gosse*
WILLIAM HAZLITT *by P. P. Howe*

FICTION

CAKES AND ALE *by Somerset Maugham*
ANGEL PAVEMENT *by J. B. Priestley*
ANTIC HAY *by Aldous Huxley*
THE HORSE'S MOUTH *by Joyce Cary*
SONS AND LOVERS *by D. H. Lawrence*
THE SAILOR'S RETURN AND BEANY EYE *by David Garnett*
SHERSTON'S PROGRESS *by Siegfried Sassoon*
THE SHIP *by C. S. Forester*
THE HOUSE IN CLEWE STREET *by Mary Lavin*
A HIGH WIND IN JAMAICA *by Richard Hughes*
THE WHITE HORSES OF VIENNA *by Kay Boyle*
THE RAINBOW *by D. H. Lawrence*
THE BEAUTIFUL YEARS *by Henry Williamson*
ODD MAN OUT *by F. L. Green*

THE JOURNAL OF A DISAPPOINTED MAN

by W. N. P. Barbellion

674

FROM the age of thirteen to the time of his death at thirty 'W. N. P. Barbellion' (whose real name was Bruce Frederick Cummings) kept a diary, and from the twenty large manuscript volumes in which he wrote it this selection was published shortly before his death. He was by profession a naturalist on the staff of the Natural History Museum at South Kensington. From childhood he had suffered acute ill-health, and in early manhood it was discovered that he was doomed to an incurable and progressive paralysis. Yet through all these misfortunes he maintained a vivid and passionate interest in life, and in this *Journal* he set down his responses to hundreds of major and minor experiences and events. He reinforced the scientist's power of detached analysis with a poetic intensity, and he could bring both qualities to bear on such different themes as an Albert Hall concert or the symptoms of his disease. In one passage he says, 'I could swallow landscapes and swill down sunsets or grapple the whole earth with hoops of steel', and it is this quality of passion which animates the *Journal* even in its most sombre entries. He had a gift of incisive and candid comment, which he applied to an immense variety of matters – to his discoveries in the laboratory or a ramble on the Downs; to his likes and dislikes in books, music, people and the theatre; or to problems of science, religion and ethics. There was a considerable strain of the introspective in Barbellion, and many of the most moving entries in the diary are those in which he puts his own complicated nature under the microscope. He was that rare combination, the man of science and the man of letters, and although he died young, his *Journal* is an expressive memorial to his genius.

Double Volume 2/-